Adam's deep voice betrayed nothing but sincerity

So much generosity was overwhelming, especially in the face of her standoffishness. "It's kind of you but I can't accept."

"Why not? Give me one good reason."

Hayley's hand hovered over the key in the ignition, itching to turn it. She didn't have a good reason. But she had her pride. "You don't even know me and you're inviting me to live in your cottage."

"Not knowing you is all the more reason to keep a close eye on the therapist who's treating my daughter. What do you say? You'd, of course, be free to come and go, and do whatever you normally do."

It was so tempting. Her garage would be cold and dark even with candles. But accepting would mean admitting she was a stone's throw from being homeless. "No. Thank you, but no."

"Why not? It makes sense. I have this big house and a cottage and you're toughing it out in a garage."

Ah, he felt guilty. Why should she care? His guilt wasn't her problem.

Dear Reader,

In the summer of 2009, my home state of Victoria was caught in the grip of devastating bushfires known as Black Saturday. People not from Australia might think the term "bush" means small bushes, but it can also mean the forest. The toll from Black Saturday was horrendous: one hundred and seventy-three human lives were lost and over two thousand homes destroyed, plus countless livestock and wildlife.

Home to Hope Mountain isn't about death and destruction, though. It's about survival and recovery and the resilience of the human spirit. It's about the ability of the land to regenerate. And about a small community that pulls together to put the tragic past behind them and rebuild their lives. It's about the power of love to heal and to renew hope for the future.

Although I've drawn on stories of the bushfires, neither the town of Hope Mountain nor any characters or their experiences are based on real places or people.

The Horses For Hope program is real, however, and does amazing work for people suffering from a variety of mental health issues. It was this program and not the fires that was the inspiration for this book. I hope I've done the program, and the amazing bond between horses and humans, justice in my portrayal. I've taken liberties with the program's method of funding for plot purposes. Any other inaccuracies are inadvertent.

Thanks to Colin Emonson for answering my many questions and explaining how the therapy works. For more information go to www.horsesforhope.org.au/.

I love to hear from readers. To drop me a line, or to find out more about my books, go to www.joankilby.com.

Warm regards,

Joan Kilby

JOAN KILBY

—

Home to Hope Mountain

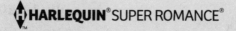
HARLEQUIN® SUPER ROMANCE®

Recycling programs
for this product may
not exist in your area.

ISBN-13: 978-0-373-60846-1

HOME TO HOPE MOUNTAIN

Copyright © 2014 by Joan Kilby

This edition published by arrangement with Harlequin Books S.A.

For questions and comments about the quality of this book,
please contact us at CustomerService@Harlequin.com.

Printed in U.S.A.

www.Harlequin.com

ABOUT THE AUTHOR

When Joan Kilby isn't writing her next Harlequin Superromance title, she loves to travel, often to Asia which is right on Australia's doorstep, so to speak. Now that her three children are grown, she and her husband enjoy the role reversal of taking off and leaving the kids to take care of the house and pets.

Books by Joan Kilby

HARLEQUIN SUPERROMANCE

Other titles by this author available in ebook format.

To the victims, human and animal, of bushfires.

To the brave firefighters and emergency workers who put their lives on the line in times of extreme danger.

And to the survivors who rebuild their lives with courage and hope.

CHAPTER ONE

ADAM BANKS DROVE down his winding, rutted driveway while his fourteen-year-old daughter, Summer, nodded to music only she could hear through the earbuds dangling beneath her long red hair.

Sunlight filtered through the canopy of eucalyptus. Birds warbled and twittered above the smooth purr of his vintage Mercedes-Benz. The open window let in a cool breeze that held just a hint of spring.

When he came to the road he looked both ways then began to pull out.

"Look out, Dad!" Summer yelled.

A horse and rider crashed through the forest and shot past right in front of him.

Adam slammed on the brakes and swore under his breath. "I saw her. Did she see me?"

The blonde woman on the dapple gray hauled on the reins, struggling to control the fiery horse. "I'm sorry. Really sorry. My horse has some issues."

Adam stuck his head out the window, his heart still racing. He'd damn near run her down and the shock of it made him rude when he wouldn't normally be. "Looks to me like you're the one with the problem."

Her cheeks flushed and her full mouth set as she straightened her Akubra hat atop her fraying braid. The horse danced and sidestepped on the gravel shoulder until the woman dug her heels into its heaving sides, and they both plunged back into the woods.

"Who the hell was that?" Adam wondered aloud as he drove off. He glanced into the forest, but the woman and her horse had already disappeared.

"Our neighbor, Hayley Someone." Summer pressed her nose to the window and gazed longingly after the horse.

"Hayley Someone needs to learn to ride." Adam gripped the wheel with both hands and scanned the road ahead for runaway horses.

"If she couldn't ride, she would've fallen off when her horse reared," Summer said. "She and her husband used to give trail rides. Mum's been on them. But Hayley's husband died in the bushfires, so I don't know if Hayley's still doing the rides." She paused. "Did you see scars all down her horse's neck? I wonder if that was from the fire?"

"Could be, I suppose." Adam had too much on his plate to be distracted by the locals. After he dropped off Summer at school he was heading into the city to meet with the Shanghai delegation about the development project the architecture firm he worked for was bidding on.

"Dad?" Summer turned to him. "I want another horse."

"We're not talking about this now, sweetheart. I told you I'd think about it." She'd been after him all weekend—horse, horse, horse—till he thought he'd go mad.

"Huh." Summer readjusted her earbuds and slouched down in her seat, allowing him to spend the rest of the twenty-minute drive going over his presentation in his mind.

Adam pulled up in front of the high school and let the car idle while Summer gathered her backpack. "Can you get the bus back to the house after school?"

"I do all the time." Summer got out of the car.

He'd only been in Hope Mountain since Friday and wasn't familiar with her routine. "Okay, well, do you have your key? An umbrella in case it rains?"

"I'll be fine." She poked her head back in through the open door, her red hair swinging. "So, have you thought about it?"

"About what?" Adam glanced at his watch. He should have been on the road to Melbourne by now. The team from Shanghai was arriving at 10:00 a.m.

"Me getting another horse."

"You only asked me fifteen minutes ago." He shouldn't have promised to think about it when he had no intention of getting her one. "I'm sorry, Summer, but the answer has to be no."

"Why?"

He honestly felt badly for his daughter—her horse, Bailey, had died in the bushfires that had swept through the area nearly a year ago. But he *had* to stand firm. "It's not a good time."

"Why, just because you say so? I'm supposed to accept that?"

He tugged at a lock of her hair in a vain attempt to wipe the scowl off her face. "Who's this sullen teenager and what have you done with my sweet-natured daughter?"

She didn't crack a smile. "Please, Dad, not another one of your stupid jokes."

"Hmm, tough audience." Being a single father was tough, too—much more difficult than he'd expected, and he'd only been at it a couple of days. Reiterating his primary reason, that he wanted to put the house up for sale at the end of the year, would only spark another argument. "Everything's up in the air. We'll talk about it later."

"You always say that."

"Honey, I have to go to work—"

"You and your work. I guess it's more important than me!" She slammed the car door.

"Summer! Don't leave like that."

She was already halfway up the path to the school. Her friend Zoe, a tall dark-haired girl, was waiting for her, no doubt with a ready ear for Summer's tale of hardship.

Adam sighed and put his car into gear, easing out of the drop-off zone and onto the street. He drove slowly through the three-block-long commercial end of tiny Hope Mountain.

Sun broke fitfully through the clouds above the mountains enclosing the narrow valley. Trees lining the wide street were budding, and daffodils were springing up in newly planted flower beds. The setting was picture-postcard pretty.

But Hope Mountain was far from idyllic.

The entire mountainside to his left was black and ruined. The remains of burned trees looked like giant charred toothpicks. The community center had burned to the ground, along with the pub, a church and half the businesses on Main Street, leaving empty, barren lots. In the public gardens a huge tent had been set up to distribute donated household goods to people who'd lost everything.

Near the rose garden workmen were erecting a memorial to the people who'd died—nearly two hundred souls. Did they really need such a reminder when the evidence was all around that Hope Mountain was in a region of high fire danger?

The place had been nearly wiped off the face of the map, yet the sounds of nail guns and saws rang out in the clear mountain air, as the townsfolk were determined to rebuild.

More fool them.

The narrow winding road out of town led down the mountain, through more burned-out forest. Twenty miles later, at Healesville, he took the turn-off to Melbourne. Only as he accelerated onto the freeway entrance and set course for the city did he breathe easily.

Three hours later he was wrapping up his presentation to the delegation from Shanghai. Lorraine, his boss, was seated at the end of the boardroom table along with five men and one woman, all in identical gray suits.

"Ladies and gentlemen, that concludes our firm's vision of the luxury high-rise apartments in the Changning district of Shanghai," Adam said. "Please, take all the time you need to review our brochure. I'm available to answer your—" he broke off as his phone vibrated inside his pants pocket "—questions any time."

The damn phone had rung five times in the past half hour. He'd ignored it until now, but it wouldn't stop.

"Excuse me. I'll just be a moment." He threw Lorraine an apologetic glance and hurried out of the room. Shutting the door, he answered his phone. "Yes, what is it?"

"Mr. Banks? This is Tom Dorian, the principal of Summer's school."

"What's wrong? Is she hurt?"

"No, she's fine. Well, not fine, but…I'd like you to come in. She's been caught shoplifting."

"Shoplifting? Summer?" He barked out a disbelieving laugh. "That's not possible."

"She was caught red-handed by the owner of the shop."

Adam pinched the bridge of his nose. This couldn't be happening. And yet it was. Did he even know his daughter anymore? "I'll be there as soon as I can."

An hour later, the company helicopter set down on the rain-wet grass of the high school football field. Adam ducked beneath the whirring rotors, his long stride breaking into a jog as he neared the front doors of the school.

Summer had never been in trouble before. Ever. She was a good student, sweet-natured—this morning's tantrum aside—obsessed with boy bands and horses…typical in every way. She'd had a rough year, with the divorce and the bushfires, but she'd never given him or Diane, his ex-wife, a moment of worry.

Until now.

Adam smoothed his hair and straightened his tie as he rushed to the principal's office.

A secretary looked up from her computer. "Good morning. Do you have an appointment, Mr.—?"

"Adam Banks. I'm expected." Through the open

door of the principal's office he saw Summer sitting with her back to him, her shoulders slumped.

He swept past the secretary, knocked once and pushed open the door. "Summer, honey, what's going on?"

His daughter swiveled on her chair and greeted him with a blank expression and a shrug.

"I can fill you in, Mr Banks." Tom Dorian was round and slightly sweaty, with short, dark hair. He rose and extended a clammy hand, then walked around to close the door before returning to his desk. "Please, sit down. I'm sorry to have interrupted you at work, but I had no choice. The shopkeeper is talking about pressing charges."

Pressing charges. The words were enough to strike fear into the heart of any parent. Frowning, Adam took the chair next to Summer. She avoided his gaze and picked at the cuticles of her ink-stained hands. "Summer, what did you steal, and from where?"

Again, she just shrugged.

"A pair of earrings from the Gift Shop Café." Tom Dorian laced pudgy fingers over his desk blotter, his earnest, boyish face serious. "It happened around 11:30 a.m. She was also skipping school."

Adam rested a hand gently on Summer's shoulder. "Is this true?"

"So I cut school. Big deal." She shrugged his hand off.

"Not that. Shoplifting. Is this about the horse?"

"I wanted something for Mom's birthday and I didn't have any money." She raised her chin and stared at him. His heart sank—now she was lying, too. She received a generous monthly allowance, and her mother's birthday had been two months ago.

"We'll talk about that later." How had she sunk to such a low point without either him or Diane noticing? Behind Summer's defiance he sensed her fear and heard her unspoken plea: *Daddy, get me out of here*.

He turned to the principal. "What happens now?"

"You need to go to the police station and talk with the arresting officer," Tom said. "Since it's a first offense the shopkeeper might let it go. But even disregarding this incident, Summer's been on a slippery slope. As you know, her attendance is poor, her grades are falling—"

"No, I didn't know," Adam said sharply.

"Summer's mother didn't mention it to you?"

"She had to leave in a hurry. Summer's grandmother is having emergency heart surgery in Sydney." That didn't explain why she'd never told him Summer was having trouble at school, but that was Diane all over—ignore problems and hope they would go away. "How long has this been going on?"

"Her problems have been gradually building since the beginning of the school year." Dorian paused.

"The bushfires affected a lot of students. It's been a difficult time."

The bushfires again. They were an unmitigated tragedy. Along with the human life lost, hundreds of homes had been burned, livelihoods destroyed and untold numbers of livestock and wildlife killed.

He'd never wanted to buy Timbertop, the two-story log home on five acres of mixed forest and pasture. Diane had fallen in love with it on a whim after spending a weekend up here with her girlfriends, riding horses. He'd purchased the property as a summer home in an attempt to save his rocky marriage but not a month later he'd found out she was having an affair. He didn't know who with and he didn't care. It had been the last straw. He'd asked Diane for a divorce, and she'd moved herself and Summer permanently to Hope Mountain.

However, things could have been a lot worse for them. Compared to some others, they had hardly been touched by the fires. "But our house was spared, thanks to the efforts of volunteer firefighters…" he said, still searching for answers as to why his daughter's behavior had deteriorated. "No close friends of Summer's were killed—"

"My horse died!"

Adam dragged a hand through his hair. "Bailey. Of course. I'm sorry."

Bailey had presumably jumped the fence, terrified by the smoke and heat, and run into the woods.

They'd never found the horse, or his remains, but undoubtedly he'd succumbed to the fire.

"And stop talking about me as if I wasn't here." Summer bounded to her feet. "Not everything is about the freaking bushfires."

"Sit down and tell me what it is about, then," Adam said.

She sank back into her chair and crossed her arms and legs, folding into herself. "You wouldn't understand. You're never around."

The barb hit home. He was supposed to have Summer every second weekend, but for the past few months work had gotten in the way. He'd told himself he was doing his best in a bad situation. The fact he didn't have a clue what was going on in his daughter's head right now sent a message as big as skywriting that his best wasn't good enough.

Adam was used to being in control of his world, moving with ease among architects, businessmen and government officials, designing and selling development projects worth hundreds of millions. Faced with one troubled teenage girl, he felt as helpless as a newborn kitten.

This was his daughter, his only child. She was the most precious thing in the world to him. And yet no one would guess it, considering how little time he'd spent with her. Diane going to Sydney to take care of her sick mother might have been a blessing in disguise, since it forced him to reconnect with the girl.

"What do you suggest?" he asked Tom. "Is there a school counselor she could talk to?"

"I've been seeing her for three months," Summer said sulkily. "She's an idiot."

"Don't be rude. Why wasn't I informed?"

She shrugged. "Mom probably told you."

"Where parents are divorced, school policy is to communicate with both mother and father," Tom Dorian explained. "A letter would have been sent to your city address as well as your home in Hope Mountain."

Adam chewed his bottom lip. Somehow he'd overlooked the communication. News of Summer's downward slide had slipped through the cracks in his life. He and Diane had both failed Summer. But guilt and shame were unproductive emotions. He thrust them aside and focused on what he could do to make up for his neglect.

"So school counseling isn't working." He eyed Summer thoughtfully. "Maybe it would be best if we moved to my apartment in the city. I'd have more time to spend with you and we could find you a good private counselor."

And they could get out of Hope Mountain. Living in a fire-prone wilderness was foolish in the extreme. Next time fire broke out they might not be so lucky.

"I don't want to live in the city," Summer said. "I don't want to see another stupid counselor. You said

I could get a new horse. I've been waiting and wait-ing. It'll never happen if I'm living in Melbourne."

Should he give in to her demand for a horse? Being lenient, giving her too much, hadn't done her any good. He'd stalled all year on the subject, hoping to convince Diane to move out of the area. She'd pushed back, citing Summer's love of Hope Mountain and her wish to let their daughter finish the school year with her friends. "Is that why you've been getting into trouble, because Bailey died?"

"No. Yes." She dropped her head. "I don't know."

Tom Dorian cleared his throat. "There's a pro-gram locally called Horses for Hope. A woman named Hayley Sorensen runs it. She and her late husband used to give trail rides, but the fires de-stroyed her stables and half her horses. Now she conducts therapy using horses."

"That's the Hayley we saw this morning," Sum-mer said.

"Her?" Now that his annoyance at being startled had passed, Adam recalled blue eyes, a full mouth and fresh, natural beauty.

"They call her the 'horse whisperer.'" Tom's voice was tinged with a hint of awe. "I can vouch for her expertise. My brother suffered from debilitating anxiety attacks after being trapped in his car by the fire. Hayley and her horse therapy healed him."

"Do you have her number?" Adam asked.

"No, Dad," Summer moaned. "She'll just be

another dopey do-gooder who tries to get me in touch with my feelings."

Behind the sullen facade Adam caught glimpses of a desperately unhappy teen, and his heart broke. How had his little girl come to this? Where had he failed her? He was floundering, with no idea how to fix her. Therapy from a horse whisperer sounded flaky, but he had to help Summer, and right now he was feeling desperate. "You'd get to be around horses."

"I want to ride, not…" She chewed on her thumbnail. "I don't even know what's involved."

Tom had been searching his computer files for the contact details. Now he wrote down the information and passed it across the desk. "She's not great at answering her phone but you'd probably catch her if you go out there."

"Apparently she's our neighbor. We won't have time to stop in today but we'll call on her tomorrow." Adam pocketed the slip of paper, then placed a hand on Summer's shoulder. "Now it's time to face the music."

"What do you mean?" She looked up at him, panicky.

"If you ever want to have another horse you have to show me you intend to clean up your act. First, we go to the gift shop so you can apologize to the owner. Then we visit the police station."

"Please don't make me go back to the shop," Summer moaned.

"Come, sweetheart," he said, tugging her to her feet. "We'll do it together."

"STEADY, ASHA," HAYLEY MURMURED to the dapple-gray mare backed against the rough-hewn log rails of the corral. Slowly she advanced across the muddy ground, gently slapping long leather buggy reins against her legs. She lowered her shoulders, relaxed her mind and tried to radiate calm.

Shane, her black-and-white Australian shepherd, lay just outside the fence, his muzzle on his front paws, his eyes alert to every movement.

Asha snorted, eyes wild. She arched a neck marred with jagged scars and danced away from Hayley, tossing her silver mane and tail. Feeling her frustration rise, Hayley stopped. Nearly a year on, she'd made almost no progress with the registered purebred Arab.

Asha's scars meant the show ring was out of the question, but she could still be bred and used in the Horses for Hope program—*if* she could be handled. Aside from the loss of income, which was certainly an issue, Hayley was hurt and baffled that she couldn't connect with her own horse—especially given that her nickname was the "horse whisperer."

Tipping back her battered Akubra hat, she pushed strands of dark blond hair off her forehead. At least no one was around to witness her humiliation except for Rolf and Molly. Her father-in-law was busy installing a hot water heater outside the garage where she'd been living since the fires destroyed her home. Earlier he'd put in a water tank to collect rain off the roof. Rolf wasn't paying attention, but no doubt her mother-in-law was watching through the single small window at the back of the garage. Molly would be sympathetic, not critical, but still...

Molly emerged from the garage carrying a steaming mug. Her rounded figure was clad in a loose floral top and stretch pants, and she stepped gingerly over the muddy ground in her town shoes. "Coffee?"

Hayley hung the coiled reins over a fence post. "Thanks," she said, accepting the hot drink. "I can use a break."

"Maybe you're pushing her too hard. That horse has been through so much. You should be easier on her."

That was Molly-speak for *You should be easier on yourself.* But Hayley had to keep trying; it was what she did. "Left alone, Asha will never get better. I'm not hurting her. I'm trying to help her."

"How is the rebuilding coming along?" Molly asked, changing the subject.

"Slowly." Which was to say, not at all. "But I'll get there."

The 1880s homestead built by her great-grandparents had burned to the ground in the bushfires along with the stables and outbuildings. All that remained was the house's brick chimney and the concrete block garage, a modern addition.

Hayley had cleared the car parts and junk out of the garage and put in a table, an old couch that pulled out to a bed and a makeshift kitchen. With the new hot water tank she would have the luxury of hot running water. A few pots of geraniums, her attempt at beautifying her dwelling, stood on either side of the door.

The fire-ravaged clearing was still charred and black in spots. Temporary horse shelters, a corral and a small paddock had been built between the garage and the dam for her five remaining horses. Besides Asha there were Sergeant and Major, who were brothers, both golden brown geldings with white socks; big old Bo, a palomino Clydesdale; and Blaze, a chestnut mare who'd disappeared the night of the fires. She'd been found three months later by a cattleman in the high country, running with a herd of wild horses. Several months had passed before Hayley realized Blaze was pregnant.

Despite the devastation, Hayley loved the property where her pioneer ancestors had homesteaded. She and Leif had started their trail-riding business here with the goal to expand to a dude ranch. Her plan to rebuild and fulfill their dream was all that kept her going.

And until that day came, she gave victims of the

bushfires therapy using horses. Like her ancestors, she'd dug her heels in and said, "My land, my home. Nothing and no one will take it away from me."

"Leif would've been so proud of you," Molly said. She and Rolf lived in town, on a small block of land that had been spared the vagaries of the fires. They'd asked Hayley to come and live with them, but although their three-bedroom brick home was comfortable, it was no place for a cowgirl.

"I need an assistant part-time in the café now that winter's over and the tourists are trickling back," Molly added. "Do you want the job? You could probably use the extra money."

Hayley adored her in-laws. Since the fires they'd been a lifeline. The hard part was keeping them from doing too much. "You and Rolf have been great. I appreciate the offer, but I couldn't fit it in around my Horses for Hope program."

"Leif wouldn't want you to struggle so hard," Molly insisted. "He'd hate seeing you all by yourself out here."

"Yes, well…" Leif had battled the fire threatening Timbertop, the big estate on the other side of the ridge, and he'd lost. She still didn't understand why he'd been there instead of at home, defending their property and their animals. Everything they'd worked for, built and loved, was gone while Timbertop's double-story log home and the surrounding forest had escaped untouched. But that had been

Leif's way, always helping others. He was a hero and she loved him for it, but… "Leif is dead."

The words fell flat on the quiet mountain air. In the blackened, twisted eucalyptus that circled the charred clearing, a kookaburra called to its mate. An answering laugh echoed deep in the woods. There was no mate and little laughter left in Hayley's life— she just felt numb. But she carried on, because that was what she did.

Molly glanced at the dark clouds gathering overhead. "I heard on the radio we're in for a storm." She called to her husband, "Rolf, are you about done? Rain's coming."

"We could definitely use it," Hayley said. The reservoirs and water tanks needed to be replenished, and the horses could sure use some grass in their paddock. The few brave spears of green that poked through the burned soil were nibbled down almost as soon as they emerged.

Shane gave a sharp warning bark and jumped to his feet at the sound of wheels crunching on gravel. Over the slight rise came a burgundy Mercedes-Benz convertible with the black top up. Fifty yards from the corral, the car slowed to a halt.

"Are you expecting someone?" Molly asked.

"Nope. It's probably sightseers gawking at the burned-out town. They get lost and come down my track once in a while."

"Don't dismiss the tourists," Molly said. "We need

the business for the town to get back on its feet. *I* need them."

"I know." Her mother-in-law's gift-and-coffee shop had been gutted by fire and had required major renovations. She'd reopened two months ago and was struggling to stay afloat.

The Mercedes had a sleek, almost retro look to it. Hayley didn't know much about cars, especially luxury ones, but she would guess it was vintage. As the male driver got out, she saw he was a luxury model, too. Tall with dark hair, he wore a suit, pants and a dress shirt, with polished black leather shoes. City clothes straight from the big end of town. He looked vaguely familiar....

Hayley was suddenly acutely aware of her dirty jeans with the rip across the knee and the soft green flannel shirt she'd owned since forever, the sleeves rolled up to her elbows to hide the fraying cuffs. She tucked honey-colored strands of her fraying braid behind her ear, resisting the urge to pull out the hair elastic and retie it. A teenage girl with long red hair, wearing the local high school uniform dress of blue-and-white gingham, got out of the passenger side. She hung back, her gaze drifting to the corral where Asha trotted restlessly.

Molly sucked in a sharp breath. "That's the girl I caught stealing a pair of earrings yesterday."

"Really? Are you sure?" Hayley's gaze narrowed.

"Can't mistake that red hair. I recognize her

father, too. Not many men around here look like they've stepped out of *GQ*."

Now she recognized him. He was the jerk who'd yelled at her the day before when she was riding Asha. "Are they locals? What did you do when you caught her?"

"I called the police, told them I was pressing charges. I didn't seriously intend to—she's only a child—but I was upset and angry at the time. I wanted to give her a scare so she wouldn't steal again. Her father brought her into the gift shop and made her apologize. I was happy with that. But he didn't stop there. He emptied his wallet into the collection jar for bushfire victims I keep on the counter." Molly turned to Hayley, her eyes round, and added in a hushed voice, "He donated nearly four hundred dollars."

"He was trying to buy you off, Molly." Who kept that much spare cash in their wallet and was rich enough to give it away without a thought? She was struggling to pay her electricity bill, small as it was now that the house was gone.

Shane stalked toward the newcomers, the fur along his spine ruffled. The stranger crouched and held out a hand, drawing the dog in closer. Shane sniffed it thoroughly then licked the hand. Having made friends with the dog, the man straightened and walked over to Hayley and Molly. He did a double take as he recognized Molly. "Hello again…. I'm sorry, I didn't catch your name the other day."

"Molly Sorensen."

"Molly. I'm sorry we had to meet under those circumstances." His gaze moved to Hayley. "Would you be Hayley Sorensen?"

Hayley wasn't as quick as Shane to give her approval. She tucked her thumbs into the loops of her jeans. "And you are?"

"Adam Banks." He held out his hand to shake.

Banks. He must be her neighbor Diane's ex-husband. She didn't have much to do with Diane, as they moved in different circles. And then there was the fact that Leif had died defending Timbertop…. Leif's death wasn't Adam Banks's fault, but she couldn't help blaming him anyway. If Adam had been at home defending his property, instead of in Melbourne, Leif wouldn't have had to do it for him. Leif might still be alive.

She tried to remember if she had met Adam before he'd almost run her over this morning. Probably not. Molly was right. She'd have remembered a man like him. Not that she was impressed by expensive clothes and a hundred-dollar haircut.

Reluctantly, she accepted Adam's handshake. It was firm and businesslike, but his warm palm and enveloping fingers reminded her how long it had been since she'd experienced a man's touch. It felt so good that she pulled her hand away a fraction of a second too soon. "Yes, I'm Hayley."

His dark eyes moved over her, openly assessing. "I understand you do some kind of therapy using horses."

"Horses for Hope. It's a government-funded program." Hayley glanced at the girl hanging over the corral railing with her hand stretched out to Asha. The dapple gray snorted and tossed her head. "Careful. She's not very friendly since the fires."

"Summer, come and say hello, please. This is Hayley Sorensen and Molly Sorensen."

The girl reluctantly left the corral and walked over, kicking up dirt with the toes of her black Mary Jane shoes. Her gaze flicked to Molly and she stopped short. She looked to her father. "I already apologized—"

"It's just a coincidence," Adam said.

"Don't worry, dear," Molly assured her. "As far as I'm concerned, that episode is in the past." She turned to Hayley. "I see Rolf's waiting for me in the truck. Think about what I said regarding the job, okay?" She gave Hayley a hug, nodded to Adam and Summer, then hurried off to the dusty red utility truck idling next to the garage.

Adam touched his daughter's arm. "Hayley is the horse whisperer your principal was telling us about."

"Hey." Summer's glance flicked briefly at Hayley, then returned to Asha. "She's beautiful."

"Summer's horse, Bailey, died in the fires," Adam said.

The sadness in Summer's hazel eyes as she gazed hungrily at the mare told a story Hayley knew all too well. Over a hundred local horses had perished in the fires. "I'm so sorry. Did he get scared and jump the fence?" As far as she knew, Timbertop hadn't been touched by the fires.

Summer shrugged and hunched deeper into her shoulders.

"We were referred to you by Tom Dorian from the high school," Adam said. "I understand you work with troubled teens."

Summer threw him a dirty look. "I'm not troubled."

Hayley ignored that and spoke to Adam. "I work with anyone who's been traumatized, not just teens."

"I'd like to enroll Summer in your program. When's the soonest she could start?"

"I'm afraid my client list is full. I suggest you ask your local doctor for a referral to a counselor. There are several practicing psychologists in the area."

"You were recommended very highly. Could we put Summer on a waiting list? Someone might drop out."

"It's unlikely. Horse therapy can be a long process, sometimes lasting months."

"Dad, forget it. She can't take me. Sorry to bother you," Summer said to Hayley and tugged on her father's sleeve. "Let's go."

"If you find you have an opening…" Adam wrote his home and cell phone numbers on the back of a business card and gave it to her. "I believe we're neighbors."

"Don't you live in the city? That's what Diane told me." Not that Hayley spoke to her a lot. Leif had usually taken her and her city friends trail riding.

"Diane's temporarily in Sydney caring for her mother, so I'm staying at Timbertop for the foreseeable future."

"So you're commuting? That's a long drive."

"I might be taking a leave of absence." Adam shrugged. "It could be worse. Spring is a nice time to be out here with everything in bloom—" He broke off, his gaze flickering around the charred clearing.

"I guess it's spring over at Timbertop." The simmering resentment in her aching chest got the better of her and she added, "My husband was a volunteer with the Country Fire Authority. He died while fighting the fires on your property."

Just in case Adam didn't know.

"I'm sorry for your loss." His dark eyes met hers. "Thank you, I guess, although that hardly seems appropriate."

She didn't want his pity. She didn't want his gratitude. And she didn't want him on her property. "If you'll excuse me, I have work to do."

Again Adam glanced around at the razed clearing, this time taking in the garage with the curtain in the window and her spare boots outside the door. "Would you consider taking Summer as a private client?"

He'd obviously summed up her situation as desperate. He wasn't far off. But she wasn't *that* desperate.

"My time is fully committed." She felt sorry for the girl, but Adam Banks was a rich dude trying to offload his problem onto someone else. Sure, he was well-spoken, handsome and polite. It was easy to be polite when people kowtowed to you all the time.

"I'll pay you double what you get from the government for your other clients."

She almost caved. God knew she needed the money. And she would have liked to help Summer. A girl who'd lost her horse—how sad was that? But she was telling the truth when she'd said she was fully committed.

Soon the trail-riding season would be here and she would be even busier. Plus she wouldn't be a good therapist if her anger and resentment toward Summer's father spilled over into sessions with her. Hayley couldn't tell Adam that, of course. He'd simply have to accept no for an answer.

"It's not possible." She turned and headed for the garage, Shane at her heels.

Shutting the door behind her, she went to the window over the sink and peered out. Adam took a step toward the garage but Summer grabbed his arm and pulled in the opposite direction. Only when they got into the Mercedes and started the engine did Hayley let out her breath. She didn't know why her heart was beating so fast. All she knew was that she was relieved when his car disappeared over the rise.

CHAPTER TWO

"WHERE DOES YOUR mother keep the brown sugar?"
Adam asked as he rummaged through the pantry.
A barbecue sauce simmered on the stove.

No response from Summer. He glanced over at his
daughter, sprawled on the couch in the great room
across from the kitchen, her eyes closed. She was
plugged into her iPod again.

The past two days had been stressful. Yesterday
there'd been his aborted meeting with the Chinese
followed by Summer shoplifting and encounters
with the school principal, the café owner and the
police. Then this afternoon he'd been unsuccessful
with Hayley Sorensen. Diane's frozen diet meals
weren't going to cut it tonight—he needed wine and
red meat, stat.

The exchange with Hayley had especially bothered him for some reason. He didn't usually have a
problem relating to women, but she'd been distinctly
cool. Her refusal to treat Summer had felt personal,
which didn't seem fair. Her husband's death was
tragic and he felt for her, but surely she didn't hold

him responsible for her loss. He hadn't even been in Hope Mountain the day of the bushfires.

Adam walked over and plucked the bud from one ear. "I'm seriously considering dismantling this thing one night while you sleep."

Summer yelped and sat up. "You wouldn't dare."

"Don't test me."

"Give it back." She made a swipe for the earbud.

He held it out of reach. "Turn this off and give me a hand with dinner, please."

She looked as though she was going to protest, then gave in. "Fine."

Back in the kitchen Adam passed her a head of broccoli. "Chop."

Summer picked up the chef's knife and whacked off the base of the stem. "I don't like broccoli."

"I'm not crazy about it, either, but it's nutritious and it's the only fresh vegetable in the fridge." He watched her shuttered face as she hacked inexpertly at the broccoli. He needed to talk to her, but it was hard to begin, to find the right tone.

"What's going on with you, Summer?" As soon as he spoke, he knew he'd gotten it wrong.

"Nothing."

Doggedly, he persisted. "I called a couple of therapists this afternoon. Everyone in the area is booked."

"I don't need therapy."

He realized he couldn't strike the right note because he was furious. And worried to death, and afraid for Summer's immediate future, and deeply disappointed—yes, all that. But also very, very angry. At himself and Diane for dropping the ball, at the bushfires for causing his family and the community grief, but right this minute, mostly at Summer for her sullen attitude.

"So, lying and stealing are perfectly normal for you?"

She tossed the chopped vegetable in the pot, not deigning to answer.

He reigned in his temper best he could. "Here's what I think should happen. Until your mother gets back—"

"When will that be?"

"A month, maybe longer. Till then we stay at my apartment, enroll you in a city school and get you a counselor. I could continue to work—"

"I thought you were taking a leave of absence."

"I called Lorraine this afternoon and she agreed I could take time off, but she's not happy. I'd really prefer to finish the project I started, but I'd still cut back my hours. It makes sense rather than stay here."

"Not to me! The school year's almost over. Plus the bushfire memorial service and dance is in a few weeks. I don't want to leave Zoe and my other friends. I don't know anyone in the city." She slashed the knife down hard on the cutting board. "I'm not going."

"Summer," he warned, "careful with that knife."

"Why, are you afraid of what I might do?" With a smile that chilled him she deliberately stuck the point of the knife on her wrist and pressed.

She was bluffing, she had to be…. He watched the flesh dip beneath the cold steel. Another fraction of an inch and it would pierce the skin. Adam snatched the knife from her. All his anger drained away. "You're scaring me."

Her smile faded and she dropped her gaze. "Sorry," she whispered. "That was stupid."

Adam went around the kitchen block and took her in his arms. "Don't ever do anything like that again." With her face pressed against his chest she shook her head. "Promise?"

"I promise." She looked up at him, tear tracks on her cheeks. "Don't make me leave Hope Mountain."

"This isn't a safe environment, sweetheart. Living in the forest is like living inside a giant stack of kindling laid for a campfire. All that's needed is a lightning strike, and these tinder-dry woods would go up in flames."

"It's been raining for weeks. The woods are hardly tinder-dry."

"They'll get that way come summer." He brushed strands of flaming hair off her forehead. "What do you call a ninja with red hair?"

"A ginga. That's so lame and you've told it a million times. Come on, Dad, promise not to make me leave here. Please?"

It would probably be a mistake to pull her out of school and add to whatever trauma she was going through. There *were* only three months till the end of the school year.

"I can't promise you'll stay here forever. But, okay, at least until school's out." Before she could continue the argument he patted her on the shoulder. "We have no sugar for the sauce, so it looks like we're eating our lamb chops plain."

"Ugh. I hate plain chops. Is there at least ketchup?"

"I didn't see any. I could go to the grocery store." He was so relieved at hearing normal, kid-type complaining he was willing to make the trip for one item.

"It closes at five on Monday."

He glanced at the clock—ten to five. Living out in the boonies was nuts. If he was at his Melbourne apartment an elevator ride would take him to street level and a twenty-four-hour convenience store ten yards away.

"In that case, it looks like another night of Diet Turkey Delight...."

Summer made a face, and he had to agree: the thought was unappetizing.

Unless he became a terrible cliché and borrowed a cup of sugar from their neighbor. Ordinarily he wouldn't hesitate, but Hayley hadn't exactly put out the welcome mat. She wasn't bad-looking with all that honey-blond hair and those big blue eyes. Her long legs were shapely even in dusty blue jeans. But she was extremely prickly.

Mind you, she had serious problems, like the fact that she was living in her garage. Maybe he'd simply caught her at a bad time. Yes, that could be it. If he gave her another opportunity to treat Summer, she might accept. He'd learned in his long career of negotiating not to give up—if at first you don't get the outcome you want, give your opponent another chance to say yes.

Not that Hayley was his opponent. But she did have something he needed—the ability to heal his daughter. If she got to know him and saw he wasn't the bad guy, she might relent.

He looked through the kitchen window, past the manicured lawn and the gum trees ringing the gravel parking area to the horse paddock. He had something Hayley needed, too. The grass hadn't been grazed for nearly twelve months and was knee-high. Sure, she'd said her program was full, but she could no doubt find another hour in her week—if she wanted to.

Hayley didn't seem like the kind of woman he could charm into acceding to his wishes, which suited him fine. This was business. He prefered straight dealing. He had the sense that she did, too. Even though he'd been disappointed and frustrated by her refusal to take Summer as a client, he liked that she'd told him no straight up, without apology.

The rain had stopped, and there was still an hour of daylight. On the way home Summer had pointed out a track through the woods from their driveway to the Sorensen property. It should take only five or ten minutes by bicycle, assuming Summer's mountain bike could handle the muddy terrain. He missed his weekly thirty-mile cycle along the beach road in Melbourne. So rather than drive the short distance to Hayley's, he might as well get some fresh air and exercise.

He turned off the heat under the pot and covered the lamb chops. "I'm going next door for a cup of sugar. How good is that track you showed me? Will I be okay on your bike?"

"I've never been down there. Mom told me about it."

"I'm going to try." He turned to go, then paused. "Maybe you should come with me."

"I have homework."

Now she had homework. Half an hour ago she was just laying around listening to music. "I don't want to leave you alone."

Her cheeks tinged with pink. "I'm not gonna do anything dumb. I was just getting at you before."

"Well, stop it. I worry about you."

She met his gaze, her normal self. "I'll be fine, honest."

Satisfied she was telling the truth, he went through the door into the garage and wheeled Summer's mountain bike outside. He raised the seat as high as it could go, took an experimental lap around the parking area then pedaled down the gravel driveway. When he saw the old fence post and the parallel dirt ruts, he turned and headed into the woods.

HAYLEY RESTED HER hand on Bo's withers, reins slack, as the big horse plodded quietly along a wildlife trail. The woods here were untouched by fire, full of the resinous scent of gum trees. Late afternoon was her time for riding, and she loved going bareback, her legs dangling and her thoughts drifting. Working with trauma victims was rewarding but it was also emotionally taxing. She needed this time to de-stress.

Today, though, her thoughts refused to drift. Should she take the job with Molly? She was barely skimping by on her income from the Horses for Hope program. What would Leif have wanted? Working in town felt like selling out on their dream, but on the other hand, she had the horses to consider. Blaze was due to foal in a few weeks. There might be vet bills. And all the horses needed to eat. Hay wasn't cheap.

Maybe she shouldn't have refused Adam's request to treat his daughter as a private patient. But he unsettled her. Partly because of his association with the bushfires and Leif's death. Partly because he was a stranger. Every man in Hope Mountain was as familiar to her as her Akubra hat. Adam was attractive and sophisticated. Rich. She didn't know how to act around him.

A muffled curse on the vehicle track to her right broke into her thoughts. She reined in Bo and peered around a bush. Speak of the devil. Adam Banks had his knees up around his ears as he made wobbly progress on the muddy track. He didn't look quite so intimidating now.

He lost his balance and thrust out a leg to brace himself only to end up ankle-deep in mud. Hayley stifled a smile. Bo shifted one of his enormous hooves and a twig broke.

Adam glanced around. "Hello? Is somebody there?"

"You need a horse, not a bike," Hayley called out. She squeezed her thighs around Bo's barrel-shaped stomach and the horse picked his way through the undergrowth. "Where do you think you're going, anyway?"

He was heading in the direction of her property. She didn't care if people strayed over property lines while hiking or riding. But she didn't want Adam Banks becoming free with the track between their places. Didn't want him popping over anytime he felt like it.

He reached into the saddlebag behind his seat and pulled out an empty plastic container. "I'm coming to beg a cup of sugar off you. Demerara would be ideal, but I'll settle for plain brown. Or even white, in a pinch."

"Sugar." She looked him over, at the designer jeans, black polo shirt and expensive white running shoes splattered with mud. "Are you making cookies?"

Was this sugar quest a ploy to talk to her again? He seemed a determined type, used to getting his own way. She wouldn't put it past him to have another go at convincing her to work with his daughter.

"Barbecue sauce. So, do you have any sugar? It would be nice to know now before I destroy my clothes and Summer's bike. I promise to repay it tomorrow."

Was that a subtle dig at her obviously straitened circumstances? The other day when she'd turned down a free movie ticket Molly had told her she was too defensive and too proud. It was hard to know anymore where to draw the line.

"I've got sugar. But you're not going to be able to ride much farther. There's a creek up ahead and the banks are a quagmire. What on earth possessed you to try to come through here on a bike?"

"I do a lot of cycling at home." Hands on hips, he surveyed the dense forest and muddy track as if wondering how he'd come to be there. "Admittedly this wasn't the brightest move."

"Are you one of those MAMILs we get up here on

the weekend?" She smirked. "They come through town in packs of twenty to thirty."

"I beg your pardon?"

"Middle-Aged Men In Lycra."

"I confess to Lycra, but thirty-six is hardly middle-aged."

She'd been joking, of course, calling him a MAMIL. He was nothing like the pot-bellied weekend warriors who puffed up the mountain, red-faced and sweaty, to collapse in the café with a piece of cake. And now that she knew he was a cyclist, she could see how he came by his lean, muscled physique. An image flashed through her mind of him in a tight-fitting jersey stretched across a hard chest, and shorts that clung like a second skin to a taut butt and sharply defined quads. No, not middle-aged. More like prime of his life.

Adam propped the bike against a tree. "I'll walk."

She doubted he would want to do that for long, either. Well, he would find out. With a nudge of her heels she turned Bo toward home.

Adam kept pace, making sure there were a couple of yards between himself and Bo. "That's a big horse."

"He's half Clydesdale. Eighteen hands and as comfy as a couch." She patted the smooth golden coat below the white mane. "You're a good old boy, aren't you, Bo." Poor beast had been a mess when Ian, the Horses for Hope coordinator, had sent him to her. Bo's coat had been falling out from mange, and he'd been so skinny his ribs had showed. With a lot of TLC, he'd recovered.

They ambled along in silence for a few moments. Hayley tilted her head, listening to the clear, ringing call of a bellbird. Leif's favorite. Adam, struggling to watch where he put his feet, didn't even seem to notice. "Have you found a therapist for Summer?" she asked.

"No, I'm still looking." Adam avoided a muddy puddle in a depression between the ruts. "Have you changed your mind?"

"No one's dropped out of the program, if that's what you mean." He didn't seem the kind of man to go for alternative practices. Maybe he didn't realize certain things about her. "I'm not a qualified psychologist, you know. I didn't go to university, and I don't have any letters after my name."

"But you get results."

"Yes, I get results," she conceded. "Why don't you buy her a horse? It might not fix all her problems, but it would help. Give her something to focus on besides herself." She didn't know what she would do if it weren't for Shane and her horses. She'd probably need therapy herself.

"Can't do that. We're not staying in Hope Mountain," Adam said. "I hope to sell Timbertop and move back to the city before Christmas."

Good. She didn't want him bringing his city ways

and his handsome face into her woods. But if she felt like that, why did she also feel disappointed?

"Summer's not happy about the idea," he went on, a troubled frown creasing his forehead. "I don't understand why, really. She's only been here a year or so."

"She'll miss her friends. And maybe she's fallen in love with the area." He looked skeptical. Hayley shook her head. "You haven't actually *lived* in Hope Mountain, have you? I understand you used to come out on weekends occasionally, but that's not living here, that's just visiting."

He threw her a glance filled with suppressed annoyance and chagrin. Had she hit a sore spot?

Diane had thrown a divorce party last year. Hayley and Leif had been the only locals, and she'd felt uncomfortable. But Diane and her friends regularly went on trail rides, so she supposed Diane was being polite.

"Even if you don't want to live here, Diane will be back eventually, when her mother gets better," Hayley said.

"I'll have to discuss it with her. She hinted before she left that she may not want to come back."

"Seems a shame to take Summer away, though."

Adam stopped walking and planted his hands on his hips. "Yes, but this is where my sweet, smart, sunny little girl has inexplicably gone haywire and turned dark and miserable."

"She's, what, about fourteen? That's a tough age."

"I don't believe it's typical teenage blues. I know I haven't been around much, but I'm her father. I can tell something is eating away at her."

"Losing her horse to the bushfires?" Hayley still felt the ache in her own heart when she thought of her dead horses—Ranger, Lady, Sham, Smokey and Bella. They'd been part of her family. Even after nearly a year she still missed them.

"Maybe it's that. I don't know. She won't talk to me."

"Patience," Hayley said. "Maybe you just need time to reconnect with her, get her to trust you."

"What do I do in the meantime when the police catch her shoplifting? Next time that might not be enough for her. She might…do anything."

Hayley's first instinct was to offer help. Her opinion of Adam had improved slightly. He wasn't just looking to off-load a problem; he was genuinely concerned about his daughter. She probably could carve out a couple of hours a week for Summer if she really wanted to.

Then the bellbird called again, reminding her of Leif. She owed Adam and his daughter nothing. Let them leave Hope Mountain. What was it to her?

The creek, when they came to it, was swollen with rain and rushing, overflowing the near bank and forming a large boggy area stretching ten yards toward them. On the other side of the creek, the coursing water had carved the bank into an undercut.

"Still need that sugar?" Hayley asked.

"No worries. I'll take my shoes off and roll up my pants."

"I wouldn't take my shoes off if I were you. There are broken branches and stones in among the muck. Might even be snakes."

That gave him pause, but only for a moment. "I didn't like these runners much anyway." He started rolling up his jeans.

"You must really want that barbecue sauce."

Adam startled and gave a shamefaced grin. "To tell you the truth, I almost forgot what I was after. I just knew I had a goal and had to reach it. I guess that sounds crazy to you."

"No, not really." She understood goals, even crazy ones. Her goal was to rebuild her house on the spot her great-grandparents homesteaded and where she'd grown up and had lived as a married woman. She was going to do it despite everyone telling her she was wasting her time and despite what little money she had.

Sell the land, her city-dwelling divorced parents said. Use the proceeds to buy a house closer to the town, or better yet, in a Melbourne suburb close to one of them. She wouldn't consider it. So, yes, she understood a man who'd walk through muck for something he wanted.

Where she and he differed was that she would never ruin a brand-new pair of shoes. When her house had gone up in flames, so had all her possessions. She clothed herself with donations and the odd new item. With so little to her name, everything she owned was precious.

"Stay here," Hayley said. "I'll ride back to the house and bring the sugar to you."

"How long will that take? I don't want to put you out."

"Twenty minutes or so, round trip."

"I couldn't ask that of you. It was my bad for not checking the pantry before I started cooking. I'll take my lumps."

Before he stepped into the mud, she raised her hand to stop him. "Wait. I'll double you."

"Beg your pardon?"

"You can ride behind me. Bo can handle it." She'd carried an extra passenger plenty of times on the big old carthorse.

"Well, all right. Thanks." He studied the problem. "That is one very large horse. How do I get up there?"

"Over here." She manoeuvred Bo to a fallen log. After a couple of tries Adam hoisted himself up and swung a leg over the back of the horse. Hayley moved forward to accommodate him. "Don't sit too far back or you'll be on Bo's kidneys. Have you ridden before?"

"When I was a kid, on my grandfather's farm." As he found his balance his hands hovered near her waist for a second before settling on his own legs.

She gave Bo an encouraging pat and nudged his sides with her heels. "Let's go home, boy."

Bo lifted his enormous hooves with their shaggy white fetlocks and started through the sinking mud toward the creek.

Hayley hadn't counted on being so aware of Adam close behind her. The heat from his body warmed her back and with every lurching step of Bo's, Adam swayed forward, his quadriceps nudging the backs of her thighs. For the first time in many months she was reminded that she was a woman and a sexual being. In close proximity was a man. A very sexy man.

It was too soon after Leif's death to even be thinking about someone else—especially Adam. He was indirectly responsible for the fact that she didn't have her husband to warm her bed at night, to work alongside her during the day and to share her dreams and goals. Sure, they'd had their rocky times, but Leif had changed and their marriage had been on the mend.

At the edge of the rushing stream Bo needed a few encouraging digs of her heels to keep moving. Slowly he picked his way across, and then scrambled up the steep bank, his big hooves sliding in the mud.

Hayley leaned forward, one hand gripping the mane. Adam started to slide backward. "Hang on."

He wrapped an arm around her waist and leaned forward, reaching for his own bit of mane. His fingers dug into her just below her ribcage and his hard chest pressed against her back. "Are we having fun yet?" he said, his warm breath close to her ear.

In the midst of feeling uncomfortable about his closeness, she laughed. Bloody Adam Banks. She should have let him get his damn shoes dirty. Or she should have gone farther upstream before attempting to cross. It was her own darn fault for wanting to make this journey as short as possible.

At the top of the bank, Bo made a final surge, crashing through the tree ferns. Adam lost his grip and slid right over the horse's rump, landing in the mud. When he scrambled to his feet, dark brown streaks covered the front of his polo shirt and his pants. Hayley hooted with laughter, then quickly covered her mouth.

Adam tried to brush off the clods but only smeared them around. "Only the truly depraved laugh at other people's misfortunes."

"Sometimes if you don't laugh, you cry."

He glanced up sharply, then smiled. "Glad I could provide you with some light entertainment."

"Want to get back up?" she asked, hoping he'd say no.

"Thanks, but I'll walk from here."

"Suit yourself." And no, she was not disappointed. Well, maybe a little. But that must only be because she truly was depraved.

All levity evaporated as they walked up the slope of the ridge. At the highest point they emerged from the untouched forest and into a stand of trees with charred trunks and bare limbs, stark reminders of the firestorm that had swept through nearly a year ago. Another fifty yards and even these blackened ghosts petered out. Then there were no trees at all. The mountain was a wasteland as far as the eye could see, down into the valley and halfway up the other side of the hill.

Adam's steps slowed, then stopped altogether. "Holy shit."

"No kidding," Hayley said grimly.

He glanced back to the untouched forest a mere hundred meters away. "So how did it happen? How did your property get razed and mine escaped with barely a singed leaf?"

"A fluke of nature."

"Tell me more. All I know is that the wind pushed the fire up the mountain."

"That's right." Hayley didn't like to relive that day. She actively tried to cast it out of her mind, but the stark landscape never let her forget. "The wind was blowing steadily from the northwest, seventy miles an hour and gusting up to ninety, ninety-five. Leif led his firefighting crew down the slope below Timbertop, clearing and back-burning to create a firebreak. During the afternoon the wind veered around to the northeast." *Just as the Bureau of Meteorology had predicted.* "It pushed the fire in the other direction." She swallowed. "Toward the volunteer fire crew."

For a moment she couldn't speak and the taut silence stretched.

"It's okay," Adam said. "You don't have to talk about it. I get the picture."

"The fire roared up the mountain like a freaking freight train," Hayley said, barely hearing him. "Jumping the break and taking out everything in its path.... Including Leif and his crew. They…they were dead before they could retreat."

Her halting recitation of the details stalled on the choking pain in her chest. *Breathe, just breathe.* After a few seconds she was able to go on. "The fire continued to advance this way. There was no one to stop it. My house and outbuildings were burned to the ground. Leif sent me a message about an hour before he died. He couldn't get out. He wanted me to head into town and stay with his parents. But I couldn't leave the horses."

Why hadn't Leif listened to the weather bureau and positioned the firebreak on their side of the ridge? Was it because the fire was heading toward Timbertop and he wanted to help their neighbor? It had been a judgment call. A fatal one.

Damn Leif. Always had to be the hero.

"Where were you when the fire went through?" Adam asked.

She turned her gaze toward him but she wasn't seeing him, she was seeing the black sky and hearing the unearthly roar of the fire, breathing in the choking smoke. "I was in the dam. Shane and I got in the dam, right out in the middle where I had to stand on my tiptoes. Shane kept wanting to swim to shore. I had to hold him in my arms. Hold him up so he could breathe. There were only three inches of air between the surface of the water and the smoke. We stayed in the dam for four hours."

Adam swore. "That must have been awful."

"I was lucky." He looked surprised. She went on fiercely, "When people commiserate and tell me how sorry they are for me, losing everything, I say, no, I was the lucky one. I'm still alive." Whenever she started feeling sorry for herself she thought about Leif, caught out in the bush with no protection from the inferno racing up the mountainside.

She had the garage to live in and her horses had shelter, albeit temporary. One day, the house and stables would be rebuilt. She would have a home again.

She started Bo walking again, and soon they came to the paddock. It was black and barren all the way from here to the garage, three hundred yards on the right.

She and Adam didn't speak again until they

approached the horse shelter, a three-sided corrugated iron box. Major emerged and whickered to Bo.

"What are your horses grazing on?" Adam said.
"There's not a blade of grass in there."

"I buy timothy-hay and have it trucked in." It was
expensive, but she was used to most of her income
going toward the horses. Some days the road back
to solvency and a normal life seemed like a mountain she was climbing, but there was only one way
she could go—onward.

She slid off Bo, removed his bridle and replaced
it with a halter before letting him into the paddock.
She would brush him down later.

"Did the horses get into the dam as well?" Adam
asked.

"No. When the fire got close I opened the gate
and let them out. They ran around the yard for a
bit and then headed into the woods." She still had
nightmares about hearing their screams as burning shards of the barn's corrugated iron roof rained
down. One had struck Asha in the neck.... "Four of
the five I have left came home one by one over the
next week. Blaze was found months later. The rest
I never saw again."

"Do you think they're alive somewhere out there?"

She cut him a scathing glance. "I'm too old to believe in fairy tales and happily-ever-afters." She'd
tried to find her horses. For weeks she'd gone up to

the high country, scouting the alpine meadows and talking to the ranchers and park rangers.

"Sorry," he murmured.

There was that pity again. Pity and charity. They had to be the two worst virtues in the world. They reminded the person on the receiving end that they needed help. That they were victims.

Brushing past him, she strode toward the garage at a fast clip with Shane at her heels. "I'll get you that sugar."

He caught up with her halfway across the yard. "Why don't you sell up and move?"

"If you have to ask that, you don't know me," she said, opening the unlocked garage door.

"No, I don't. That's why I'm asking."

She tossed her hat on a hook beside the door and toed off her boots. She could give him an impassioned speech about how she grew up riding in these woods, how Hope Mountain was in her blood, how she couldn't conceive of ever living anywhere else. But she didn't know him, so she wasn't about to tell him her innermost thoughts and feelings. They wouldn't mean anything to him. So she shrugged it off. "Guess I'm just stubborn that way."

Adam stood in the doorway, blatantly cataloguing the sparse furnishings. The shabby recliner, the old tea crate she used as a coffee table, the Indian bedspread she'd hung on the wall for color, the battered two-seater table and chairs and her pull-out couch with the extra blanket folded over the arm. If he said something cheerful about how cozy it was she just might pull out her rifle and shoot him.

"My paddocks are full of long grass," he said instead. "You're welcome to bring your horses over to graze."

"That's kind of you, but I can fend for myself." She washed her hands, then rummaged through the cardboard box that held her supply of canned goods and packets of dry food.

She felt his skepticism and ignored it. She didn't want to be beholden to the man who'd indirectly been responsible for her husband's death.

"You'd be doing me a favor," Adam went on. "I'm trying to clear away excess fuel and make Timbertop fire-safe. The grass is way overgrown. If you don't bring your horses over I'll have to get a flock of sheep."

She got an image of him herding sheep in his fancy suit and polished leather shoes. Hiding a smile, she said, "That much feed is worth a lot of sugar."

"I'm not offering it as some sort of repayment for services rendered, either now or in the future. I thought the creed of the bush was that everyone helped each other."

She straightened, holding two partial bags of sugar, one white and one brown. "True, but you're not part of the local community. You don't have any responsibility to help."

"My daughter lives here."

So she did. And Adam had dumped four hundred dollars into the community center fund. Hayley felt ashamed. Why was she pushing him away so hard? Where was her tolerance? Another creed of the bush was "live and let live."

Maybe he didn't want anything from her. Maybe he was simply being generous because he could afford to be. And maybe that was why she was so prickly. An urbane, sophisticated man like Adam Banks couldn't possibly be interested in a scruffy mountain girl like her except as a charity case. Not that she was ashamed of who she was. No, sir. If anything, she felt sorry for him because city folks were soft. Put Adam Banks in the bush without his smartphone and he would be lost within minutes.

But he had a point about reducing fuel. Come summer that grass would dry out and be tinder.

She took the plastic container from him and emptied the contents of both bags into it. Combined there was about three quarters of a cup of sugar. There went her nightly hot chocolate, one of her few indulgences. "I hope that's enough."

"Perfect." His gaze flickered at the realization that he'd taken the last of her sugar.

Before he could do something stupid like try to give it back, she said, "Well, you've just done me a favor. I've been trying to use this up so I could go on a sugar-free diet. That stuff will kill you. Better you than me."

"Come for dinner," he said suddenly. "Summer would be glad to have company other than her father for a change."

Lamb chops with barbecue sauce. Probably mashed potatoes and green beans or salad. For a moment she was so tempted she actually salivated. If she stayed home she'd be dining on canned tuna and toast. Or lentil soup, which was tasty enough and nutritious but uninspiring after the third or fourth night in a row. "Thanks, but I can't."

He waited for more. She shrugged and smiled but didn't utter another word. She didn't owe him an explanation. And frankly, she didn't have one. She was no martyr. If anyone else had invited her for dinner she would've gone in a heartbeat, just for the company. But Adam, well…

He looked pretty tasty himself.…

Admit it, you're attracted to him.

No, no way. She was *not* attracted to him.

He was generous and kind. *And hot, don't forget hot.* But that didn't mean she was attracted. He didn't belong here and he couldn't wait to get away. He'd said so himself.

Leif hadn't been gone a year. Getting involved with the man whose property he'd died defending when that man hadn't even bothered to show up would feel like betrayal. She and Leif hadn't made love for six months before he died, but so what? Despite their problems, she'd been loyal in life and she was loyal in death. And what would Molly and Rolf think if she started seeing someone so soon? Hurt and disappointment wouldn't begin to describe their reaction.

It was only dinner, not a date. Don't overreact, she told herself.

Finally Adam raised his hands in surrender. "Okay. If you change your mind you know where we live."

She was relieved he didn't press her to come. The fact that he didn't proved he was only being polite. "I'll drive you back."

"You don't need to," he began, then stopped as he realized the alternative was her doubling him again on Bo. Heat flared in his eyes, kindling an answering response from her. For a moment they just stared at each other. She recalled the press of his thighs against hers, the feel of his arm around her waist, his legs tightening around her butt.

Then he shook his head. "Actually, I'd appreciate a lift. Next time I won't wander into the woods so impetuously."

Nope, he clearly didn't want a repeat of that kind of togetherness any more than she did. Hayley released her breath.

He held up the container of sugar. "Thanks for this. I owe you."

She gave him a tight smile and grabbed her truck keys. What he owed her, he couldn't begin to repay.

CHAPTER THREE

"Thanks anyway," Adam said, and scratched the last name off his list of potential counselors. "You have my number if you get an opening."

He tried Diane for the fifth or sixth time. After leaving another message he pushed back from the desk in his study and went upstairs to knock on his daughter's door. "Summer?"

"Yeah?" she said in a distracted, muffled voice.

He peeked in and found her lying on her stomach in bed, still in her pajamas, her red hair spilling across her shoulders. She didn't even look up as her fingers flew over her phone, texting.

"Hey, kiddo. What do you call a lazy baby kangaroo?"

"Dunno."

"A pouch potato."

She groaned. "You need new material."

"Can you give me a hand outside?"

"I'm talking to Zoe."

"Say goodbye for now. I want to move the woodpile away from the house." And he figured Summer would benefit if she got outside and did something physical instead of moping around indoors.

"That's dumb. We'll just have to walk farther to get wood for the fireplace during winter."

He hoped she wouldn't be living here next winter, but he wasn't foolish enough to mention that. "It's a hazard in the event of a bushfire. Come on."

"Do I have to?"

"Yes, you need to do something to earn the exorbitant allowance your mother gives you."

"Hey, I do the dishes and clean my own room."

"Wear sturdy shoes or boots and get yourself a pair of gloves from the toolshed."

"Oh, all right." With a heavy sigh she put down her phone.

Adam had moved two wheelbarrow loads from the house to a new woodpile he'd started beside the barn by the time Summer shuffled outdoors in Ugg boots and a hoodie. She waited with her hands tucked into her sleeves for him to trundle back.

He began loading wood, sparing a brief nostalgic thought for the old days when she'd been eager to help Daddy. "Come on, then."

Slowly she pulled the gloves out of her back pocket and put them on. Then she picked up a chunk of firewood by her fingertips and dropped it into the wheelbarrow. "There are probably spiders in the woodpile. Maybe even snakes."

"They're more afraid of you than you are of them."

"I didn't believe that when I was five and I don't believe it now."

He chuckled, and her sullen expression cracked into a reluctant smile. "Fair enough. If you see a snake or spider you're allowed to run screaming. Until then, pick up the wood like you mean it."

"I don't think it's something you can 'mean.' You just do it."

"Ever heard of mindfulness?" He wasn't even sure where he'd picked up that expression. Probably from overhearing the women in the office talking. But it made sense. He'd done chores on his grandfather's farm when he was a kid. He'd forgotten how enjoyable it was to focus on a simple, repetitive act like hauling wood. Doing reps on a weight machine at the gym just wasn't the same.

"Mom's the yoga person in the family." Summer tossed three chunks of wood on the pile so hard one bounced out of the barrow. "Oh, I forgot. We're not a family anymore."

Twelve months had passed since the divorce. Adam had hoped Summer wouldn't be feeling so raw by now. They'd never really had much opportunity to talk about his and Diane's breakup. Since they'd moved out, his access visits with Summer had been movie-and-dinner combos with stilted conversation.

He picked up the fallen piece of wood and replaced

it on the pile. "Sounds like you're still pretty angry about that."

She shrugged. "Whatever. It doesn't matter."

"How you feel matters to me."

She stared at him, unsmiling. "What're you going to do about it?"

He'd never felt so helpless. And that made him angry. "Not much I can do, I guess. The marriage is over and we all have to deal with it."

"Why didn't you and Mom try marriage counseling?"

"It wouldn't have done any good." He'd promised himself he would never say anything bad to Summer about her mother, but it was so tempting to set the record straight. Diane had been unfaithful and unrepentant. "Never mind."

"Yeah, that's right, brush off any talk of her. If you hadn't been working all the time, maybe Mom wouldn't have—"

"Maybe she wouldn't have what?"

Summer looked away. "Nothing."

Wouldn't have had an affair? Was that what she'd been about to say? Adam picked up the wheelbarrow even though it was only half-full and pushed it quickly across the grass to the barn. Damn Diane for not being more discreet. It was bad enough that she'd cheated on him but to be so careless, so sleazy, around their daughter...

He didn't know who her lover was and he didn't

want to. It didn't matter. But he'd found evidence a few times when he'd come up for the weekend. Secretive phone calls, disappearing for unexplained long periods, an air of excitement that he knew darn well wasn't about him.

"Hey, Dad, wait." Summer caught up with him, panting from running. "Sorry."

"You've got nothing to be sorry for." He tipped the barrow and the wood tumbled out. Reaching for a piece, he wedged it into position on the top layer. "Place it bark-up and point-down, see?"

He simply couldn't talk to Summer about the five-hundred-pound gorilla in the room. It was possible she didn't know about her mother's lover. Maybe all Summer had meant was that if he'd been around more her mother wouldn't have left their city apartment. Maybe she simply wished he'd cared enough to ask Diane to stay....

As angry as he was with Diane, he *was* guilty of working long hours. He didn't want Summer to have bad feelings about her parents—or at least no more than any normal teenager. He'd known when Diane moved to Timbertop and he stayed in the city that their marriage was over. He wasn't concerned about her affair for his sake, only for his daughter's.

"I am though. Sorry." Summer kicked at the ground and dislodged a pebble. "I've caused you both problems."

"The divorce wasn't your fault." He'd said it a million times before but he kept saying it because he wasn't convinced she believed it. Otherwise, why else had she gone off the rails? He didn't think it could be only about Bailey.

"I know."

"Do you?" He searched her face.

"Yeah. 'Course." She lifted her chin, cocky and defiant. "It's never the kid's fault. That's in all the books and movies. It's the grown-ups that mess things up."

He gave her a wry smile that was more of a grimace. "And kids never do."

She dropped her gaze as a tinge of pink crept over her cheeks. "I said I was sorry."

"Oh, Summer." He pulled her into a clumsy hug. She hesitated, then her arms circled his waist. "I just wish I knew what was bothering you so much."

"Nothing's bugging me." She pulled out of his embrace and turned away, dashing her gloved hand across her eyes. "I'll push the wheelbarrow."

Adam let her have a few minutes by herself and stacked the wood he'd just dropped. When he got back to the woodpile she seemed calmer, if no more talkative.

"I haven't been able to find a therapist nearby," he said, trying to sound matter-of-fact. He never knew what would set her off. "On Monday I'll start phoning around in Shepparton and Healesville."

"It would take forever to drive there and back."

That was a slight exaggeration but it would be a hassle. "It's either that or move into the city."

"No." She redoubled her time moving logs.

They loaded wood in silence for a moment. When the barrow was full, Adam paused and said gently, "If you talked to me, maybe you wouldn't need to see a therapist. I'm on your side, Summer. Can't you tell me what's bothering you?"

Her face looked as if it was about to crumble and he started to reach for her, to give her another hug. Surely now she would tell him what was worrying her. Then she drew in a breath and her features hardened into a brittle mask that was so unlike his young daughter he instinctively took a step back.

"For the last time," she yelled, her hands clenched at the end of rigid arms. "There's nothing wrong and I'm not hiding anything."

She stomped back inside the house, slamming the kitchen door behind her so hard the windowpane over the sink rattled.

Adam stared after her, feeling sick. Her intensity, her fury—or was it fear?—was downright frightening. Something was seriously wrong. And she *was* hiding something.

HAYLEY EMERGED FROM the woodland trail on Major and dismounted in her yard. She tied him to the fence, removed his saddle and slung it over the top rail. Then she brushed him down, wiping away flecks of sweat and removing tiny burrs. Hopefully with better weather coming she would get some trail rides. It wasn't easy exercising all the horses by herself.

Hayley bet Summer Banks would love to ride. She had nothing against the girl and would happily have her help exercise the horses. But how did she ask when she'd turned down Adam's request so brusquely?

"All right, big fella. You'll do," she said, giving Major a scratch behind his golden ears. She exchanged his bridle for a halter and put him back in the paddock with the others.

Carrying the saddle over one arm, Hayley headed back to the garage, Shane at her heels. As she went through the door her phone rang. She placed the saddle on its wooden peg and pulled her phone out of her breast pocket, hoping the caller wouldn't be her friend Jacinta or her mother or anyone who wanted a long chat. She barely had time for a quick lunch before her therapy session with Dave, a retired man in his sixties.

"Hello?" she said.

"Hayley, hi." It was Ian Young, the director of the Horses for Hope program. Based in Shepparton, he coordinated the funding for her and two other horse therapists in the state.

"Hey, Ian." She dropped the saddle next to the door and shrugged out of her jacket. "I hope you're not calling because you have another rescue horse for me. I can barely afford to feed the ones I've got."

She was only joking, as Ian well knew. If another horse needed saving she would be the first to put her hand up. However, she was down to her last ten bales of timothy and didn't have a clue where the next lot was coming from. She probably shouldn't have been too proud to take Adam's offer of grazing. If it had been anyone else she would have jumped at it.

"No, it's not another rescue horse. But how's Bo doing?" Ian sounded down and distracted, unlike his usual upbeat self.

"Excellent. The mange has cleared up and his new coat is coming in nice and glossy. Drop in next time you're up this way. Are you coming to the bushfire memorial next month?"

"I'll be there." His parents had lost their home and Ian had lost a good friend. The bushfires had touched so many lives. Everyone had lost someone, it seemed, or knew someone who had. "Hayley," he began haltingly, "I'm sorry, but…"

"What?" A chill settled over her shoulders. Instinctively she knew he was no longer talking about the memorial service.

He cleared his throat. "The program is finished."

"I beg your pardon?" She walked over to the couch and sank onto a lumpy cushion.

"The government cut our funding."

For about two seconds she couldn't move, couldn't

speak. Then she got to her feet but she didn't know where to go. "In the middle of the program? They can't do that."

"They did. Nearly a year has passed. People have forgotten. The state wants the money for something else, a new highway or a railway crossing. Who knows?" Ian sounded defeated.

"What about my clients? What am I going to tell them? These people need help."

"They can still access social services for counseling."

"They'll be shunted onto a waiting list." Needing air, she opened the door and wrapped an arm around her waist against the chill. "If they can see a regular therapist why can't they see a horse therapist?"

"You know what it's like, Hayley. The bean counters move their columns of numbers from one ledger sheet to another and suddenly they're able to balance the budget even though no more money has come into the coffers. It's sleight of hand."

"But why pick on Horses for Hope?"

"According to the official letter I got it's been deemed 'nonessential.'"

"Nonessential?" Hayley repeated forcefully. "Tell that to Dave Green, who suffers survivor's guilt because he couldn't save his wife and granddaughter. Working with Bo has given him a reason to go on living." Hayley went outside to pace the muddy yard ringed by the charred skeletons of trees. "Or Samantha, who spent six hours huddled in her car while the forest blazed around her. Her anxiety attacks make it impossible for her to work."

"Hayley, calm down," Ian said. "You don't need to convince me of the program's importance."

"Who do I talk to in the government to restore funding? Tell me and I'll be down there in Melbourne tomorrow on the steps of Parliament."

"It won't do any good. I've talked to them all. There's simply no money left."

"Are there any other agencies that might fund the program? I could get testimonials from my clients."

"I'm pursuing other options. So far nothing has panned out. I'll keep you updated."

"So how long can I continue before I have to pull the plug? Next week, the week after?" Ian didn't reply and his silence told the story. "Oh, you're kidding me. Right away?"

"I'm sorry," he said again. "We've been operating in the red for the past month, waiting for the next check. Now we find out it's not coming. You need to call your clients now, today, and let them know there won't be any more sessions."

Hayley tried to catch her breath around the tightness in her chest. As well as her concern for her clients, there was the impact on her. Her primary livelihood was over as of this minute. Trail rides were few and far between, partly because it was too early in the season and partly because so many of the trails had been burned out.

And then there were her horses to think about. What would happen if she couldn't afford to feed them? If she had to sell one or two, which would she choose? She loved them all. Asha was her own special horse, though she couldn't ride her without difficulty. But how could she get rid of her when she'd been through so much? And Bo and Blaze, Sergeant and Major. All were so dear to her.

"I have to go," Ian said heavily. "I've still got a few phone calls to make."

Hayley said goodbye. She needed to call Dave. He was due here in half an hour. She couldn't make herself do it, couldn't bear to hear the sound of his disappointment.

Listlessly she picked up her mail. There was a notice from the electric company, warning if she didn't pay her bill within two days she'd be cut off. Wonderful. The icing on the cake.

She glanced at the clock. She couldn't put this call off any longer. Feeling sick in her heart, she reached for the phone and dialed. "Hey, Dave."

"Not late, am I?" he said gruffly. "I was just about to head out to your place."

Hayley pressed the phone to her chest and tried to pull in enough breath to continue.

"Hayley, you there?"

"I'm afraid I have bad news...."

Adam dropped Summer off at school and continued on toward the main street shopping district, passing empty blackened lots interspersed with intact houses. He slowed as he passed a charred sign reading Hope Mountain Community Center. In the cleared area a large tent had been erected where donated goods were being redistributed.

He drove on, ruminating over how huge the loss of the community center was to a small town. His grandparents had relied on theirs as a hub of local social life. His grandmother in particular had spent a lot of time there with the Country Women's Association.

His phone rang as he pulled into the grocery store parking lot. He glanced at the caller ID. Diane, finally. "I see you got my messages. Thanks for calling back."

"Sorry I've taken so long," Diane said, sounding harried. "I'm at the hospital day and night."

"How's your mother doing?"

"Not great. They're trying to stabilize her blood pressure and sugar levels before they operate. It's now going to be a quadruple bypass rather than a triple."

"That's rough. Give her my best. I guess a box of her favorite chocolates wouldn't be a good gift just now."

Diane gave a weary laugh. "No, and no flowers,

either. She's developed hay fever from all the bouquets in her room."

"I've been trying to call you to talk about Summer."

"Is she still going on about getting another horse? I told her you'd have to approve it."

"She wants a horse, yes, but that's not the problem. She was caught shoplifting. She stole a pair of earrings from the local gift shop. Luckily the owner didn't press charges, but this is serious."

"She's going through a phase. All kids do at that age."

"Not all kids shoplift. She's got real problems that need to be addressed. I can't understand why you haven't talked to me about her before this. Apparently she's been in counseling at school for months."

"You would have gotten a letter, same as I did."

"I'm not absolving myself of responsibility. But hell, Diane, this is our child. Regardless of our own issues we have to do what's right for her."

"What do you suggest?" A note of tension crept into Diane's voice. "I've got all I can handle taking care of my mother. There's not much I can do for Summer from Sydney."

"I don't expect you to do anything. I just wanted to let you know what's going on. I'm trying to find her a counselor outside school." He paused, searching for tactful wording. "Is there anything else should know about, anything going on in your life that might be upsetting Summer?"

"No."

"Are you sure?" He'd never asked for details of her affair and he didn't want them now—unless they were relevant to Summer. "That person you were seeing—"

"That's over," Diane said sharply. "And it had nothing to do with Summer. She's fine, just moody like all teenagers. It's hormones."

"She won't talk to me."

"She barely speaks to me, either. Don't worry about it. Listen, I've gotta go. The cardiologist is coming to see Mom and I want to talk to him about the operation."

"Wait a sec. Do you have any idea when you'll be back?"

"Recovery from this kind of operation is measured in months. Hopefully by Christmas, but I don't know. I'm seriously considering moving back to Sydney to be closer to Mom."

"That's the impression I got before you left. How would you feel about putting the house up for sale once school's out? I'd just as soon get rid of it. The fire danger makes this an unsafe area."

"Hope Mountain's okay once you get used to how small it is. But do what you like. I'm over the place."

She'd bought the property on a whim and abandoned it without a second thought. Even though her change of heart fell in line with his plans, he asked, "What about Summer? She seems attached to the town, and she's desperate for a horse."

"She'll love Sydney, too. Once she sees the beaches she'll forget all about horses. Oh, there's the cardiologist. Say hi to Summer for me and tell her I'll call her soon."

Adam said goodbye and hung up. He doubted Summer would forget her love for horses that quickly. Diane had been less than helpful where their daughter was concerned, but he supposed she was preoccupied with her mother. At least he had her blessing to sell the property.

He went inside the grocery store and pushed his shopping cart around the aisles, stocking up on fresh fruit and vegetables and consulting his list for staples they were low on. He wasn't much of a cook but he would have to learn. Man could not live on Diet Delight alone.

He threw in a couple of frozen pizzas and some chips to keep Summer happy and on impulse added extra items to drop off at the distribution center. At last he proceeded to the checkout.

"Hey, how are you goin'?" The thirty-something woman at the till had a high black ponytail, bright red lipstick and a cheerful smile. Her name tag read Belinda.

"Not bad, Belinda. Yourself?" He unloaded the

groceries methodically, putting the cold things together, next the cans and finally the fruit and vegetables.

"Oh, I'm okay. Or I will be once I sell my house and blow this crazy pop stand."

Ah, someone else besides him who didn't go into raptures about Hope Mountain. "You don't like it here?"

She snorted. "It's the pits. What's so beautiful about burned-up mountains?"

"The fire danger's a real concern," Adam agreed.

"You're telling me. Every house on our block went up in flames except ours. My husband went out and bought ten lottery tickets. Me, I called Mort."

"Who's Mort?"

"The real estate agent. Thank God his office didn't burn. I listed our house first thing. Bob, my husband, thinks I'm a coward. I told him, 'You can stay but I'm getting out.'"

Diane had been working part-time for a local Realtor before she'd gone to Sydney—Mort must have been her boss. "Well, Belinda, I happen to think you're smart for not wanting to live in a fire-prone region."

"Thanks very much. You're pretty smart yourself." She scanned a box of cereal and bagged it. "Are you a local? I figure you must be with all the groceries you're buying. No one buys four bags of sugar for the weekend. But if you don't know Mort…" She trailed off, waiting for an explanation.

"I live here for now."

"How long are you staying?" Belinda seemed to have all the time in the world to chat. And apparently she thought he did, too.

"I don't know. Four or five months. Six tops."

She swung the filled bag over to the loading area and started on the next. "I'd say that makes you a local."

"No, really, I'm just passing through."

She cocked her head with an infectious grin. "But slowly."

He smiled back at her. "Yeah, slowly."

Too slowly for his liking. In business he was the hare, not the tortoise. He moved quickly and decisively. Now he had to put on the brakes and wait for Summer to heal.

Belinda cracked her gum. "So what's the deal, are you trying to sell your house and not getting any bites? Join the club."

Now she had his attention. "Are that many people leaving? There seems to be a lot of building going on."

"People are either determined to stay or determined to leave. It all depends. So what's holding you up?"

"It's complicated." Did people really spill their guts to complete strangers in this town? He never had conversations like this with the guy at the convenience store below his apartment building. He liked Belinda all right, but he wasn't sure he wanted a heart-to-heart with her.

"Hold your cards close to your chest, don't you? That's okay. We all got personal shit going on. I won't even ask you about all the sugar."

Adam smiled. "Two bags for me. Two for a friend."

"Sweet on her, are ya?" Belinda winked at him.

He chuckled. Not likely.

"If you ask me," Belinda went on. "The government should buy us all out and bulldoze the town. Everyone should move someplace where the firefighters have a chance to put out the fire and where residents can get out safely. There's only one road in and out of this place. It was cut off in three spots. People were trapped."

"But there were warnings of extreme fire danger," Adam said. "People should have left earlier."

"Maybe so. But folks have a legal right to stay and defend their property." Belinda stacked the last grocery bag in the cart and rang up the total. "That'll be one hundred and fifty-five dollars and twenty-eight cents. Any cash out?"

Adam handed over his credit card, then checked his wallet. He had only sixty dollars on him. "I'll have an extra hundred, thanks."

She rang it through and passed him two fifty-dollar bills. Adam dropped them both into the bushfire rebuilding donation jar on the counter. "I can't believe the town is relying on spare change to fund a new community center."

"There's a long list of stuff that needs replacing. The primary school, the maternal health clinic, half the police station…" Belinda shrugged. "It's all going to take time, I guess. They have to start somewhere."

He threw in another fifty from his wallet, leaving himself ten dollars.

Belinda's eyes widened. "Thanks, er…"

"Adam." He gathered up his bags. "Nice to meet you, Belinda."

"Same." She grinned widely. "See you around."

"I hope not." When she looked surprised, he added, "If I don't, it'll mean you sold your house and got out."

Belinda laughed and cocked a finger at him. "Gotcha."

Adam piled the groceries into the car and continued on down the main street, brooding on the state of the town. Nine months on there was still the faint whiff of burned wood in the air. Or was that his imagination?

He wasn't a coward, dammit. People like him and Belinda were being sensible. Why didn't more townsfolk cut their losses and start new lives elsewhere?

Spying the real estate office, he parked out front and went inside.

A balding man with a perfectly pressed dark suit and a white smile rose from behind a desk, buttoning his jacket. He held out a hand. "G'day. Mort Brooks. What can I do for you?"

"Adam Banks. I live out of town at a place called Timbertop. Diane Banks is my ex-wife. I believe she used to work for you."

"Yes, nice to meet you," Mort said. "I was sorry Diane had to leave. Although business isn't exactly booming so it's probably for the best. How is she? How's her mother doing?"

Seemed like the whole town knew your business if you spent any amount of time in the place. To be fair, Mort genuinely seemed to care, and that was kind of nice. "As well as can be expected. She hasn't had the operation yet."

"If you talk to her, tell her I said hey."

"Will do." Adam glanced around the empty office. "Diane doesn't plan on returning to Hope Mountain, and I don't intend to stay long. I'd like to have Timbertop valued and put up for sale this summer."

Mort's smile dimmed. "You and a hundred other folks in the area. Nothing's moving in this glutted market."

"My place isn't burned. It's intact. Great location with views, horse stables and paddocks, five acres…" He trailed away as Mort, looking more like a funeral director than a Realtor, shook his head glumly.

"I'll value it for you and I can put it on the market, no problem. But fantastic properties are going at bargain-basement prices. The question you have to ask yourself is—are you willing to take a bath on the place?"

Adam thought about it for all of five seconds. "I'll take whatever I can get for it. It'll be worthless to me if it burns to the ground."

"Is it insured?" Mort asked.

"Yes, of course, but I wouldn't rebuild." He dragged a hand over the back of his neck. What if he was stuck with this white elephant? It wouldn't hurt him too much financially, but the house was part of Diane's divorce settlement and she would need another place to live. Morally speaking, he didn't owe her another house, but he still felt responsible for her. And of course he was responsible for Summer.

Unless Summer could be persuaded to live with him.

He hadn't realized until he'd come back to Hope Mountain just how much he missed his daughter and how nice it was to have her around, even in her black moods. They'd grown estranged over the past year and he wanted to reconnect. If she moved to Sydney with Diane he'd have an even harder time seeing her.

But she would stay with him if he kept Timber-top....

No way. The trees hadn't suddenly grown asbestos bark.

Mort made a note in his day planner, a big book open on the desk. "I'll come out next week and take photos. You never know. There are people picking up properties simply because they're cheap. And there's talk of a government buy-back scheme. You might qualify."

"Can you time your visit during school hours? My daughter doesn't know yet that I'm planning to sell."

"No worries."

No worries. He wished. Not telling Summer his intentions felt like a betrayal. Would she want to live with him after he sold the home she loved—even if he was doing it for her own good?

He drove back through town past the many construction sites. The townsfolk determined to rebuild were misguided. It was like building on a flood plain or in an earthquake zone. Just plain dumb. And yet people did it over and over again—that was how strongly they felt about a certain geographical location they called home.

A tiny part of him admired their resolve. Maybe he just wished he had a place that felt like home no matter what. Having a father in the armed forces, he'd been uprooted as a child more times than he could remember. The closest he'd come to a permanent home had been his grandparents' farm. He and his brothers had spent most summers there with his mom while his dad was serving overseas.

Later, after he'd married, he and Diane had owned two houses in the city. Diane was into decorating, and they'd felt more like showrooms than homes. Give him a lived-in look any day. His apartment… well, he didn't spend enough time there for it to look lived in.

Someday he would build his dream home. He'd designed it in his head many times, changing small details as he refined his ideas. It would be by the ocean, with a special place for him to put his drafting table. Mostly he worked on computers, but he still liked drawing by hand. The house would be filled with light from floor-to-ceiling windows. Bifold doors would open the house to the elements and let out onto a huge deck looking onto the water.

He pulled into the parking lot next to the distribution center and unloaded two bags of groceries. He carried them through the group of people milling in front of the counter. One half of the tent was given over to clothing, kitchenware and smaller items like books and even CDs. In the back were the major appliances. A man was trying to wrestle a fridge off a dolly and into place next to a washing machine.

Adam caught the eye of a fifty-something woman who was volunteering behind the counter. "Where do I put these?" he asked.

"I'll take them." She peered into one of the bags. "Meat, eggs, cheese… Fantastic. Thank you so much, er…?"

"Adam Banks. No big deal." He nodded at the man with the fridge. "He looks like he could use a hand. Should I?"

"Oh, please do. There's a whole truckload of heavy appliances to bring in. People have been so generous that some days we don't have enough manpower to sort and store stuff."

Adam thought of his own groceries growing warm in the trunk of his car. It wasn't a hot day. How long could it take to unload a truck? The milk and meat would keep for an hour. Too bad about the ice cream. "How do I get back there?"

HAYLEY PARKED HER truck in the main street, on the diagonal, outside Molly's Gift Shop Café. Shane sat up beside her in the passenger seat. He went everywhere with her, and she was especially glad of his moral support today. Sensing her discomfort, he put a paw on her leg and gave her a soulful look.

She ruffled the fur around his neck. "I'm okay, Shane. Just girding my loins, so to speak."

Working with horses was what she did—lessons, trail rides, therapy. Selling postcards and pouring coffee was a big step backward, to the days before she'd found a way to make a living working with horses and being outdoors.

Being in town wouldn't be so bad. At least there were the cheerful sounds of rebuilding going on. The clock tower in the middle of the main street had already been repaired and colorful petunias had been planted around its base. The pub on the corner was nearly ready to welcome locals back for counter meals and karaoke nights. It would be good for her to be around people more often.

"Hayley!" A petite brunette with shoulder-length curls rapped at her window. Jacinta, her best friend and the town librarian, motioned to her to roll down the window.

"What are you doing roaming the streets in the middle of the day?" Hayley got out of the truck and gave her friend a hug. As they moved to the sidewalk Shane bounded through the open door and sat at Hayley's heel. "Aren't you supposed to be at the library shushing someone?"

Jacinta laughed. "Between the resident poet holding forth every lunch hour and the book club ladies yakking, the place is pretty darn noisy."

"Guess it's a while since I've been to the library. I don't have much time to read these days."

"We haven't caught up in ages." Jacinta touched Hayley's shoulder and lowered her voice. "You okay? Your eyes are all puffy. You haven't been crying, have you?"

"Horses for Hope's funding got cut." Yesterday had been one long tear fest as she'd rung client after client, giving them the bad news. She'd told Dave she would treat him for free until funding came in from somewhere. He'd thanked her and refused, pointing out that she would need to get another job. She'd started to protest before realizing he was right.

She wasn't even going to mention to Jacinta that her electricity had been cut off, too—a day earlier than threatened. Bastards. Well, she'd lived without power for a month in the immediate aftermath of the fires. She could manage again. Which reminded her: she needed to buy candles.

"That's terrible. I'm so sorry." Jacinta hugged her again. "I could go for an early lunch if you want to talk."

"I'd love to, but I've got something I need to do."

Jacinta saw the direction of her gaze, to Molly's shop, and frowned. "You're not going to move in with Leif's folks?"

"No." She noted the quickly hidden relief on her friend's face. "Why don't you like Molly and Rolf? They're wonderful. I'm closer to them than to my own parents."

"They're great. I have nothing against them. It's just that…" Jacinta rubbed Hayley's arm soothingly. "I know you're still grieving and everything, but I'd like to see you move on at some point."

"I am moving on, really. Molly and Rolf are friends, not just my in-laws. I don't know what I'd do without them."

"Sure, but they keep you in the past."

"I'm not going to cut them off." They were practically the only people she saw regularly these days.

"Hey, I have a date on Friday with Jeremy, a pharmacist from Healesville. Do you want me to see if he has a friend?"

"Thanks, no. I'm good."

"Hayley, you never get out anymore," Jacinta accused. "You're in danger of turning into a crazy horse lady, sitting home cleaning your bridles and knitting pullovers."

"I'll call you soon." Hayley eased away from Jacinta, toward the Gift Shop Café. "We'll get drunk and dance with cowboys."

Grinning, Jacinta pointed a finger. "One of these days we are *so* going to do that."

Dancing with cowboys in bars had been a joke between them since high school. Jacinta was an academic type and would sooner ride a bucking bronco than date a cowboy. And Hayley had been with Leif since graduation. Party girls they were not. But they'd never worried about it, being content with their lives. Now, as they closed in on their mid-thirties and Jacinta was still single and Hayley newly so, the joke seemed a tad less funny.

Hayley waved goodbye, then braced herself to go inside. She couldn't dwell on the past. She had to look to the future. She was alive and healthy and determined to write her own story, not give up or blame fate for her misfortune. And how could she complain when she had a job she could just walk into for the asking?

"Sit, Shane." The dog sat obediently. "Stay."

Hayley took a deep breath and entered, setting the bell over the door jangling. To the right was the café with a meal counter, tables along the window and a small kitchen out the back. On the opposite side was the gift shop selling local handicrafts, paintings and Australiana. The place was empty except for Molly, who was behind the counter putting price stickers on koala key rings.

Molly glanced up at the bell and her round face brightened. "'Morning, Hayley. So nice of you to stop by."

Hayley returned her mother-in-law's warm smile. Truly, she had more blessings to count than things to complain about. "I'd like to accept your offer of a job, after all."

"Oh, that's wonderful!" Molly leaned over the counter and gave her a hug, scattering the key rings.

They got coffee and sat in the café and talked about the job. Molly was terrific, telling Hayley she could have as many or as few hours as she wanted, making Hayley wonder if she really needed help or if this was a form of charity. But she couldn't afford to be proud, so together they worked out a schedule that suited both of them.

"It's a darn shame about the Horses for Hope program," Molly said for the twentieth time, as Hayley prepared to leave.

"It is what it is." Hayley shrugged. "Nothing I can do about it." She'd racked her brain all night on possible sources of funding and had come up with nothing but a headache. "Thanks again. I'll see you Wednesday morning."

Molly walked her to the door. "I'm so glad we'll get to spend more time together. Ever since Leif… Well, it isn't the same without you around. At least with you, Rolf and I can talk about our boy and remember all the good times we had."

"Yeah." Hayley's smile faltered. Maybe Jacinta had a point. Sometimes with Molly and Rolf, she felt as though she was living in the past. She'd loved Leif and wanted to honor his memory, but some memories hurt.

Occasionally, in the morning before she was fully awake, she would forget what had happened and reach for him only to find the other side of the bed cold and bare. She'd open her eyes and see the roller door and the tools hanging on the walls, and reality would crash in on her. All that kept her going some days was her and Leif's dream of building a full-time dude ranch. She loved the horse therapy, but she'd held that other dream so long it would feel like failure if she didn't carry it out.

"Stay for lunch?" Molly said. "I made Thai green curry for today's special."

"Tempting, but I can't. I've got another stop to make this afternoon." If she wanted to keep her dream alive, she had to swallow her pride and take care of her horses. Simple as that. Desperate times called for desperate measures.

CHAPTER FOUR

HAYLEY PASSED HER own driveway and carried on to Timbertop. Entering Adam's green and leafy forest she felt like Dorothy leaving black-and-white Kansas and landing in the colorful land of Oz. The untouched bush was so beautiful it almost hurt.

She pulled up in front of the two-story log home and sat in her truck for a moment, taking in the house, barn, detached garage and guest cottage. A wave of resentment washed over her. Every building was intact, untouched by fire. The paddock was lush with tall grass, watered by winter rains. Then she remembered the paddock and barn were empty and her resentment was tempered by sadness for Summer's horse, Bailey.

She climbed down from the truck and headed toward the house before she chickened out. Shane jumped out and followed her, a perpetual shadow at her heels.

Adam came around the side of the barn, a brush cutter balanced in his gloved hands. His sleeves were rolled up, exposing muscled forearms. With a smear of dirt on his square jaw and his dark brown hair windblown, he looked less like an office worker and more like a man who tended the land. "Hayley, what brings you out?"

She removed her hat and pushed back the strands of hair that had come loose from her braid. "I'd like to take you up on your offer to graze my horses on your property. That is, if you meant it."

"I meant it. Better that than brush-cut the whole outdoors." His gaze roamed over her and she was glad she'd worn her blue blouse tucked into clean, relatively new jeans and her good cowboy boots. "What made you change your mind?"

"I…" she swallowed at the humiliation of coming cap in hand, then glanced at her hat, literally in her hands, and jammed it back on her head "…just hate to see good pasture go to waste. But I don't want something for nothing. I'll treat Summer in exchange for the feed."

"That would be great. But I insist on paying your usual fee. Did someone drop out of the Horses for Hope program?"

"I can do it, is all." What difference did it make what her reasons were? She didn't want to tell Adam all the stuff going on in her life and let him inside her head. She might start crying again.

"Okay," he said. "Well, bring your horses over anytime. When could you begin the therapy?"

"Soon. Tomorrow afternoon, even. I suggest

alternating a day on and a day off. Give both horse and girl a rest."

"Wonderful. Come inside and have a cup of coffee. We can tell Summer together, talk about what she can expect."

"There's not much to talk about. When I do talk, it'll just be with Summer." He looked taken aback at her blunt statement. Damn. Her nerves were on edge and she couldn't even manage common civility. "I work with horses, but it's still therapy," she explained, aiming for a nicer tone. "Everything that passes between Summer and me is confidential."

"I'm her father. I have a right to know what's going on." Adam hefted the brush cutter in one hand, freeing up the other. Not threatening but… assertive.

Hayley, trained in body language, noticed. She made a conscious effort not to take a step back. Things weren't going to be smooth between them. She needed to get used to that. And not care.

"You have a right to expect that I'll do the best job I can, and that I'll work with Summer until she no longer needs me. Beyond that, you'll know whatever Summer chooses to tell you."

He looked like he wanted to protest further but instead he shut his mouth and nodded. "Whatever you say. I'm grateful you've found time for her."

She had to admire his ability to be gracious under duress. "Well, see you tomorrow— Damn."

"What is it? Is there a problem?"

"No, not with Summer or the horses. I just forgot to buy candles when I was in town." She glanced at her watch. "If I hurry I might make it before the store shuts."

"Diane has a million tea lights and scented candles. You're welcome to them. Come inside."

She started to protest, then stopped. She wasn't going to quibble about a few candles at this stage. "Well, all right. Thanks." Hayley followed him up the shallow steps onto the veranda and into the kitchen, telling Shane to stay outside.

Adam found a plastic bag and filled it with candles from a drawer. He tossed in a lighter. "Why do you need these? Has your power gone out? Ours is still on."

"Yeah, well, it's kind of a limited outage."

"When will it be back on?"

This guy asked way too many questions. "As soon as I pay my bill."

He laughed, then stopped when he saw she wasn't smiling. "Are you kidding me?"

"It's no big deal. I'll sort it out soon."

"I can pay you for Summer's first session up front—"

"No, that's totally unnecessary. I've got money." Coming in the future, once she'd done two weeks' work and Molly paid her wages. Molly would give her the money early if she requested but she wasn't going to ask. Hayley reached for the bag of candles. "I'll get out of your hair and let you get back to work."

"If your power is out you won't have any heating, either," he said, scratching his head.

"I don't need heat. Thanks for these." She wished she'd never mentioned the electricity. That was what happened when you asked for even the smallest thing. People got a window into your life, and damn if they didn't peer inside and have a good look around.

"Wait. I have something else for you." He opened the pantry and handed her another two bags. "Sugar."

A bag of white and one of brown, just as he'd promised. Her stiffness melted right away at his thoughtfulness. Oh, boy, was she in trouble. He was making it impossible to dislike him. "Thank you."

He badgered her all the way to her truck. "Do you have any place to stay until it's sorted? Friends, family?"

"Of course. But I can't leave my horses." She opened the truck door so Shane could jump in, then she climbed into the driver's seat and started the engine.

Adam put a hand on the open window, effectively preventing her from driving away. "I've got an idea."

"Whatever it is, it probably won't work." She appreciated his help but hated seeing pity in his eyes, just like with the volunteers who manned the food

and clothing distribution. Lining up for basic sustenance after the fires had been the most humiliating
experience of her life.

"Is that the kind of advice you give your clients?
How immensely you must help them."

His teasing dragged a reluctant smile out of her.
"Okay, now you're channeling Oscar Wilde."

"I was channeling a smart-ass. Why Oscar
Wilde?"

"You're kidding me, right? *The Importance Of
Being Earnest*." It was one of her favorite books
among the hundreds she'd owned. All gone, burned
along with her house. While Leif watched his sports
on TV she would curl up with a book. It was no coincidence that her best friend was a librarian. She
and Jacinta had bonded as ten-year-olds over *Harriet
the Spy*. "You should try reading sometime. Broad-
ens the mind."

"Good advice, I'm sure." The hint of laughter in
his voice invited her to continue the banter.

Banter? How had they gone from her thinly veiled
antagonism to bantering?

"I'd better get back and organize the horses. If
they're going to graze for a couple hours and get
back before dark I have to start now."

"First, listen to my idea. Why don't you move
into my guest cottage while you're working with
Summer? Your horses can use my stables as they
eat down the grass, and Blaze can give birth in the

comfort of a straw-lined box stall. In fact, they can have the hay stored in the barn. Now that Summer's horse is gone I have no use for it."

His steady gaze and deep voice betrayed nothing but sincerity. So much generosity was overwhelming, especially in the face of her standoffishness. "It's kind of you but I can't accept."

"Why not? Give me one good reason."

Her hand hovered over the key in the ignition. She didn't have a good reason. All she had was her pride. "You don't even know me and you're inviting me to live in your cottage."

"I thought neighbors helped each other in Hope Mountain. You'd be free to come and go and do whatever you normally do."

It was tempting. Her garage would be cold and dark even with candles. But accepting would mean admitting she was a stone's throw from being homeless. "No. Thank you, but no."

"Hayley, it makes sense. I have this big house and a cottage and you're toughing it out in a garage."

Ah, he felt guilty. Well, his guilt wasn't her problem. She tightened her grip on the steering wheel. "What are you, my fairy godmother?"

"Why are you so prickly? Are you like this with everyone?" He touched the back of her hand where it gripped the steering wheel and his voice dropped to a lower register. "Or is it just me?"

His touch sent a shiver up her arm. Mostly, it was

him. She resented him, resented needing his help, but she was attracted, too, even now when he was right in her face. He confused the hell out of her. She didn't know if she wanted to drive over his feet or grab his face in both hands and kiss him. "I don't do charity. No more than I have to, that is."

He met her gaze, his mouth set in a determined line. "Your husband died defending my property while you lost everything. I know the circumstances were complicated but I feel responsible in a way."

It was what she'd been thinking for the past year but as soon as he said it aloud she saw how wrong the notion was. She prided herself on being fair, but she hadn't been fair to Adam.

"Leif died because the wind changed and he and his crew were trapped. It could've happened anywhere. As for my place burning while yours survived, that occurred throughout the community. You see it in town, one house in every three left on a street. It's like when a tornado goes through, the path is unpredictable and capricious." She struggled for the next words but she had to say them, both for his sake and because she couldn't be anything less than fair. "You're not responsible."

His breath released in an audible sigh. "Thank you for saying that. For a while I thought you might have blamed me."

She dropped her gaze. For months she'd been hanging on to the idea that Adam was responsible for Leif's death, building up anger and resentment in her head.

It had been easy to hate Adam Banks when he'd been distant and unknown. Confronted by the kind, generous man himself, it wasn't so easy.

Jacinta was right; she was in danger of retreating into the past, cocooning herself in grief. That wasn't her way. Maybe if she let the anger go and admitted how wrong she'd been, her life would open up again. Suddenly, her desire to move forward tugged at her more strongly than her desire to retreat.

She looked up and met Adam's eyes, moved by the compassion there. Some of her stored anger and resentment melted away. "I guess it's not charity if we help each other."

"Exactly. That wasn't so hard, was it?" Adam extended his hand through the open window and wrapped his fingers around hers. "It's a deal, then."

"Deal." His kindness and strength flowed through his palm and into her, seducing her into letting down her guard. She hoped she hadn't made a big mistake. If she didn't have anger and resentment to hide behind, she was opening herself up to being truly vulnerable.

ADAM UNLOCKED THE door to the guest cottage and flicked on the light. He wanted to make sure the place was ready for Hayley before she moved in. His nose wrinkled at the musty smell, so he pushed the door wide and held it open with a chair. In the sitting room an old magazine lay on the coffee table. He glanced at the date—two months before the bushfires.

He carried the magazine to the recycling bin in the laundry room, then went back to the kitchen. The sink needed to be scrubbed and the floor could use a good cleaning. Two coffee cups sat in the sink, one with lipstick stains on the rim. Why hadn't Diane cleaned the cottage after her guests left?

The fridge held only a single bottle of boutique beer. Five empties sat in the cardboard six-pack on the floor. Continuing his exploration, he peered into the cupboards. Plenty of dishes and pots and pans but not much in the way of staples. Would Hayley be offended if he stocked the fridge and pantry? He'd like to help her out. Maybe her situation wasn't any of his business but she was struggling and he was her neighbor.

Even though she'd said he wasn't responsible for the fires, he did feel guilty that he hadn't suffered any damage while her property and horses—her whole life, in effect—had been wiped out. Worst of all, she'd lost her husband. He would have been devastated if Diane had been killed, even though their marriage was over. How much worse for Hayley, who clearly loved her husband?

Adam wandered down the hall to the main bedroom. The bed had been slept in and not remade, the covers crumpled and pulled back. He quickly stripped the sheets and tossed them into the hall to take up to the house to wash. Then he remade the bed with fresh linen.

It would be nice having another adult around to talk to. Okay, not just another adult; an attractive woman—albeit a different type than he was used to. Hayley intrigued him. She was a puzzle and a challenge rolled into one. What would it take to break through that hard shell? On the rare occasions when she smiled the effect was dazzling.

He moved on to the bathroom en suite and was pulling used towels off the rack when he saw a glint of gold on the edge of the bathtub, partially hidden by the shower curtain.

It was a gold Rolex watch worth thousands of dollars. Strange that whoever lost this hadn't come looking for it. He turned it over and found an inscription. Holding it up to the light, he read the fine italic script.

For Leif, my sexy mountain man, from your red-hot mama.... The date was Christmas of the previous year.

Leif. The name gave him a jolt. What had Hayley's late husband been doing in the bathroom of this cottage? Hayley mentioned they'd come to one of Diane's parties. Maybe they'd stayed overnight rather than driving home after drinking. He thought back to the two cups in the sink, one with lipstick stains.

Hayley didn't wear lipstick. Maybe she did to a party. Or maybe…

Adam sank onto the edge of the bathtub. Diane had been seeing someone. He'd assumed the man was a friend from Melbourne. But what if he wasn't? What if Diane had been having an affair with Hayley's husband? A sick wave washed over him as the pieces fell into place. Now it made sense that she just had to buy a house in Hope Mountain. And not any house but one right next door to her lover.

Leif wasn't a common name. The odds of there being two men in this neck of the woods called that were slim. As for the watch, Diane spent money like water and wouldn't think twice about buying her lover an expensive gift.

Did Hayley know? He hated to even think about that. She seemed so innocent. Not naive, but somehow unspoiled. Natural, in a way Diane could never be.

The sweep hand was still ticking off the seconds. The gold casing was as shiny as new, smooth and cool beneath the pad of his thumb.

What if he had it all wrong? Maybe Hayley had given Leif the watch. She was poor now but they may have been well-off before the fires. If that was the case then Adam should give it back to Hayley.

But if she didn't know anything about the watch, being presented with a gift to her husband from his mistress would cause Hayley a lot of pain. Should he even tell her about it? What was the right thing to do?

Adam's mind was spinning and then another thought hit him. If Hayley knew her husband had slept with another woman in this very guest cottage she wouldn't want to stay here. Already he felt as if he was enticing a wild deer out of the blackened forest, offering sustenance so she wouldn't perish. That was probably a false impression on his part. He suspected she was tougher than he was in many ways. But knowing about the watch might even put her off treating Summer.

Damn Diane for going after another woman's husband, a woman she'd invited into her home and been friendly with. He was angry but not surprised. Diane had her good points but she was also rich, bored and selfish. But what was wrong with Leif that he would cheat on Hayley? She had more character in her dirty fingernail than Diane had in her entire spa-pampered body.

Adam fished in his pocket for his phone and punched in Diane's number. The call went to voice mail. He swore again. He left a message for her to call him back as soon as possible.

He rose and pocketed the watch. Until he had some facts he wouldn't speak to Hayley about it. He didn't want to upset her or screw up Summer's therapy over what might turn out to be nothing.

But as he finished cleaning the cottage, dark emotions stirred up by the watch churned to the surface. Even though he hadn't been in love with Diane for a long time, it was still humiliating that she'd had an affair. And not with another architect or a lawyer or a businessman but with *her sexy mountain man*. Leif had been a rugged individual, at home in these woods in a way Adam couldn't begin to compete with.

Her sexy mountain man. Had Hayley seen Leif that way, too? Of course she would have because Leif had been *her* man. Another spurt of anger rushed through him. How could Diane and Leif have done that to Hayley?

As Adam finished cleaning the cottage he tried to put the whole problem from his mind. But he couldn't stop thinking about Hayley and how he had no right to keep secrets from her. He also had an unexpectedly strong urge to protect her from more pain, which was a bit strange. She was only his neighbor, after all. And his daughter's therapist. Yes, he found her attractive and he enjoyed a little harmless flirting, but there were too many roadblocks to them becoming more than friends to even think in those terms.

He grabbed the dirty laundry basket and shut the door on the cottage, the watch a heavy weight in his pocket. The whole situation was becoming way too messed up and complicated.

"GEE UP!" HAYLEY SLAPPED Blaze on the rump. The pregnant mare trotted through the gate into Adam's paddock, where Asha, Bo, Sergeant and Major already had their heads down, tails whisking as they eagerly tore into the succulent young grass.

She'd ridden Sergeant and led the others in a string along the road and up the driveway, avoiding the still-muddy bush track. Then Adam had driven her back to pick up her truck and the rest of her things.

He'd gone inside while she'd tended to her horses, supposedly just to get the key to the cottage, but that was half an hour ago. Didn't matter. She'd been busy scrubbing and filling the old bathtub used as a water trough. Then she'd positioned the salt lick below the broad eaves of the barn where it wouldn't melt away in the rain.

Now she sank onto the lush grass outside the paddock and watched her horses crop the juicy green stems with brisk swipes of their tongues. The steady chomp of the grinding molars was a sweeter sound than a songbird in spring. Her horses were being nourished. Blaze, her fat round belly gleaming in the sun, would have a safe and comfortable place to have her baby.

Thanks to Adam, she and her horses had been transported almost magically into a land of luxury and plenty. The barn was full of hay and sacks of oats and grain. Her horses could live on that for months. As soon as she could afford it, she'd pay Adam back. Until then she wouldn't be lying awake at night wondering if she would have to sell any of her horses, and which she would choose if it came to that. Knowing she and her animals were safe felt as if a huge weight had rolled off her shoulders.

Shane bounded through the grass to flop at her feet, panting, after his exploration of the yard and the buildings. Hayley scratched the black-and-white fur behind his ears. "Pretty swish, eh, Shane? We're living high on the hog now."

Why would Adam want to leave such a beautiful environment and live in the city? He had a big house, a guest cottage, a barn with a hayloft, a tack room and a box stall as well as shelter for the other horses. There was a lunge ring, a tool shed and a three-car garage. As reluctant as she'd been to accept his offer, now that she was here, she couldn't stop grinning.

The screen door on the kitchen banged and Adam strode across the grass, a set of keys dangling from his fingers. "Sorry I took so long. I got a call from work. Seems they can't quite do without me after all."

Hayley jumped to her feet and brushed bits of grass off her jeans. "No worries."

"I'll show you where you'll be staying." He led

her across the lawn to the cottage set back among the trees. "It's small but comfortable."

"I'm sure it'll be great." She quelled the urge to skip and instead walked sedately at his side.

"Dad!" Summer came running out of the house, her long coppery hair flying out behind her. "Why didn't you tell me the horses were here?"

"You were plugged in to that mp3 player, as usual." Adam stopped to let his daughter catch up to them.

Hayley smiled at Summer. The girl was different today, excited and happy. "Are you ready to do some horse therapy?"

"Will I be riding?" she asked eagerly.

"That's not part of the treatment, but you can ride another time. I'm going to look at the cottage. How about we meet at the lunge ring in, say, half an hour?"

"Okay. But first, what are the horses' names?"

"The gray one is Asha, the pregnant chestnut is Blaze, the big palomino is Bo and the two gold-brown horses are Sergeant and Major," Haley said. "They're brothers."

"How do you tell Sergeant and Major apart?" Summer asked. "They look like identical twins from here."

"Sergeant is taller and heavier and a darker red-gold color," Hayley explained. "Major has four white socks instead of three and is a lighter gold."

"Cool."

The girl ran off.

"That's the most excited I've seen her in weeks." Adam turned back to Hayley, his dark eyes filled with warmth. "You're doing her good already."

His deep brown eyes framed by thick arching brows were magnetic. Her gaze clung to his a good two seconds longer than was seemly. Combined with the approval in his voice and words, he was hard to resist.

But resist she must. She was basically his employee—they could be friends at best. "It's not me, it's the horses. I, uh, I'd better put my stuff inside so I can meet Summer."

She strode to her truck, full of saddles and other tack, plus her clothes and miscellaneous items. She dragged out the first box that came to hand.

Adam swung out her duffel bag and led the way up the flagstone path to the cottage. He opened the door and stood back to allow her to enter. "There's no laundry, but you can use the washer and dryer in the house. Sorry for the inconvenience."

"Hey, don't apologize. This is awesome. And it beats going into town to the Laundromat."

"If you need anything at all, just ask. I want you to be comfortable here."

Hayley walked into the living room and set the box on the coffee table. Then she turned in a slow circle, taking in the comfortable furniture, the fireplace, fresh flowers on the dining table and the kitchen fitted out with new appliances.

And windows, lots and lots of windows, through which the warm afternoon light streamed, coloring everything with a golden glow. Gratitude expanded in her chest, filling her to aching point. Maybe she was doing Adam a favor, but he was doing her a far bigger one. He'd given her a home.

"Is it okay?" Adam dropped her duffel bag inside the doorway.

"It's just fine." She didn't dare look at him for fear of betraying how close to tears she was and acknowledging how desperate she'd been. She could have survived in the garage even without electricity. It wasn't comfortable, but it was a roof over her head. But her straitened circumstances meant that sooner or later she would probably have had to sell her horses. And then what would she have done? Who would she be without her horses? She didn't even want to think about that.

"I'll let you get settled," Adam said, retreating to the porch.

Hayley came to the door. It occurred to her that Diane might not appreciate Hayley living in her guest cottage. The other woman was unfailingly polite, but their acquaintance had always felt strained for some reason. "Diane won't mind me being here?"

"I'm sure she won't. She actually may not be coming back except to pack her things. She's talking about moving to Sydney. Since the fires she's not so keen on the area."

"Outsiders usually do want to leave after something catastrophic. Those of us who grew up here can't bear the thought of living anywhere else."

"You've lost so much. Your home, your husband…" He searched her face. "You never think about getting out?"

Occasionally, yes, in the night, when she was alone and lonely and the wind whistled through the cracks between the walls and the roof. Then she would fantasize about giving up the struggle and the hardship and going to live in the suburbs of Melbourne in a normal house with a normal job and a regular paycheck.

The lure of security called to her when she felt weak. When she didn't think she had another ounce of strength left to heal anyone. Molly had asked her once, *Who's healing you?* She didn't need healing. She was resilient. She soldiered on. And sure enough, even after a bad night, come morning she would gaze out over the mountainside and the valley below and feel her heart swell with a feeling of home and belonging. She would wither anywhere else.

"No, I never think seriously about leaving. No matter how bad things are I know they will eventually get better. I've got a job and now a proper roof over my head, thanks to you. Even if it's only temporary it's a huge help. Spring is here, the grass is growing, birds are nesting. Every day I'm a tiny step closer to getting my house rebuilt and the dude ranch started."

"What about the horse therapy?"

She hesitated. "I didn't tell you. The funding ran out sooner than I expected. It's a shame but I never thought I'd be doing it long-term."

"That's too bad. Everyone says you're so good at therapy."

"I loved it. It's been incredibly rewarding to see how people and horses respond to each other, to see them go from hurt and closed off to opening up and feeling strong." She sighed and glanced away.

There was no point pining after what was lost, though. Turning back, she said firmly, "The dude ranch is the real goal. Leif and I had our hearts set on it." To be completely accurate, Leif had come up with the idea but she loved it, too. A couple needed common goals for a strong marriage. Fulfilling their dream was a way to keep Leif's memory alive.

"I hope you get what you're after." Adam stepped off the porch onto the paving stone pathway. "I'll let you unpack."

"I'll finish later. Summer's waiting for me. Could you tell her I'll be out in a few minutes?"

Adam nodded and left, then walked over to the paddock where Summer was perched on the fence, mooning over the horses.

Hayley went back inside, unable to resist quickly

exploring the rest of the cottage. The bedroom had a king-size bed with a patchwork comforter, a chair by the window, a dresser and a closet. The bathroom gleamed with cream tiles and gold fixtures. She couldn't wait to take a proper shower and fill the cabinet with her toiletries instead of having them crowded around the sink where she washed dishes.

The kitchen was compact but complete, with all the basic appliances. She opened the fridge to make sure the freezer worked. Had to have her ice cream—

She pressed a hand to her chest. The fridge was stocked to the brim with fresh food. Milk, eggs, cheese, butter, jam, salad makings, fruit. In the freezer was meat and, *oh, my God,* ice cream bars.

Hayley blinked hard. Damn Adam Banks. He was too nice. How could she keep her distance when he was so welcoming and generous? She didn't want to hate him. But neither did she want to owe him. She'd been here less than a day and already she was deeply in his debt simply for the way he'd made her feel safe and secure again. It wasn't about money; it was about having a home. To him it was only a guest cottage, but to Hayley it was a palace. It reminded her of how much she'd lost and how desperately she wanted her own house again, and a sense of permanence.

She drew in a breath and wiped her eyes on the back of her hand. Then she went to the front door and pulled on her boots. There was one way she could repay him. She would give his daughter back to him, whole and healthy.

CHAPTER FIVE

ADAM TOUCHED SUMMER'S shoulder as he joined her at the fence. "Hey, sweetheart. I wonder which one you'll be working with."

"I don't know. I hope it's Asha."

"I hope not. She's trouble. Hayley even has problems controlling her."

"That's because she was hurt in the fires. She's traumatized."

If Hayley couldn't cure her own horse, how did she manage with people? But she did. Tom Dorian had been very convincing and all the counselors he'd spoken with had recommended Hayley very highly as an alternative to conventional therapy.

"Mom called while you were helping Hayley bring her stuff over," Summer went on. "Grandma's having her operation this afternoon. I hope she's going to be okay."

"I'm sure she will be. Did your mother say if she was at the hospital right now?"

"She said she'd be in and out for a while." Summer rested her chin on her crossed arms atop the fence. "Dad, do you really think there's something wrong with me?"

What could he say? She was perfect in his eyes despite whatever issues were making her act out. But that was such a "dad" way of reassuring her. She wanted absolutes and he didn't know enough to give her that. "What's big and gray and doesn't matter?"

"This isn't a joke." Moisture filmed her eyes. Then her curiosity got the better of her. Grudgingly she said, "What?"

"It's irrelephant."

She didn't even smile. "What do you mean?"

He touched her cheek. "I love you. No matter what."

"But you don't really know me."

"I've known you since you were born."

"You don't know me now, the things I feel inside."

"I might if you would talk to me." Hadn't they had this conversation already?

"Hayley's coming." Summer blinked and knuckled her eyes.

"Everything's going to be all right, sweetheart. I promise." He squeezed her shoulder. "Have fun." Fun? Possibly not an appropriate term for what she was about to experience.

Hayley's path crossed his in the middle of the yard. "Everything okay for you in there?" he asked.

"It's amazing. Thank you for making me feel so at home. All the food, everything, I didn't expect—"

Her smile broke free. "Ice cream bars! How did you know?"

"Lucky guess." The radiance of her smile practically melted his insides. "I'm glad you're here. For Summer's sake." He paused a beat. "And mine." Her gaze met his and a ripple of awareness passed between them. When he was with her it was hard to remember why he had to keep his distance.

"I mean, it's nice to have another adult around. To talk to, that is. I'm suffering culture shock being away from my workplace and friends in the city. I usually go out a lot but here, not so much. I've become quite the hermit."

Like a babbling brook his words kept flowing. Now the look in her eyes had turned to amusement. He forced himself to stop. "I'll let you go. Summer's waiting, and I need to make a phone call...."

"We'll chat later," Hayley suggested.

"One more thing," Adam said quickly. "I've got to take all the brush I've cut down to the tip. By any chance would I be able to borrow your truck?"

"Sure, no worries. Hang on a tick." She ran back inside the cottage and came out with her car keys.

"Thanks." He watched as she strode off toward the paddock, his gaze dropping to the neat fit of her jeans shaping her hips. Then he shook his head and did an abrupt one-eighty, heading for the house. All he needed was for her to turn around and catch him watching her.

Once inside he grabbed the phone and punched in Diane's number—she answered with a brisk greeting. "I can't talk long. Mother's being prepped for surgery. What's this about Summer having horse therapy?"

"Your neighbor, Hayley Sorensen, treats trauma victims using horses." He pushed aside the curtains to peer out the kitchen window. Hayley and Summer were sitting in the grass outside the lunge ring, talking. "It's unconventional, but apparently it works."

"Hayley from next door? How is she going to do Summer any good? She seems a bit…unsophisticated. What are her credentials?"

"She has credentials." So what if she didn't have a piece of paper with a degree? "And she's got testimonials as long as your arm. But that's not what I called about." He paused, allowing himself a second to make the mental shift. "I found a gold watch in the guest cottage."

"Oh?" Diane was suddenly wary.

"It was inscribed, *For Leif, my sexy mountain man, from your red-hot mama.* Do you know anything about that?"

There was a long pause. "Why would I know anything about it?"

"Come on, Diane. Just tell me the truth."

"Leif is dead," she said flatly. "There's no sense raking stuff up."

"You had an affair with him, in the guest cottage,

didn't you?" There was no disguising his bitterness and anger. "He's the one you were seeing while we were still married."

"What difference does it make?"

"It makes all the difference. I could've put up with your overspending and your flirting and your frivolous ways. I could have even stuck out a lukewarm marriage till Summer was through school. But infidelity was the one thing I refused to tolerate. But forget about me. How could you have fooled around in front of Summer?"

"He never came while she was home," Diane said quickly. "I always made sure she was at school, or out with her friends."

"Very thoughtful of you," he said drily. "From things she's said, I think she suspected. Oh, and did you spare a thought for Hayley and about what you and Leif were doing to her?"

"She was clueless. Anyway, Leif and I didn't plan it. It just happened."

"Right, like a thunderbolt from heaven. You couldn't help yourselves."

"Exactly. He was a real man's man, you know?" Diane sounded almost dreamy. "He had calluses on his calluses. And that Marlboro Man squint from beneath his cowboy hat."

Oh, but that was cruel. It was almost as if she was trying to hurt him. Had he somehow brought that out in her? He glanced at his own strong but clean hands, which generally wielded a pencil and ruler. They were blistered from all the yard work he'd been doing, and that only emphasized how smooth they normally were. Was that why his marriage had failed—because he had clean fingernails?

"Yeah, a man who cheats on his wife is a real prize."

"He was there for me, Adam," she said sharply. "Every time you weren't. And in every way."

Ouch. That barb was valid and it stung.

"Do *not* tell Hayley about this," Diane added. "There's absolutely nothing to be gained."

"I'll have to think about that. It's a big secret to keep from her."

"She won't thank you," Diane warned.

"I've got things to do," Adam said abruptly. "I'll talk to you later." He started to hang up when he remembered to add, "Give your mother my best. Let me know how the operation goes."

He went back outside and began to move the pile of brush from behind the toolshed to Hayley's truck. Hayley and Summer were still sitting in the grass, talking. What about? He hadn't had that long a conversation with Summer since she'd believed in fairies.

Despite the blisters, he didn't mind getting his hands dirty. Making a tangible difference to his surroundings gave him a totally different type of satisfaction than designing buildings. Both were good, but the physical activity was more immediate. And it got him outside his head.

But he couldn't avoid thinking about Hayley and the watch. Was Diane right? Was there no point in burdening Hayley? Was it better that she mourned Leif with his memory untarnished?

Even if she'd known about the affair, if Adam gave her the watch then she'd know that *he* knew. No one liked to be humiliated in front of others. The knowledge that Diane had slept with another man while they were married stung. The difference was that he'd already fallen out of love with her. Hayley was still devoted to her late husband.

It was a no-win situation.

He hated to admit it, but Diane was probably right. He shouldn't tell Hayley.

And yet, keeping the affair a secret seemed wrong. How could he be a friend to Hayley if he didn't tell her? But how could he stay her friend if he *did?* It was human nature to shoot the messenger.

Adam heaved a bundle of saplings onto the truck.

For now, he would keep quiet and leave the watch where he'd put it in the sideboard with the silver. He didn't want it in his room, and it was too valuable to leave lying around. Hopefully over the next few weeks he'd figure out the right thing to do.

He retraced his steps to the brush pile, hoping to see Hayley and Summer working with a horse by now. He had no idea what the therapy involved and he was curious. Surely no one would object if he watched from a distance.

They were still sitting cross-legged outside the fence. One of the golden-brown horses was inside, nibbling at the grass growing around a fence post. Was it Sergeant or Major who had four white socks?

Hayley seemed to be doing most of the talking. Summer had her head down as she tore a blade of grass into long strips. Adam took a drink from a water bottle. He'd give anything to know what she was saying.

As he watched, Summer glanced up at Hayley. Her face, initially impassive, grew cloudy, then stormy. She said something sharp. Adam heard the tone if not the words. Then she rose and started to stalk off.

Should he interfere, tell Summer to get back out there and cooperate? Before he could make a move, Hayley jumped to her feet and went after Summer. She put a hand on the girl's shoulder. Summer spun around, her eyes flashing and her mouth drawn into a deep scowl. His daughter's next move was usually to shout something about being picked on and take off again. He wouldn't blame Hayley if she quit on the spot.

To his surprise Hayley pulled Summer into a hug. Summer stiffened, her arms rigid at her side. Hayley released her but kept a hand on her shoulder, speaking steadily and calmly. Her body language was authoritative but open and compassionate. Miracle of miracles, Summer wasn't running away. She was still frowning, but she was listening.

"WHY DID YOU get upset when I asked if anyone you knew died in the bushfires?" Hayley held Summer on the spot with her steady gaze and a calming hand on the shoulder. Out of the corner of her eye she saw Adam watching them from the toolshed. She mentally shut him out so his presence didn't distract her. She knew he was concerned, but he needed to understand this was private between her and Summer.

Summer had been chatting to her about the music she liked, which had led her to mention a concert she'd been to in Melbourne last year. Hayley had then asked her about the friends she'd gone with. They'd talked about them for a while and how her girlfriend's aunt had died in the bushfires. Casually, Hayley had asked if Summer had known anyone else, perhaps a close friend, who'd died.

The girl had gone ballistic, shouting that of course she knew people who'd died. One of her teachers, her friend's aunt, the guy who'd delivered the gas bottles for the house, and three classmates. Oddly, Summer hadn't mentioned Leif, whom she must've met either at the divorce party or when her mother had gone on trail rides.

Were any of these people close friends? Hayley gently probed, trying to discover the trigger for Summer's anger.

That was when Summer had jumped to her feet. Fight-or-flight was the reaction to stress. She'd started out fighting, and now she was in flight mode. Hayley went after her, giving her what she needed even if Summer didn't realize it herself—a hug. Comfort, connection, sympathy and an acknowledgment that whatever the girl was reacting to was real and scary.

Summer was too tightly wound to relax and tell all, but at least she'd stopped running and was listening. Hayley told her about Leif and what his loss meant to her. It was painful to talk about, but sharing her story of loss and grief was the quickest, surest way to establish a bond between her and Summer.

"He and three other men were trapped in their fire truck," she told Summer. "The fire was all around them. There was no escape."

"So they burned," Summer whispered. Her eyes fell shut and her throat worked as she seemed to struggle to control her emotions. She opened her eyes again. "W-were their bodies found?"

Hayley swallowed. Sometimes therapy was harder on her than on her clients. "Bones. Teeth. The dentist identified Leif's molars."

"That's so awful." Summer looked as if she was going to be sick. "I'm sorry."

Hayley put her arm around Summer's shoulder. "Did you have a close friend who was lost?"

"Not killed but burned badly." Tears filled Summer's eyes. "But…we're not friends anymore."

Hayley took a stab in the dark. "A boy?" Summer nodded. "What's his name?"

"Steve. He has scars on his arms and some on his face. He keeps calling me. I don't want to talk to him, but not because of the scars…." She broke off, crying.

Hayley handed her a tissue from the packet she kept in her pocket during therapy. "Why don't you want to talk to him?"

Summer shook her head, her nose buried in tissue. "It's personal."

Red alert. This boy, whoever he was, was of significance. Hayley didn't often stumble onto the source of a client's anxiety so quickly, and she had to tread carefully so Summer didn't shut down again. "Did you tell your mom and dad about Steve?"

The girl lifted her head, wiped her eyes then sighed. "Mom doesn't like him because his family is poor and his father's out of work. Dad wouldn't like him, either, not because of that, but because—" She broke off, sniffing.

"Is there some reason you don't want your father to know about Steve? Was he your boyfriend?"

"I'm too young to have a boyfriend, according to Dad. Anyway, it's over now, so it doesn't matter."

"If the thought of him still bothers you, maybe he does matter," she said gently.

Summer blotted her red-rimmed eyes with the soggy tissue. "You're friends with my dad. If I say anything, you'll tell him. He's good at making people talk about stuff."

"I won't tell him anything you don't want me to." Was she friends with Adam or were they just helping each other out? There was also something more, an awareness so tangible she knew he must feel it, too. She'd seen it in his eyes and heard it in the flurry of unnecessary words earlier. He didn't strike her as a man who usually lost his cool.

Yes, she'd admit to a slight attraction, but it wasn't going anywhere—in a few months he'd be leaving Hope Mountain for good. Anyway, this wasn't about her. She had to concentrate on Summer and gaining the girl's confidence. "Please trust me, Summer. Anything you say to me during these sessions is completely confidential."

"Like a doctor-and-patient thing?"

"I'm not a doctor but, yeah, like that. I won't make you talk about anything you don't want to, although sometimes I might push a little if I think it will help you. I know it's painful, but you're only going to get well if you open up."

"I'm not sick. And I'm not crazy!" Summer flipped on a dime, back to anger. "Why should I open up? I don't even see why I have to do this. The only reason I agreed to therapy was so I could be around your horses."

Hayley knew her snappishness was defensive and it was time to back off. "Let's go see Major, then. But I'd like you to calm down first. Horses sense when you're upset and angry. They don't like it. It makes them anxious."

Summer glowered mutinously but reluctantly followed Hayley to the lunge ring. "Why would how I'm feeling make Major anxious?"

"Horses are a bit like dogs in that they are herd or pack animals. They want to follow a strong leader, and they see humans as their leaders. If they sense a person is weak, then they become afraid something will happen to them. Like humans, sometimes their reaction to being fearful is to become angry instead." She paused, throwing Summer a sideways glance to see if the point sank in. "Does that ever happen to you?"

"You mean, do I get afraid and cover it up with anger?" She thought about it. "I don't know about afraid, but I get pissed off a lot."

"What about?"

Summer shrugged. "Stuff. My dad's always on my case. Having my iPod up too loud, not doing my homework, cleaning my room…"

Adam's concerns might be valid but Summer's problems didn't stem from trivialities like homework and a messy bedroom. "Maybe you're afraid of another bushfire."

"I don't think so. We were safe here. It was in other places, in the bush and the town, that people got killed."

Hayley forced herself not to react to the girl's naïveté. Or was it denial? She would have liked to dig deeper, but she didn't want to make Summer angry again. Instead, she focused on the horses.

"If you come to a horse upset or angry, the horse will react badly. You need to control your emotions for their sake. Eventually you'll be able to control your emotions at other times. To do that, you need to learn to identify what triggers those out-of-control feelings." She paused. "Feelings like the anger you felt just now when I asked that question."

Summer leaned on the railing and watched Major with her chin resting on her hands. "How do I do that?"

"First, rate your anxiety level right this minute on a scale of one to ten."

"Why?"

"Just do it. I'll tell you why afterward."

Summer ducked her head and mumbled, "Nine."

"And what would you rate your inner smile?"

"Inner smile?" Summer's brow crinkled in confusion. "I don't have one."

"Maybe a two?"

"Sure, whatever."

"Okay, let's remember that. Now, before we go into the lunge ring, we'll do breathing exercises. Turn around." Hayley took Summer's hand and placed it on the girl's stomach. "Breathe in from your gut. Do you feel your hand rise? Good. Now let it go, slowly. In through your nose. Out through your mouth. Drop your shoulders. Right down." Summer lowered her shoulders under pressure from Hayley's hands and took a couple of long, deep breaths. "How do you feel?"

"Okay." Summer continued to breathe. "A bit calmer, I guess."

"Good." Hayley smiled reassuringly. "You're doing great. Keep breathing, slow and deep, while I explain some things. Horses have a racial memory about creatures with eyes facing forward, like humans. They see us as predators, so their natural instinct is to be afraid of us."

"Bailey wasn't afraid of me."

"Because he knew you. Major doesn't know you. He has fears, too. He ran into the woods when I opened the gate during the fires. Some people caught him a couple of days later. They meant well but they scared him by throwing a lasso around his neck. Now he associates strangers with fear and pain."

Summer turned to Hayley, her eyes huge. "That's so sad. But how can Major help me if he's traumatized?"

"You help each other. Do you want to try that?"

Hayley glanced over at the brush pile. Adam was still hauling branches but she had a feeling he was *very* attuned to what they were doing. "Does it bother you that your father's around?"

Summer bit her bottom lip. "He's so pissed at me."

"He's concerned about you. I don't think he's angry."

"I've let him down. He's had to take a long break from work in the middle of a big project. He doesn't say anything, but I know he's disappointed in me." She blinked rapidly and glanced away. "I don't want him watching me in case I don't do it right."

"He won't know if you're doing it right since he doesn't know what it is you're *supposed* to be doing. He's on your side, Summer—that much I do know. But don't worry about what he's thinking right now. You just worry about yourself and Major, okay?"

"Okay," Summer said. "What do I do?"

"Go into the ring."

"By myself?" Summer looked anxiously at the horse who was chewing on the top railing of the fence, a nervous habit he'd taken up since the bush-fires.

"I'll be with you the first time. Here, put these on." She handed Summer a padded safety vest and a riding hard hat. "Before we go in, tell me again how you're feeling. Rate your anxiety level on a scale of one to ten."

"Eleven?" Summer said, buckling up the vest.

Hayley smiled reassuringly. "I'm betting you a horse ride that you'll cut that in half by the end of the session." She picked up the long leather buggy reins looped over a fence post. "The aim is to make the horse feel safe around us. We do this by mimicking the role of leader. Did you know that horses communicate with each other? In every herd there's a leader who tells the others where they should graze."

"How can I be a leader to a horse? I can't speak their language."

"It's all about body language." Hayley led the way inside the ring, then shut the gate behind Summer. "Stand in middle of the yard in a strong, open body stance. Project strength, not anger." She demonstrated by standing very tall, with her shoulders squared. She started slapping the leather reins on her thigh as she walked toward Major. "First, you get the horse to run. You want them to respond to your energy. See how his head is high and his ears are flicking? He's afraid but he senses I'm trying to communicate."

Hayley kept walking forward, slapping the strips of leather. Major trotted away from her, along the fence line. "By getting him to run away from you you're proving you're in control of him. In a minute he'll see you don't mean to hurt him and he'll stop being afraid. Here, you try." Hayley handed the reins to Summer. "I'll be right behind you, holding the back of your safety vest. If anything goes wrong—not that it will—I'll pull you out of the way."

Summer gathered the coiled loops of leather and awkwardly slapped the loose ends of the reins against her leg.

"Go toward Major," Hayley urged, lightly gripping the back of Summer's vest. "Make him move away from you. Dominate him the way a leader horse would."

Major turned the other way, his ears flattened back as he kicked out to the side. "He's mad," Summer said. "Is he going to bite me?"

"He's scared. Look at his inside ear, see it flicker? He's listening to us, trying to figure out what's going on."

Major kicked out again.

"I can't do this. He's scaring me." Abruptly, Summer threw down the reins and ran back to the gate. She didn't stop to open it, just scrambled over and tore across the yard, into the house. The door slammed shut behind her.

CHAPTER SIX

HAYLEY PICKED UP the spilled loops of leather and brushed off flecks of chip bark. Major dropped his head and slowly walked over. She stroked the animal behind his ears. "You're a good boy to put up with this time after time. Be patient. Summer needs us."

Adam cut across the yard to the ring. "Is there a problem?"

Hayley continued to stroke Major, drawing calm from the horse. "The first session can take time. Summer was agitated when she went in there."

"Because of what you two were talking about?"

"I'm not telling you what we talked about so there's no point in fishing." She gave a small smile to soften her refusal. "You can ask her to come back out. We're not finished."

Adam dragged a hand through his hair. "Don't you think since she's upset, she needs a break?"

"Following through with her therapy is part of learning self-discipline. She's not going to make progress if she's allowed to run away when she doesn't like how she feels." Adam still looked dubious, so Hayley added, "I know it might seem harsh, especially to a parent. But I want her to take responsibility for her anger and modify her behavior."

Adam absorbed that, leaning an elbow on the fence and pulling at a splinter in the wood. "I get that we want her to control her anger, but can you explain how behavior modification will fix what's wrong with her?"

"Sure," Hayley said. "There are basically two responses to trauma. Flight, or hyper, mode which manifests as anger."

He nodded. "Summer, to a tee."

"Or shut-down mode, which is all about anxiety. A person can't or won't talk about what's bothering them because their brain is protecting them from fear."

"That sounds like Summer, too," Adam said. "Although she pretends she just wants to be left alone to listen to her music."

He looked baffled and worried. Hayley could only imagine how hard this must be for Adam, coming into the scenario late and finding his daughter troubled in a way he couldn't fix.

"Her general levels of anxiety are probably quite high," Hayley said. "In any given day she might have fifteen occasions when she could act out but she only gives in to it once. The other fourteen times she's able to tame her anxiety to an extent. The horse therapy builds on that, teaching her to manage her emotions from a position of strength, not weakness. Working with the horse helps her focus on calming herself."

"I still don't get how the horse figures in," Adam said. As if on cue Major wandered back and nudged Hayley's hip with his nose.

She found a stub of carrot in her pocket and fed it to him. "You can't fool a horse. They can read a person's emotions better than a body language expert."

"He seems very calm," Adam observed. "Is that because you're calm?"

"Exactly. If Summer's angry or anxious, the horse will sense it and react accordingly." Hayley scratched the animal's neck as he crunched the juicy treat. "But if she can control her strong emotions, then the horse will be in a calm state also. It's about gaining the horse's trust and respect—projecting strength without aggression. And getting control over herself will boost her self-esteem in all areas of her life."

Adam shook his head as if still not quite believing. "If you and the horse can do all that, it'll be nothing short of a miracle."

"We've done it before, and there's no reason to think Summer won't respond to the therapy." She tipped her head apologetically. "But it might be better if you weren't out in the yard. Do you mind?"

"No, I can see how she would need to focus." He pushed away from the fence. "I'll go get her and then I'll take a load down to the tip. Thanks for explaining."

"No worries." She fiddled with the ends of the buggy reins. "I'm sorry if I was curt with you before. I usually offer an explanation to parents of clients before I begin therapy. I'm sorry—I should've done the same with you."

"It's okay. You've got a lot on your mind right now." Smiling, he squeezed her arm lightly, his hand lingering for a second. "I'll see you later." He turned and headed for the house.

Hayley laid her palm over where Adam's fingers had left a warm imprint on her arm. His touch was brief, but it sealed the connection they'd gained from their conversation and forged a common goal—helping Summer heal. It also sent a buzz of excitement through Hayley.

Adam was a strong, virile man with dark good looks and a hard male body. His touch sparked feelings she hadn't had for a long time. A connection over Summer was one thing, but she would have to watch herself.

Adam reemerged from the house, waved to Hayley, then drove off in her truck. The screen door slammed again and Summer came out and slowly walked over, shoulders drooping. She was clearly feeling bad about herself. Instead of castigating her, Hayley draped an arm around her and squeezed. Maybe it wasn't orthodox behavior for a therapist, but in her book comfort and compassion never went astray. "I'm proud of you, coming out so soon, ready to try again."

Summer responded warily. "You're not mad at me for running away?"

"No, I'm not. Your anxiety is created by sensitivity, which is good, not bad. But you need to manage it so it doesn't manage you."

The girl's skeptical expression reminded Hayley of Adam. "Trauma actually changes brain function. You're frustrated by your inability to behave and react as you used to. Do your teachers or your parents ever tell you to just 'act normal'?"

Recognition sparked in Summer's eyes. "Yeah, like, all the time."

"The changes in your brain mean you aren't able to, which frustrates you, and the frustration manifests as anger."

Summer nodded. "I'm angry a lot. At nothing. At everything. I don't know why and I can't stop it."

"Sometimes anger is justifiable, like when you see someone mistreating an animal. But when you're angry for no apparent reason, or your anger is over the top, it suggests an inability to manage strong feelings like unhappiness, sadness, frustration…"

"But I can't control the anger. *Or* the frustration."

"That's what we're going to work on." The quickest way to get Summer feeling better was for her to accomplish something. "Major might look scary at times, but he won't hurt you. *If* on the off chance he tries, I'll move between you and him so fast you'd think I was Superwoman flying across the chip bark."

Summer giggled. "I'd be running so fast you'd think I was Supergirl."

"I already think you're super." Hayley smiled warmly. "Now, breathe deep and slow, and let's try again. Tell me, Summer, what makes you feel calm and relaxed?"

Summer didn't even have to think about it. "Listening to music."

"Close your eyes, put yourself in that space. Lower your shoulders and breathe out. Mentally hum a few bars of your favorite song." She waited while Summer closed her eyes and did as she asked.

About thirty seconds passed. Summer opened her eyes again. "Okay, I'm ready. I think."

Hayley led the way back into the lunge ring. "He's going to be agitated at first," she reminded Summer. "But he'll settle down if you stay strong and in control. Be calm for him. Make him feel safe. When he stops trying to run away and lowers his head, that means he respects and trusts you." She gently pushed Summer forward. "Off you go."

Slapping the reins back and forth on her legs, Summer took a hesitant step toward Major. The horse snorted and sidestepped away, head high in the air.

"Stand tall. Shoulders back and down," Hayley said. "Keep breathing, slowly, deeply, from your abdomen."

Summer straightened her back and kept going, following Major when he trotted away. Soon the horse was running in a circle around the perimeter of the ring, as if he had a whip flicking him along. His neck was damp with sweat and his nostrils flared.

"That's excellent," Hayley said. "Now, slow down and stop slapping the reins. Stand still. Maintain your calm focus on Major. Let him know you won't hurt him."

"Can I talk to him?"

"Sure. Low tones. Soothing but strong."

"It's okay, boy," Summer said. "You're okay. You're safe now. I'm gonna take care of you. Nothing's going to h-hurt you." Her voice broke.

Hayley's heart tugged. Was Summer remembering that she hadn't been able to keep Bailey safe?

"Take a breath," Hayley advised in a low voice, herself caught up in the palpable emotion of the moment. "Stay calm, keep your body energy low. You're doing great."

Summer continued to murmur to the horse. Gradually Major slowed to a walk and then stopped altogether. He swung his head left, then right, scenting the air, watching the girl.

"What do I do now?" Summer whispered, standing very still.

"Turn around slowly, away from the horse. Drop your shoulders and head. Then just wait."

Summer turned and lowered her head, chin to chest. Major stopped moving and watched the girl. Then, with measured steps, he walked over and stood behind Summer, his head lowered, too.

"Major is right behind you," Hayley said quietly. This part never failed to thrill her. "Turn around."

Summer turned, saw Major standing there, calmly and obediently. Her mouth fell open and her face lit as if she couldn't believe what she saw. She glanced at Hayley for guidance. "Now what?"

"Pat him gently. Tell him he's a good boy. Use smooth soft movements."

Summer raised her hand to let Major sniff her. The horse dropped his head lower still and gave her a gentle head bump.

"That means he respects you," Hayley said softly.

"He's beautiful," Summer said delightedly. The horse rubbed his nose along her hip. She patted his neck. "Good boy, Major."

"Now turn around and walk away," Hayley said.

"Oh, no. Really? Do I have to? He's accepting me."

"Just do it."

Summer gave Major one last pat then turned around. Hayley held her breath. This was the moment of truth. The small miracle never failed to occur but each time she felt the tension. Summer took a step, then another, and looked over her shoulder. Major flicked her ears from front to back.

"Keep going," Hayley said. "You have to trust, too."

Summer faced forward again and started walking. Major hesitated, and then began to follow, head down. When she reached the far side of the ring Summer stopped. She looked over her shoulder and saw Major right behind her. Her eyes filled with tears even as a smile spread across her face. She glanced at Hayley in wonder.

Hayley's chest filled with an ache that was familiar but ever new with each person she treated. This feeling was why she persisted in spite of all the difficulties and setbacks. Knowing that she and her horses made a difference to someone's life was amazing.

Summer walked over to Hayley, her face streaming with tears that collected in the creases of her ear-to-ear grin. Major followed. When she stopped, Major stopped. He nibbled delicately on her shoulder.

"That means he trusts you." Hayley's own smile spread.

"This is so awesome."

"How's your anxiety level now? On a scale of one to ten."

Summer put her arms around Major's neck and hugged, rubbing her cheek against the glossy golden-brown coat. "Three, maybe."

"And your inner smile?"

Summer laughed out loud. "Eleven!"

ADAM PULLED BACK into the yard just in time to hear Summer's whoop of joy. He climbed out of the truck and headed over to the lunge ring. To hell with staying out of the way, he wanted to see what had caused his anxious, angry daughter to sound like she was going down the big hill on a roller coaster.

He rounded the corner of the barn to see Hayley and Summer locked in a tight hug. Summer's eyes were scrunched shut and her cheeks wet with tears but her smile lit the cloudy day like a beacon. Major—or was it Sergeant?—was resting his chin on Summer's shoulder. The long buggy reins used in therapy were folded and hung over the fence. The session appeared to be over.

"How's it going?" he asked.

"Dad, Major followed me! I turned around and walked away and he just walked right after me."

"Fantastic." He tweaked the end of her hair, an old endearment she hadn't welcomed of late. She smiled wider and broke free of Hayley to put her arms around his waist.

Adam squeezed her tightly, his chest filling with wordless gratitude and relief. Was the nightmare over already, and so easily? He glanced at Hayley. "So…?"

She seemed to know what he meant. "Progress, good progress. Everyone gets the horse to follow them at the first session. It's exciting and very emotional. But it's not the end, by any means."

"But it's a good beginning."

"It's an excellent beginning," Hayley said, smiling.

"I'm going to go text Zoe." Summer pulled away and ran off to the house.

Hayley's smile lingered as her gaze followed Summer, then she turned back to Adam. "There will be setbacks, so don't be disappointed when that happens. Two steps forward, one step back—and sometimes three steps."

"I can live with that as long as the net result is ultimately a move forward." Adam glanced at his watch. "It's almost five. I have to start dinner. I hope you'll join us. Nothing fancy, just barbecued chicken."

She didn't answer right away, and he could almost hear her mental debate. Was she thinking about the awareness that had sprung up between them and didn't want to encourage those feelings? Had he held her gaze too long or had his innocent touch made her uncomfortable? Okay, not so innocent. He wanted to touch her. But at the same time, he didn't. Was this feeling of attraction going to build to the point where they wouldn't be able to ignore it? He wanted to find out. And he didn't. It was an added complication to an already complicated situation.

When she still didn't reply the invitation started to seem more fraught than it should have. Attraction aside, he wanted to express his gratitude, and he had a feeling Hayley was one of those people who sometimes forgot to eat. He wanted to…nourish her. He wasn't sure where this impulse came from. She was as self-sufficient as anyone he'd ever met, but she was doing it tough and she deserved a little pampering. If he didn't do it, who would?

Was that naive on his part? For all he knew she might have a boyfriend. Her husband had been dead nearly a year….

Not that he was trying to start anything. That would be foolish, considering he'd be leaving in three or four months. He didn't know Hayley well, but she didn't seem like the type to go in for casual relationships. For that matter, neither was he. But he did want her company for dinner—that part was simple.

All these thoughts flashed through his mind in the seconds it took for Hayley's inner struggle to play out over her face. At first he thought she was going to agree and then she said, "It seems a waste when you've stocked my fridge full of such good things."

"You'll have plenty of opportunities to use them. Summer would really like it if you came. She's sick of me and my lame Dad jokes."

"I'm just not sure it's a good idea. You're essentially my employer—"

"Can't we be friends, too?"

A half smile lifted one corner of her full mouth. "You don't like people saying no to you, do you?"

"It's only dinner, not a trip to Paris." He smiled easily, hoping she would capitulate. Because she was right, he didn't like people saying no to him.

Her half smile turned into a full grin. "If you offered me a trip to Paris I might say yes."

"Okay, let's go. I'll call my travel agent right now."

That made her laugh out loud. "You're crazy." He was feeling pleased with himself until she said, "Thanks, but no. I need to pick up a few more things at my place." She gathered up the looped reins and started walking toward the barn.

Adam went after her, surprised at how quickly she moved with that long stride of hers. "I'll help." He wasn't sure why he was being so insistent. Clearly the woman didn't want to spend time with him.

"No." This time her tone was as final as her words.

It took him a moment to process. Hayley wasn't

a woman to sugarcoat a rejection. "All right." He backed away, hands up. "Another time."

BACK AT THE garage, Hayley threw her record books for Horses for Hope into a box, furious with herself. Why was she standoffish to the point of rudeness with Adam? He'd only invited her to dinner. He was simply being polite and friendly.

What was she afraid of? So there was a minor buzz happening between them. They were both smart enough to know they'd be dumb to act on it— she was grieving and he was leaving. Plus, her treating Summer was reason enough not to see where the attraction might lead. Already the girl had confided things that Hayley couldn't tell Adam. Better to keep her distance.

She carried the last box out to her truck, then went back to the garage for a final check. She had her fireproof lockbox, her knitting and Shane's bowl and bag of dog food…. Then she spied an old photo her mother had sent not long ago, fallen behind a pot of parsley on the windowsill. It was of her and her younger sister, Marta, with their grandparents in front of the old house on this very property.

The house was lit by the setting sun and the whole clearing was a golden glow. She and her sister were laughing at something their grandfather had said. Grandma was smiling, as always. Happy days. Hayley slipped the photo into the box with her other papers and left.

Back at Timbertop she parked in front of the cottage. It was about the same time of day in the photo, when buildings and trees glowed. Through the open window of the big house came the soft strains of instrumental music. The enticing aroma of barbecuing chicken wafted from the deck at the front of the house. Suddenly she wished she'd said yes to Adam. Not for the food but for the company. What kind of fool was she to turn down a simple invitation to dinner?

She could see him moving around the kitchen. He was one seriously hot dude, even in a barbecue apron. Classic broad shoulders tapering to narrow hips, his shirtsleeves rolled up to his elbows. That thick dark hair falling over his forehead as he bent to…what, read the cookbook, rinse something in the sink…?

Then Adam looked up—their gazes locked. Shit. What was she doing, gazing into his window like the Little Match Girl, longing for a home and loved ones? With a jerky nod of her head she ducked inside the cottage.

Damn, damn, damn. Now he would think she really wanted to come but didn't because she was afraid of spending time with him. She was, but she didn't want him to know that.

She began unpacking a box. On top was a framed

photo of her and Leif on their wedding day that Molly had given her after she'd lost all her photos in the fire. She rubbed the dust off the glass with the sleeve of her shirt and placed it in the center of the mantelpiece.

Oh, Leif. She was such a jumble of emotions where he was concerned. If he'd lived would they have sorted out their problems? She really wanted to believe they would've, but…

Suddenly, she wasn't in the mood to unpack. Thinking about the past always made her restless and angsty and…lonely. A knock sounded at the door. Probably Summer. She touched her fingertips to her eyes and cleared her throat. "Come in. Door's open."

Adam's tall frame filled the doorway. He carried a plate of bruschetta piled with diced tomatoes and basil. "I thought you might want a snack. I had extra."

Hayley salivated at the savory treat, but Adam's solid presence and deep, rumbling voice was even more welcome, pulling her back to the present. "Are you trying to lure me up to the house for dinner?"

A glint came into his dark eyes. "Is it working?"

She bit the inside of her cheek to stop from smiling and cocked her head on the side as if deliberating. "What else have you got?"

"Chicken with peri peri sauce and veggie kebabs."

She tapped her cheek. "Sounds good. I'll have to think."

"Try one of these. It might help you make up your mind." Adam set the plate of bruschetta on the breakfast bar and strolled around the room.

Hayley reached for a slice and bit into it, tasting garlic and fruity olive oil. Yum.

Adam stopped in front of the mantelpiece to study her wedding photo. "So this is Leif, your late husband. He's certainly a handsome devil."

"Huh. Most people say something about what a lovely bride." She grinned to let him know she was joking but she was a bit confused. Was that an edge to his voice? Leif had died trying to save his damn property. "Did you know him?"

"No, but Diane did. She and her girlfriends were a bit gaga over him." Adam glanced over his shoulder as if checking her reaction. "I hope I'm not being untactful."

"Not at all," Hayley said stiffly. "Everyone loved Leif."

Had Adam somehow clued in to the troubles between her and Leif? Had he heard gossip in the town? Leif had given her cause for concern, and twice she'd come close to leaving him. But he'd regretted his actions and had promised never to do it again. She'd believed him. She had to. The alternative would have meant the end of her marriage, the end of her and Leif's dreams. She couldn't have handled that. Home and family were everything to her, and she'd invested her whole adult life in Leif.

"Leif and I were solid. Women flirted with him all the time but it meant nothing." Her mouth twisted. "Sorry, I didn't mean to imply that Diane flirted with him."

In fact, at her party Diane had hardly spoken to Leif, almost to the point of ignoring him. Hayley remembered being miffed at that, since Leif had gone out of his way to take Diane and her friends on an extralong trail ride.

Adam turned away from the mantelpiece, his gaze bland and unreadable. "How long were you married?"

"Eight years. But we'd known each other since high school." She allowed herself a tiny sigh. "I'd always loved riding but thought of it as a hobby. Leif made me believe I could make a livelihood out of horses. We were going to build a dude ranch. I still want to do that."

"It must be nice to have a common goal with your partner."

Unlike Adam and Diane? Had he and his ex-wife led separate lives? Again, there was so little expression in his face or voice she couldn't read him. "Hope Mountain is a long way from the city where you work," she ventured. "Hard to have common goals when you're so far apart."

"Our marriage was over long before we bought this property. I just didn't know it."

He sounded as if it didn't matter, but he must have his own share of grief and anger. "I'm sorry, Adam."

"Don't be. I regret how our breakup affected Summer, but… Never mind." He walked back to the kitchen where she was tackling another bruschetta. "So will you come for dinner? I've been on this cooking jag since I've been in Mount Hope, and I'm getting pretty good."

Hayley couldn't disagree as she swallowed another delicious mouthful. She was relieved that the conversation had taken a new turn. "How will Summer feel about it? After our therapy session she might be uncomfortable being in a social situation with me."

"Who do you think demanded I bring the appetizer down?"

Hayley licked a drop of juice off her thumb. "In that case, I'll come, thanks. I'll wash up and be there shortly."

"I'll see you soon, then." He smiled into her eyes and added softly, "You were an extraordinarily beautiful bride." Then, while she was blushing to the roots of her hair, he let himself out and went back to the house.

All her confusion came swirling back and she felt like running after him and saying she couldn't make it after all. But after that chat about Leif she'd rather not be alone with her thoughts this evening.

She took a deep breath. This was crazy. She needed to get control of her emotions, damp them down, tame them into manageable proportions. It was just dinner. Just a meal with a nice man and his daughter. Not a date with a hot guy who set her pulse racing every time he looked into her eyes. Not, not, not.

But she hummed to herself as she took a shower and brushed out her hair. She started to pull on a clean pair of jeans, then changed her mind, instead opting for a sundress. It would get cold once the sun went down, so she grabbed a bulky cardigan she'd knit herself.

She carried a half bottle of Molly's cumquat liqueur as a contribution and went out into the balmy spring evening, repeating her mantra: *This is not a date*. Not even close. Just two people sharing a meal. Three people. Summer would be there the whole time. They would eat, have some light conversation and she would go back to the cottage. What could possibly go wrong?

"She's coming," Adam told Summer as he entered the kitchen through the back door. He recognized the undertone of excitement in his voice and tried to quell it. "She'll be here shortly."

"Goody." Earbuds in, Summer practiced a dance

move on the sun-drenched hardwood floor in the great room.

Adam opened a bottle of pinot grigio he had chilling in the fridge and got out two wineglasses. *Play it cool.* This was just a simple meal. He had plenty of food and he was sharing? Really? So why had he shaved and put on a clean shirt before going down to the cottage?

Okay, it felt a bit like a date. But he was glad he'd tried again. Seeing her outside with her face aglow in the sunset, he'd caught a disconcerting glimpse of yearning and conflict beneath her outward strength and optimism. She wanted to come just as much as he wanted her to. All she'd needed was a gentle push in the right direction.

And he had to admit the watch was bothering him. A lot. He wanted to give it to her, but he didn't want to add to her pain over her late husband. If he got to know her better, he might be able to decide what to do.

He went outside to check the barbecue, shifting the partially cooked chicken to one side and adding skewers of vegetables. He hoped she liked eggplant. He wasn't sure he did, but the color went nicely with tomato and zucchini.

Footsteps sounded as Hayley came around the side of the house onto the veranda. "I thought I'd find you back here."

Adam dropped the lid on the barbecue with an unintentional bang. Hayley's honey-blond hair swirled loose around bare shoulders, and a blue paisley cotton dress clung to her slender curves and bare legs. Miles of legs, still pale from winter, but oh, so shapely. At her sandal-shod heels trotted her black-and-white dog.

"Sorry I made you jump." She clutched a bundled sweater under one arm and waved a bottle half-filled with orange liqueur. "For later. My mother-in-law makes it."

"Thanks. I'm so glad you decided to come." He took the bottle and put it on the round glass outdoor table. "Would you like a glass of white for now?"

"Sounds lovely." Her wavy hair, still slightly damp, sent a whiff of lemony shampoo in his direction. "Is it all right if Shane is here? He's used to going everywhere with me."

"He's fine. Have a seat." He poured her a glass from the bottle in the wine cooler, then turned down the barbecue so they would have time to talk before dinner.

Her fingers curled around the stem of the wineglass. Her nails looked freshly scrubbed, pink and clean. "Sorry about before, Adam. I must have seemed pretty rude."

"You have a problem accepting the kindness of strangers?"

She gave him a rueful smile. "I'm out of practice with socializing."

Adam angled his deck chair to face her. "Admit it, the bruschetta changed your mind, didn't it?"

"It was pretty amazing," she conceded, smiling.

"If I'd known food was such a chick magnet I'd have taken up cooking long ago."

Laughing, she made a face. "Chick magnet?"

"Not cool, huh?" He winced. "I'm out of practice, too." This was his cue to tactfully ask about her love life. But he could just imagine how crass that would sound. *So, have you hooked up with anyone new since your husband died?* The pause stretched into seconds.

"It must be lonely for you up here, not knowing anyone," she said, as if picking up on his thoughts.

"I'm okay with my own company. Temporarily, at least." He added as gently as he could, "And how are you coping, with your husband gone?"

Hayley glanced into her glass and shrugged. "I'm fine." Then she smoothly changed the subject. "I guess with all that time on your hands it makes sense to do some spring cleaning around the property."

Okay, so her husband was off-limits. "I'm getting the house ready to go on the market. But don't repeat that to Summer, if you don't mind."

"You two should try talking to each other. You both might benefit."

"I've tried. She goes ballistic when I mention moving. I promised we'd stay till school's over. I hope by then you can get to the bottom of whatever's bothering her. She and I used to have a great relationship. I hope we will again." He paused. "We shouldn't talk about her when she's not around. I don't think she'd like it."

"You're right." Hayley sipped her wine. "So, what can we talk about? Work? What do you do for a living?"

"I'm an architect."

She brightened. "Do you do residential work? You've no doubt noticed there's plenty of construction going on in Hope Mountain. You could keep busy if you wanted."

"I work on large developments, mostly overseas. I was in the middle of designing a luxury apartment complex in Shanghai when I was called away to look after Summer."

"Wow, that's big. How is moving out here impacting your project?"

"Working from home part-time is no problem in the short term. But this project is supposed to pave the way for me to become a partner in the firm. Naturally, I'd like to get back to full-time work as soon as possible."

"I guess you wouldn't be interested in drafting plans for the rebuilding of my house. Small potatoes compared to what you're involved in."

"Well, I wouldn't dismiss it out of hand. A project like that might be fun. It's been ages since I've designed a single-family dwelling. Do you have any idea what you want?"

"I want to re-create my grandparents' house." She crossed her legs, drawing his gaze down to her smooth bare calf. Circling her ankle were tiny tattooed horses. One, two—

"There are five." Her smile flashed on, then off. "The ones I lost."

He dragged his eyes back to her face. "Do you have photos or a sketch of the floor plan?"

"I have one photo taken of the front of the house when I was a child. I could draw a plan from memory."

"Do that when you have a spare moment and I'll take a look."

"Thanks." Her blue dress rode up over her knee as she leaned back, her arms loose and relaxed. "I'm really racking up items on the IOU list. You don't have to do this—I don't expect anything."

"Seeing Summer so happy this afternoon puts you firmly in the black." He topped up their wine and set the bottle back in the cooler. "Are you serious about rebuilding in the same location? You're not worried about another fire?"

Her face closed up and she tugged down her skirt. "Fire is a fact of life in the Australian bush. Hope Mountain is my home."

"I see." She was making a big mistake in his opinion, but hey, it was none of his business. Clearly nothing anyone could say would stop her, let alone him.

The sliding glass doors slammed open and Summer emerged, a glass of cola in her hand. "Hi, Hayley." She turned to Adam. "When's dinner?"

"Soon. I'll turn the barbecue up again. Summer, maybe you could make a salad?" He waited for the inevitable groan of resistance to any suggestion of work.

Before Summer could say anything, Hayley rose. "I'll help you if you like, Summer."

"Okay," the girl said eagerly.

As he adjusted the flame under the grill, Adam listened to them talking about horses as they worked in the kitchen. Apparently Summer was excited about Blaze's imminent birth, and she was already thinking of names for both colts and fillies.

He turned the chicken pieces over and moved the vegetable skewers around. Would Hayley get the vet to attend, or was she concerned about the bills? He hadn't had to worry about basic expenses in so long it was sobering to consider things from her perspective.

Hayley's life was a microcosm of the whole community up here. At the time of the bushfires he'd watched horrific newscasts on TV. Many people across the nation, including himself, had donated money for the victims of the fires—then promptly put the misery out of their minds. Even now, as he emptied his pockets into collection jars all over town, being in Hope Mountain had made him realize that wasn't enough.

These people needed practical help, such as when he'd unloaded the truck at the donation tent. Maybe he'd see if he could do something else while he was here, like join a volunteer group to clean up the burned-out church. This wasn't his life and he wouldn't be here if not for Summer, but like it or not, he was part of the community for the foreseeable future. Work needed doing, and he wanted to get involved.

He transferred the cooked chicken and vegetables to a platter, which he placed on the table. The tableau in the kitchen made him pause. Hayley's blond head and Summer's bright red hair glowed in the dying light of the sun. They were laughing together as Hayley chopped a red bell pepper and Summer tipped washed and torn lettuce into a big wooden bowl.

Hayley had told him to be prepared for setbacks and he was, but nothing could take away from seeing his little girl smiling again. After the storms and gloom of the past week her face shone like a rainbow, full of promise.

"The food is ready," he called. "Bring everything outside and we'll eat on the veranda." Summer carried out plates with cutlery balanced on top. He slung an arm around her. "How're you doing, kiddo?"

Instantly she tensed beneath his touch. "I'm fine."

Uh-oh. He was trying too hard. He knew he should withdraw his arm, but he wanted so badly to hang on to the good vibe that he didn't. "Did you have a good day with the horses?"

"Why, did Hayley say something?" Summer's gaze flickered with anxiety, suspicion and guilt. "She promised me our sessions were confidential."

Guilt? Surely he was mistaken. But alarm bells were ringing. What was going on with his daughter, and why did he have the feeling he was going to be the last to know?

"Hayley didn't say anything," Adam said. "If she told you it was confidential I'm sure she'll keep her word." He paused. "Would you like to tell me anything? I promise I won't be angry or upset."

"How can you promise that when you don't know what I might say? What if I told you I'd murdered someone?" The notion was ludicrous but Summer's mood had done one of its quick flips. She was sharp and intense, not joking.

"I wouldn't believe you."

"Maybe you don't know me as well as you think you do."

"All the more reason to talk, right?" he said lightly.

She shook her head and ducked out from under his arm. "I'm going to set the table."

CHAPTER SEVEN

ADAM WAS STILL smarting from Summer's brush-off when Hayley came out with the wooden salad bowl.

"Everything okay?" she murmured. "Is Summer upset?"

He watched his daughter fling down the knives and forks. "As you say, one step forward, two steps back."

"Don't worry." She touched his arm. "It'll all work out."

"I hope you're right. Let's eat."

They sat around the table, and the next few minutes were quiet as everyone filled their plates. Below in the valley, shadows had fallen. On the far mountains the spiky profiles of trees rode the ridges, etched against the pink-and-orange sky.

"I would love to have this in my new house," Hayley said, sweeping her arm in a wide arc. "A big, wide veranda with comfortable chairs where I could watch the sun set."

"Did the original homestead have a veranda?"

"Only a small one. But I was thinking while Summer and I were getting the salad ready. This is my chance for a do-over and it makes sense to improve on the past. I doubt my grandparents would've chosen sentimentality over practicality—life was hard enough in their day. They would have taken every improvement they could get their hands on."

Adam speared a piece of marinated eggplant. It didn't look so pretty now. "I take it you won't be going back to using an outhouse?"

"No, I think I can live without that."

"How about a gazebo with a hot tub instead?"

"Now you're talking." She laughed and then sighed, as if she was only dreaming. "Put it on the wish list."

He would get such a buzz out of making her wish list come true. "If you like, I could incorporate the best of your old house with modern elements for a structure that's practical but homey."

"Are you sure you have time, what with your other work and getting this place ready for…" she glanced at Summer "…the bushfire season?"

"It'll be fun." He poured her more wine, keeping an eye on Summer. She was checking her phone beneath the table. He didn't allow the phone at the table and she knew it.

"Eat up before your food gets cold," Adam said to her.

"I'm looking up horse names for the foal." Summer turned to Hayley. "What about Trixie for a filly, and Blade for a colt?"

"I haven't really thought about names yet," Hayley said. "Why don't you start a list and put those on it?"

"Cool." She tapped away on the keypad.

"Put the phone away till after dinner, please," Adam insisted. A ping signaled an incoming message. Summer started to read it. Frustrated, he said, "Summer."

She didn't seem to hear him. Her face went white, making the freckles on her nose stand out. Then color flooded back and she stabbed at the phone to turn it off before tossing it across the table.

"What's wrong?" Adam asked.

"Nothing." Summer's hand trembled as she reached for a piece of chicken. He didn't say anything else but he continued to watch her, concerned and helpless. She glanced up, eyes blazing. "Quit staring at me!"

"Sorry," he said quietly, not wanting the scene to escalate. Hayley gave him a sympathetic glance but didn't offer any comment.

Adam turned his attention away from Summer. He was learning it was better not to keep asking her questions when she was in this mood. Instead he quizzed Hayley on her lifestyle and her practical needs, and inquired about her other interests. Turned out she liked to knit.

"I always think of people who knit being elderly, like my grandmother," he said.

"You are so wrong." Hayley tucked into her

chicken. "I belong to a knitting circle. We meet twice a month, and not one of us is over forty. Well, Lisa is forty-eight but she only admits to thirty-nine."

"Did you make your sweater?" Summer asked, nodding at the soft multicolored garment on the back of Hayley's chair.

Adam relaxed a little. If his daughter was back in the conversation it meant she'd calmed down—by herself. Maybe the horse therapy was starting to have an effect.

"I knit it out of scraps of donated wool," Hayley said.

Adam envisaged a nook beside a fire with one of those armless rocking chairs and Hayley sitting there, knitting. "What else do you do for relaxation?"

"I read, watch movies. I like to dance."

"A ballroom might not fit in a standard-sized home but I could try." He enjoyed seeing her quick smile. "How many bedrooms, three or four? Do you want to make room for future children?"

The smile froze on her face.

Hell. He wasn't normally this clumsy with women. Treading the narrow line between friendship and flirting was throwing him off balance. "Sorry, that's too personal."

"I… No, that's okay. I would like to have kids someday, but…who knows if, or when, that will happen."

"Some lucky man will snap you up. When you're ready."

She flushed and reached for her glass, taking a big gulp of wine. "I don't know."

"I do."

More frozen silence. Damn. All he'd intended was a gallant compliment to the effect that she was too desirable a woman to stay single for long. He couldn't say that in front of his daughter so his words had come out as even more suggestive, as if *he* had designs on Hayley.

Inside the house, the phone rang. His first impulse was to go answer it and escape the awkwardness but then he had another idea. "Summer, can you get that?"

She scraped back her chair and went inside. Her animated voice indicated the call was for her. Adam reached for her cell with a quick glance at Hayley. "Don't judge me."

She held up a hand and silently shook her head.

He tapped into Summer's message log. The latest was from someone named Steve. *I want to talk to you.* Seemed harmless enough, so why the dramatic reaction? "Has she mentioned anyone named Steve?" he said to Hayley.

"You know I can't tell you. Please don't ask."

Adam set the phone carefully back where he'd found it. "If this boy or man hurts my daughter…" His words trailed away as he realized he was implying it would be Hayley's fault. She was only trying to help them both. He scrubbed his hands over his face.

Hayley reached across and touched his shoulder. "Don't worry so much. I don't think she wants to talk to him."

He looked into her eyes, so blue and serious. She was willing him to trust her. And he did, instinctively. It eased his mind a bit, except…she knew something he didn't.

"Dad?" Summer was back. "Can I be excused? *Puberty Blues* is on TV, and Zoe and I are going on Twitter to talk while we watch."

"You're not finished eating."

"I've had enough. Please?" She jiggled up and down with impatience.

"Okay, off you go. Take your plate with you. And thanks for helping with the salad."

"No problem. See you later, Hayley. I'll show you my list of names tomorrow."

"I'll look forward to it. Good night."

Summer grabbed her phone and her dirty dishes and left.

Adam put the last few minutes out of his mind and rewound to where his and Hayley's conversation had left off. Ah, yes, they'd been mired in awkwardness thanks to his foot-in-mouth attack. "Um, we were talking about the number of bedrooms."

Hayley cleared her throat, her features composed. "Three would be fine."

Damn Leif. What had he been thinking to cheat on her? Adam wished the man were alive so he could knock his block off.

Hayley was strong, but there were moments like earlier when he glimpsed the vulnerability beneath her tough exterior. How would she ever let another man in while she was still clinging to her husband's memory?

Maybe it was Adam's duty to tell her the truth. If the situation were reversed, would he want to know? He thought so, but on the other hand, what one didn't know didn't hurt them. Who really knew what went on in a marriage? Outwardly, he and Diane had looked solid, too.

If he wanted to help Hayley, he should stick to drafting house plans and giving her horses shelter, not poke into her private life. The last thing he wanted was to hurt her. She was fresh, natural, unaffected. Not innocent, naturally, but not jaded, either. Despite everything she had an optimism that he found admirable and inspiring.

"Were you able to save anything from your house of sentimental value—photos, keepsakes…jewelry?" he asked.

"No, I was in the dam. Where would I have put anything?" she said mildly.

"Of course," he murmured. "It's a shame you have nothing left to remember your late husband by." Like a watch.

"I have the wedding photo my mother-in-law gave me. But I don't need it to remind me of Leif. I can picture him easily."

"Images fade with time." Adam knew. His memory of his grandfather was hazy now, consisting mostly of the smell of tobacco and a pair of weathered hands hoisting him onto the back of a horse when he was about five years old.

The fundamental thing was that he had no right to hold on to her late husband's property. How could he assume she wouldn't want to know the truth? And how could he deprive her of a valuable item when she was clearly hard up for money? She could sell the Rolex and buy a new saddle or something.

Hayley leaned across the table and touched his hand. "It's okay, Adam. I don't need Leif's child to remember him, if that's what you're thinking. And if I end up never having kids it won't destroy my life."

He realized he'd been staring at her soberly, intently, trying to sort out his own dilemma about Leif's watch while she thought he was worried that he'd embarrassed her over her lack of children and a partner to start a family with.

The bottom line was, having the watch in his possession and not giving it to her felt dishonest. Regardless of what had gone on between Diane and Leif, regardless of Hayley and Leif's relationship, what he cared about was *his* relationship with Hayley. Whatever that turned out to be, whether simply boss and employee, or friends, or a flirtation, he wanted it to be based on honesty. He'd had enough dishonesty with Diane to last a lifetime.

A gust of evening breeze lifted Hayley's hair. Shivering slightly, she drew on her sweater. "It's getting late. I'll help you clean up, but then I'd better go back to the cottage."

"We haven't tasted Molly's liqueur," Adam said. "Stay a little longer?"

She hesitated and then said, "All right."

Together they carried the remains of the meal inside. Adam put the kettle on and over his protests, Hayley stacked the dishwasher. It was a quiet domestic scene, peaceful and with a feeling of good will. Hayley seemed more relaxed than he'd seen her since they'd met. Clearly, being in a home again and having her horses secure was good for her.

And now he was about to blow her world apart.

HAYLEY CAST SIDELONG glances at Adam as he poured small glasses of golden liqueur. He'd been lovely at dinner, relaxed and funny and sweet, trying to draw her out as he figured out the best plan for her house. Yes, there'd been a couple of awkward moments when she hadn't known how to react to his questions, but it had been a long time since a man had hung on her every word and been so interested in what she did, thought and wanted.

And if that was a sad commentary on her marriage, well, so be it. She and Leif had been so busy building the trail-riding business—and he'd had his volunteer firefighting—that they hadn't spent a lot of quality time together those last few months. That had been about to change, though. He'd promised that this spring they would take a trip somewhere, maybe a cruise to Tahiti or Singapore. It would have been a second honeymoon.

There was no point crying over what couldn't ever come to pass. *Like having a family.* Leif used to say he wanted kids, but whenever she'd broached the subject of trying for a baby, he'd always had some compelling reason why they should wait another year. Poor Adam had looked so upset at the thought of hurting her feelings that she'd made out like she didn't care about not having children. When in fact, she cared. A lot.

Adam handed her a glass of liqueur, then went to the sideboard in the dining room and removed an object from the drawer. His expression was so serious she almost felt alarmed. What could possibly make him look like that?

"I found this," he said, holding out a watch. "It belonged to your husband."

She gave it a quick glance. "No, it can't have been Leif's. He wore a brushed metal timepiece, and this is a gold Rolex. Leif never owned anything so valuable."

"Read the inscription."

Even before she turned the watch over she got a prickling over the back of her neck. Then she saw the words. *For Leif, my sexy mountain man, from your red-hot mama.*

Oh, no. Oh, hell. She couldn't breathe, couldn't catch her breath. He'd started up again with someone else. He'd promised. The date on the inscription was Christmas of the previous year. Two months before he'd died.

Bastard. He'd humiliated her again, this time in front of a virtual stranger, but a man she liked and respected and whom she wanted to think well of her.

Very carefully she set her tiny glass of cumquat liqueur on the table. "It's not Leif's," she heard herself deny. "There's a mistake. It must belong to another man with the same name."

"Hayley, I'm afraid there's no mistake." Adam's eyes were warm and dark with compassion. "I confronted Diane. She admitted she and your late husband had an affair. I'm sorry."

Why was he doing this to her? What was the point? Who did it serve? No one.

"She's lying, maybe to hurt you," Hayley said stiffly. "I don't know. I don't know her very well." But she could well believe Diane had seduced Leif. Or Leif had seduced Diane. Those two were similar in some ways, skating along the surface of life, indulging in their own selfish wants and desires.

Well, they weren't going to take away what little dignity she had left.

She pushed the watch back into Adam's hands and he was forced, reluctantly, to take it. "Leif loved me. He would never have cheated on me."

Adam's expression was carefully neutral. "You could sell it, use the money for your horses."

The thought of profiting from Leif's affair made her want to throw up. "Give it back to Diane."

"She doesn't want it."

Hayley wanted to walk out the door and pretend this conversation never happened. But her curiosity got the better of her. Like probing a festering sore, she had to know how deep the wound was and how painful the poison. "Where did you find the watch?"

"In the bathroom."

Hayley's facial muscles felt tight. Her hands clenched in her lap. Leif had promised not to do it again. She'd been fool enough, weak enough, to believe him. No, it was worse—she'd wanted to believe him so she wouldn't have to do anything about her sham of a marriage. She hated what that said about her. Weak. Spineless. No self-esteem.

This thing with Diane was no one-night stand, as he'd claimed the other two betrayals had been. No woman, even one as rich and frivolous as Diane, gave a man a gold Rolex after one night. Looking back, there'd been times when she'd wondered where Leif was and he couldn't give her an answer. Times when she'd caught him out in a small lie. But she'd stayed quiet, not confronting him. She'd been willfully blind, wanting to believe the best of her husband, not wanting to think he would cheat on her again. Not wanting to see herself in the role of the wronged wife.

She couldn't admit that to Adam. Leif had hurt and humiliated her in life—he wouldn't do it in death, too. "I have no idea whose watch that is, but it wasn't my late husband's. Leif wouldn't do that to me."

A horrible thick silence fell between her and Adam. He patently disbelieved her but was too polite, too kind, to say so. Hayley couldn't meet his gaze. She felt so brittle she might shatter if she moved. Her fingers curled into her palm so tightly the nails dug in. Shane whined and licked her knuckles.

It was enough to wake her up. "What are you doing inside the house, boy?" She had to get out of here before she broke apart. "I'll say good-night. I have to work at Molly's café in the morning."

"I'll walk you down to the cottage."

"It's okay, I can manage." But she was so stiff she tripped on the edge of the dining room carpet. Shaking off his hand, she walked carefully to the door.

"Take a flashlight, at least. It's dark out." He handed her one from the windowsill, then followed her to the veranda. "I'm sorry."

"What for?" She managed a smile. At least she hoped it was a smile and not a grimace. "I hope you find whoever lost that watch. I'm sure they'll be missing it."

"Hayley…"

"Thanks for dinner." With the flashlight bobbing across the gravel driveway she stumbled toward the cottage, missing the flagstone path because her eyes were blurred, and wetting her sandals in the dew-covered grass. Adam stood in his open kitchen door, watching her progress.

How could he be so calm and indifferent? Didn't he care that his ex-wife had had an affair with her married neighbor? Did marriage mean nothing to him?

For Leif, my sexy mountain man, from your red-hot mama.

The words ought to be etched on Leif's memorial headstone so the whole world would know what a lying, cheating jerk he had been. But, a small voice inside her head insisted, then the world would also know that Leif had played around because she wasn't enough woman to hold on to her man.

That was plain wrong, and she knew it. She had to fight that voice. Leif had been the one with the problem, not her. She'd spent so much time trying to be worthy of him that she hadn't stopped to wonder if he was ever worthy of her. He wasn't. He just wasn't.

The cottage door wasn't locked, thank God, or

she didn't know how her numb fingers would have managed the key. She started to go into the bedroom and balked at the threshold. When she'd asked Adam where he'd found the watch he'd hesitated for a fraction of a second and his eyes had flickered. She'd assumed he'd meant the bathroom in the house.

What if he hadn't shared the whole truth? What if Leif and Diane had been together in the guest cottage, making love in the bed she was to sleep in? It made sense if Diane wanted to keep evidence of her affair away from her daughter. *Oh, dear God. It had to be.* Hayley wouldn't get a wink of sleep, imagining Leif and Diane together, naked....

No, she wasn't going to conjure painful scenarios. With an effort she thrust the images from her mind. Tonight she would sleep on the couch. Tomorrow she would move back to her garage—

But she couldn't, not after she'd insisted the watch hadn't belonged to Leif and that he'd never had an affair with Diane.

Stuck, she uttered every curse word she knew. That made her feel a tiny bit better, enough to go through the motions of brushing her teeth and washing her face.

She grabbed the quilt off the bed and took it out to the love seat. Punching the pillow, she curled into a fetal position, willing herself not to cry. The evening had been perfect until Adam had brought out the watch. Great food, delicious wine and excellent company. Now she didn't know how she was going to face Adam in the morning.

Would he tell Summer? No, of course he wouldn't. Unless Summer already knew. Maybe she'd walked past the cottage and heard her mother and Leif inside—

Hayley flipped onto her back, legs bent at the knee, trying to get comfortable. She sat up and switched on the table lamp. Maybe a cup of camomile tea would help.

She got up and threw on a light dressing gown and hunted for tea bags. Sure enough, there was a small stash of herbal teas in the cupboard. She stuck one in a mug and leaned against the counter, waiting for the kettle to boil.

She should never have moved into the cottage. She could have just come during the day to feed the horses and give Summer her therapy. That was what she would have done if she hadn't been seduced by the luxury of windows and furniture and a real bathroom. She was getting soft.

A shadow passed across the curtains and a second later there was a knock at the door. For a moment she didn't move. She couldn't bear for Adam to see her so fragile, so broken.

He knocked again. "Hayley, are you all right?"

She went to the door but didn't open it. Instead she pressed her hands to the wood for support. "I'm fine."

"I saw your light on. Are you having trouble sleeping in there?"

"I got up for a cup of tea. Don't worry about me. I'm a night owl." Her voice was pitched an octave too high as she told the lie. She was up at dawn every day of the year and crashed early. Tomorrow she would be a mess on her first day at the café.

"Can I come in?" he said. "Just for a moment."

He wasn't going to let her deal with this on her own. Reluctantly she opened the door. He came in, bringing a waft of cool night air. She pulled her dressing gown tighter, her bare toes curling on the polished wood floor. "Why are you here?"

"I came to apologize for springing the watch on you like that. I should've softened it, or waited, or kept it to myself. I feel terrible about this."

She kept her chin high and her gaze firm. "Thanks, but I don't need your pity."

His eyes flashed. "I don't pity you. I'm angry at Leif and Diane. Do you want to talk about it?"

"Not really. I'd like to get back to sleep."

He glanced at the blanket and pillow on the couch and back at her. Damn. He must realize she'd figured out that Leif and Diane had their rendezvous in here. Suddenly she was weary of pretending. All through her marriage she'd played her role in the facade of a happy, united couple, holding her head high and smiling when her heart was crumbling. Now she had to face the truth. Leif didn't deserve her loyalty.

She raised an arm and let it drop heavily to her side. "You're right. You win. The watch belonged to Leif."

Adam reached for her hands. She hadn't realized how cold her fingers were until they were sandwiched between his large warm palms. He chafed them gently, rubbing circulation back into them. "It's okay."

"Yes, I'm fine." Maybe not fine enough to sleep in the bed of betrayal, but she had just enough strength not to collapse into a quivering, weeping wreck. "Why didn't you tell me right away, Adam? You don't need to protect me."

"I wasn't sure I should tell you at all. I didn't want to cause you pain." He gave her a small, rueful smile. "And if I'm going to be perfectly honest, I figured you wouldn't want to stay in the cottage if you knew the truth. I didn't want you to leave."

"For Summer's sake. I get it." And she did. Adam would do anything for his daughter. She would be like that, too, if she had a child.

"She's made such a good start with her therapy I'd hate to see that derailed." He hesitated then looked at her directly, his gaze frank. "But I don't want to be another man who lies to you. We don't know each other well yet, but I hope we can be friends. I told you in the end because I wanted to be honest with you."

Friends. Honesty. The backs of her eyelids pricked. "That sounds good."

He came a step closer and placed his hand on her shoulder, squeezing gently. His heat seeped through the thin cotton of her dressing gown and warmed her. Something flickered in his eyes, and for a moment she thought he would pull her into his arms. Her breath stopped, and she realized in that terrible instant how much she longed to be held, how desperate she was for the simple human comfort of a caring embrace.

Which was crazy because she got hugs all the time, from Molly and Jacinta and her therapy clients. So it must be a man's embrace she wanted. And maybe, just maybe, Adam's touch in particular.

So part of her was disappointed when he simply squeezed her shoulder again and let go. Another part of her was grateful he reverted to briskness. "You can stay in the spare room up at the house." When she started to protest, he held up a hand. "That couch will break your back. There's plenty of room and it's no trouble."

If she hadn't had to work at the café tomorrow she would have refused. But it was past midnight and she needed sleep. "Okay. Tomorrow I'll go back to my place. It won't affect Summer's therapy, I promise."

"We'll talk about that in the morning. Get your

things and let's go." A few minutes later they left the cottage behind, making their way across the yard.

The house was dark but for the light over the stove. Adam flicked on a hall lamp and led the way up the curving staircase to the gallery on the second floor. Hayley tiptoed down the carpeted hall, looking around at the paintings on the wall and the dried flower arrangement on a narrow table at the head of the stairs. At the end of the hall was a large round window that, judging from the direction the house faced, would flood the corridor with morning light.

"This is Summer's room," Adam said in a low voice as they passed a darkened door. "The bathroom is next door and you're on the other side. The master bedroom is there—I don't use it. My room is at the end of the hall." He stopped at a linen closet and found a set of sheets. "I don't know who stayed in the spare room last."

Summer's door opened a crack and her tousled head peered out. "Dad? What's going on?"

"Hayley's going to sleep in the spare room," Adam said. "Go back to bed."

"I thought she was staying in the cottage," the girl said.

"There's a mouse running around in there. She's scared."

"Oh. Okay. 'Night." Summer retreated into her room and shut the door.

Hayley held her outrage until they were in the

bedroom. She whipped off the coverlet to expose a bare mattress pad. "A mouse? I've never been afraid of a mouse in my life."

"Sorry, I should've said a rat." His eyes danced as he spread the bottom sheet.

She huffed as she tucked the elastic corner around the mattress. "I can take on a rat with one hand tied behind my back. And don't bother suggesting a snake—I can deal with them, too. Once a black snake found its way into the garage when I left the door open."

A hint of a smile tilted Adam's mouth. "I suppose you killed it with a shovel and barbecued it for dinner?"

"Nope."

"Strangled it with your bare hands?"

"No way. A black snake can strike faster than you can blink. I got the hose and flooded the garage. He floated right back out the door."

Adam paused, the top sheet in his hands. "You're not kidding, are you?"

"Why would I joke about that?"

He flung the sheet across and she grabbed it with both hands as it fluttered down. For a moment their gazes met across the stretched sheet. How did she feel about her snake of a husband now that she'd found out about his affair?

As if she'd caught the direction of his thoughts,

she said almost fiercely, "You *are* feeling sorry for me. Stop it. I'm not brokenhearted."

"I'm glad." He let a beat go by. "Did you know about Leif and Diane?"

Hayley tucked in the corner, wrapping it tightly. "No, but there'd been others before her."

Adam swore softly as he tucked his side. "Why did you stay with him?"

Tears sprang to Hayley's eyes and she sat down on the half-made bed. She didn't speak, just clenched her fists on her thighs. Adam came around the bed and sat beside her.

"I wanted our marriage to work," she said at last, her voice tight and watery with unshed tears. "I thought if I tried hard enough, was a good wife, did my best to 'understand' him and be tolerant, he would be faithful. He kept promising to be." A tear fell on her white knuckles. "I was an idiot to believe him."

Adam put an arm around her. "Don't be angry at yourself. Be angry at Leif."

She brushed away the moisture in her eyes. "It's my fault, too, for putting up with his behavior. My parents split up when I was little." From nowhere came a spurt of intense anger. "Out of the blue they announced they were getting a divorce. They didn't even try to work things out. After the divorce I went to live with my grandparents. I hardly ever saw my father after that."

"It probably wasn't out of the blue," Adam said. "But maybe they didn't fight in front of you."

"Maybe," she conceded. Her dad had been out of work and couldn't get another job. He wanted to leave Hope Mountain and her mother had refused to go. When he left, she'd had a nervous breakdown and ended up leaving, too.

Why couldn't her parents have been like Grandpa and Grandma? They'd had a wonderful marriage that lasted sixty-five long and happy years. Hayley had wanted that for herself, had believed in it as hard as she could. Seeing Molly and Rolf's happy marriage cemented that desire.

Had she lost faith in the possibility of happiness? She wiped her eyes. "Adam, when do you think it started?"

"You mean Leif and Diane? I'm not sure. The first time she and her girlfriends came up here for trail riding was a year and a half ago, in the autumn."

"She rode a lot that winter, with Summer or her friends. Lots of times it was just her. And Leif, of course." Hayley reached for a tissue from the box on the nightstand. "I didn't think anything of it. I was such a fool."

"When this house came on the market Diane pressured me to buy it as a holiday retreat." Adam shook his head. "I thought if she was happy maybe we would be happy as a couple. Not long after that she moved out of our city house permanently. I knew then she was seeing someone but I didn't know who, let alone that he was married." He paused. "Were you ever suspicious?"

Hayley shook her head. "I trusted him. He'd promised to turn over a new leaf. He made a joke of it. Leaf, Leif." Her mouth twisted in a bitter smile. Then she turned her head to look at Adam, her eyes filling again. "We had dreams. That's what I was hanging on to. The dream we had together."

"You'll have new dreams." Adam gathered her into his arms. She rested her forehead against his chest. The embrace wasn't at all sexual, and yet she was very aware of the unacknowledged current that hummed between them. So tempting to raise her face to his for a kiss. To feel his warm lips on hers and his hands on her body. To run her hands into his thick hair to see if it was as silky as it looked. To pull him down onto the bed…

She couldn't go there, couldn't even let her thoughts head in that direction. She'd had a nasty shock tonight. Anything that happened would be a reaction to that and not out of a true desire between her and Adam.

As if sensing her thoughts, or maybe he was feeling the same, he eased away. "I should let you get to bed."

Before he left, he flung the fluffy quilt over the top of the bed. She walked him to the door. He hesitated, then dropped a light kiss on her temple. "Sleep well."

"I will now. Thanks."

Hayley closed the door and bowed her head against it. Adam had brought her into his home out of compassion and she'd come gratefully, little thinking of how his close proximity would affect her. How would she feel facing him across the breakfast table, meeting him in the hallway between their bedrooms, or sharing a cozy evening in front of the fire?

Adam, Summer, the beautiful big house… All of it too closely resembled the happy home she'd been longing for all her life. But it wasn't hers.

CHAPTER EIGHT

THE RADIO ALARM dragged Hayley out of a beautiful dream that evaporated upon waking but left her feeling good. Soft linen brushed her cheek as she stretched out in a big bed. For a moment she didn't know where she was, but it felt delightful.

Then the night before flooded back. The watch. The anguish of learning Leif had had an affair with Adam's wife. The shame, the sick sense of betrayal.

Ruthlessly she shut those emotions down. A new set rushed forward. Sharing midnight confidences with Adam, his arms around her, him kissing her forehead. The way her body had responded to his. She'd come so close to offering herself to him. After the emotional turmoil of the evening she'd wanted nothing more than to seek oblivion in his body.

Bad idea. Thank God she hadn't given in. Even after simply thinking inappropriate thoughts she didn't want to face him this morning.

She sprang out of bed and rushed through dressing, desperate to be out of the house before Adam got up. She felt awkward about all that had passed between them last night. Awkward and exposed.

She crept downstairs and out of the house. Shane fell into step at her heel as she strode through the wet grass toward the paddock. Asha whickered, and condensed breath streamed from her nostrils in the chilly morning air. Bo whisked his tail and plodded toward the rail. Sergeant and Major, cropping at the grass, lifted their heads and came forward, too— Major in front, as always, while Sergeant brought up the rear. Blaze was inside the barn in the single box stall.

"Hello, my beauties," Hayley said, stroking velvety noses on the brown-and-gold heads stretched over the top railing. They crowded in, jostling hooves and bumping shoulders to get close to her. Asha kept apart as usual, trotting a few paces away, her silver tail lifted and gray neck arched.

Hayley went into the barn to get buckets of oats. Blaze was dozing in the stall, one back hoof cocked and resting in the straw underfoot. Her round belly gently expanded with each breath.

"Not long now, sweetie." Hayley tipped a special mixture of chaff and mineral supplements into the manger. Then she added a flake of alfalfa and carried the rest of the bale outside to spread it over the ground for the other horses. While they ate, Hayley leaned on the fence. Dawn was breaking, and mist clung to the tall, straight mountain ash marching up the hillside.

Whatever Adam had intended with that chaste

kiss—and it probably was nothing more than comfort—her response had been more complicated.
Could she possibly be falling for a man she'd known
barely a week? That brief touch of his lips to her
forehead had been balm to her aching heart. But
she wasn't good at hiding her feelings, and now she
was living in his house.

She didn't want to feel anything for Adam. Not
only was he leaving Hope Mountain, but their circumstances were vastly different and would make
for an uneven relationship. Being poor and forced
to accept his help put her at a distinct power disad-
vantage. Not a good foundation for a relationship,
even supposing he was interested in her in that way.
The sole reason she was here was to heal Summer so
Adam could move away. She had to remember that.

But it was impossible not to like the man. He was
a good father and had been incredibly generous to
her. And he was honorable. In spite of the pain of
knowing about Leif and Diane, she was glad Adam
had told her. How much worse would she have felt
if he'd known and kept it from her? He'd made the
right call. It couldn't have been easy for him, either.

As for Leif, there was no point being angry or
hating or blaming him now. She'd lived with the
knowledge of his infidelity for years—nothing had
changed, really. So why were her hands clenched so
tightly on the top rail of the fence that her knuckles

were white? She needed to *do* something instead of stewing on her problems.

There was a good hour before she had to be at the café, enough time to do some work with Asha. She got a bridle out of the tack room in the barn and went into the paddock. The gray mare was nibbling on the last bits of hay strewn over the grass. Hayley ran a hand down her neck over the ridges of scars and took hold of her halter, clipping on a lead rope. Asha immediately jerked her head up and pulled back, lifting her forelegs a few inches off the ground.

"Whoa, girl. It's okay." Hayley led the horse through the gate and over to the lunge ring, Asha sidestepping and pulling the whole way. She tied the quivering horse to the fence and wrangled a bridle over Asha's tossing head. As Hayley threw the saddle blanket over her back, Asha put back her ears and tried to nip her on the butt.

"Hey! What is wrong with you, Ash?" Hayley gave a sharp jerk on the lead rope, then blew out a long breath. Getting mad wouldn't do any good. But it was frustrating.

Asha used to have a calm, even temperament. Since the fires she had been skittish and unpredictable. Some days she would allow Hayley on her back; other days she bucked and reared, using all her tricks to throw her off. Today was one of those bad days. In fact, this was the worst she'd ever been.

Hayley attempted to straighten the blanket and

Asha sidestepped abruptly, knocking it askew again. Hayley nudged her over to the fence so she couldn't move sideways, but Asha lunged backward, pulling on the rope so hard Hayley worried she might break the fence or hurt herself.

It was no use. She wasn't getting anywhere with the horse today. She untied Asha from the post and led her prancing and sidestepping back to the paddock. This had gone on too long. She needed to work with her using the slapping reins technique and become the horse's leader again. Poor Asha clearly had more recovering to do.

Hayley went back into the house and ran upstairs as quietly as possible to change into clothes more suitable for the café: a peach-colored knit top and black pants. Then she brushed out her hair in front of the mirror and braided it. She was *so* not the type of woman Adam was used to—women like Diane, immaculately groomed and expensively dressed. No doubt she had nothing to worry about where he was concerned—except covering up her own feelings.

She still had a few minutes, so she sat at the small desk in her room and quickly sketched a rough plan of her old house on a piece of paper she'd found in the drawer. As she went back downstairs she heard Summer in the shower and down the hall the sound of a closet door shutting. Adam was up, too.

She placed the sketch and the photo of her and her sister in front of her grandparents' house where

Adam could see it. Then she grabbed an apple from the fruit bowl and headed out to her truck. She didn't want to get in the way during their morning routine. Her hasty escape had nothing to do with avoiding Adam—no, sir.

"SUMMER, HURRY UP or you'll be late," Adam called up the stairs before grabbing his keys from the occasional table. "I'll be in the car."

"Coming," she yelled over the sound of the hair dryer.

He backed out of the garage and waited, keeping the motor idling. Hayley's truck was gone—she'd left half an hour ago—but he'd seen her earlier from the upstairs hall window, moving between the barn and the stables, carrying flakes of hay and tossing them over the fence, scattering them so the horses could all feed at once.

She was so strong yet graceful, every movement of her long legs and arms economical and balanced. He hadn't been able to look away. And when the sun rose above the barn roof and a shaft of light turned her dark honey hair to a golden halo… Breathtaking.

Last night all that beautiful hair had been flowing loose around her shoulders in a hundred shades between cream and old gold. And when he'd held her, it was all he could do not to bury his face in the fragrant silky mass. He could still feel her in his arms, her slender frame strung tight as a bow. He'd have given anything for her to melt against him.

He'd barely slept last night, knowing she was just down the hall. He'd tortured himself imagining knocking quietly at her door, her soft voice inviting him in, then the both of them slipping beneath the covers…. Would it be so wrong for them to find comfort in each other's arms?

The passenger door opened and Summer climbed in, dropping her backpack on the floor with a thud. "What're you all moony-eyed about? Let's go. I'm gonna be late."

Adam put the car into gear. What was he thinking? He had no intention of starting something with Hayley. Since he and Diane had split up he'd dated a few women, but no one serious. He'd needed a rest from all that emotional turmoil. Now that he was finally feeling better about his life, he needed to focus on priorities—get Summer sorted out, sell the house and return to his real life in the city, building major developments.

It was a life Hayley would want no part of. She might have lost her husband, but she was still wedded to the bush. The proof, if he needed it, was in the floor plan and photo she'd left for him on the kitchen counter. She still had her dream of rebuilding on Hope Mountain, and it was stronger than ever.

He pressed a button to lower the roof.

"Da-a-ad," Summer wailed. "My hair will fray."

Instead of her usual ponytail, she'd done her hair in a crooked French braid. Looked like someone else had a crush on a certain cowgirl.

He tossed her a cap from the backseat. "It's the perfect morning to put the top down. I smell spring in the air."

Summer smirked. "What you're smelling is horse manure."

"Ha, ha, very funny." But his heart lifted that she'd actually joked with him. "Are you still feeling good about what happened with Major?"

"Sure," Summer said, suddenly acting wary. "Why?"

"Just wondering." Who was Steve? He let a beat go by as they slowly bumped down the potholed driveway. "What did you and Hayley talk about yesterday?"

"It's confidential." Summer swiveled in her seat. "She didn't say anything, did she?"

"No." It was frustrating not being in on the therapy. Didn't a father have a right to know what was going on with his fourteen-year-old daughter? "Did you get all your homework done?"

She made a face. "Most of it. I had trouble with algebra."

"Ask me for help next time. I'm pretty good at math."

As they approached the road, a country fire authority truck rumbled past. Adam thought of Leif's watch back in the drawer in his sideboard. What was he going to do with it? Hayley didn't want it. Would it be crass for him to sell it for her and give her the money? It seemed ridiculous to throw away such an expensive watch.

"Dad, you just passed the bus stop." Summer craned her neck to look back.

"That's okay. I'll take you to school." At least she couldn't leave the car, so there was more opportunity for conversation. "Hey, I've got a good one for you."

"Uh-oh."

"Two buffalo are at home on the range. A tourist walks up and says, 'Those are the mangiest-looking buffalo I've ever seen!' One buffalo turns to the other and says, 'I think I just heard a discouraging word.'" He chuckled.

Summer groaned, but a small smile lurked as she said, "Don't quit your day job."

Adam fell silent as the thick forest transitioned into a burned area and they passed charred stumps of trees. Summer went past this twice daily on the bus to and from school. Did it make her think of Bailey?

As if she'd caught the direction of his thoughts, Summer said, "Hayley's gonna let me ride Sergeant or Major whenever I want." She sighed. "I wish I could ride Asha."

"Even Hayley has trouble with that horse. Asha must've been very traumatized by the fires."

"She almost died. She had fifty-eight stitches in her neck." Summer's mouth turned down. In an abrupt change of mood, she tugged her cap low and slumped in her seat.

Adam thought of Hayley huddling in the dam for hours, shivering and traumatized herself, emerging to find her horses dead or missing and her favorite badly wounded. She must be unbelievably resilient to have recovered so well.

He pulled up in front of the high school. "I'll pick you up this afternoon and we can go for ice cream."

"For cripe's sake, Dad. The ice cream shop burned down! Where's your head?"

"I didn't know—"

"You don't know anything." She jerked open the door and grabbed her backpack. "Don't bother coming. I'll get the bus."

He started to call her back but it was too late. She'd merged into the stream of students entering the front doors.

All the sunshine drained out of the day. He put the clutch back into first gear. Summer had a ways to go before she was back to her old self. Hayley had warned him so. With a sigh, he headed home. Twenty minutes later he pulled into the driveway at Timbertop.

Early on, when he'd still thought he and Diane might share this house, he'd set up an office for himself with a drafting table and supplies. He grabbed himself a cup of coffee and settled in. Once he got a design that Hayley liked he could put it on the computer on AutoCAD.

It had been a long time since he'd designed a single-family residence, but knowing that Hayley would live in this home made the process unexpectedly appealing. He smoothed out the paper and studied her rough drawing. The house appeared to be a miner's cottage with the addition of extra bedrooms, a storage room and an extended kitchen.

What the hell, why not add stables and a covered lunge ring for her horse therapy? It would be fun designing Hayley a dream home and equestrian center. Whether any of it would come to fruition he had no idea, but if he could, he'd love to give it all to her—if anyone deserved to realize their dreams it was Hayley.

He worked for several hours, breaking twice to field calls from his office about the Shanghai project and once when Mort arrived to take photos of the property so he could prepare a listing. The Realtor gave him a ballpark figure that was substantially less than Adam had paid for the house nearly two years earlier. He didn't care. He'd drop the price further if he had to. Not only was Timbertop in a fire-prone area but he would never be able to forget that Diane had had an affair here. As far as he was concerned, the property was tainted.

Soon it was time to pick up Summer from

school—before she could get on the bus. He really wanted to have as normal a life as possible with his daughter. Maybe if they acted like everything was okay, it would be. He didn't believe for one second that she'd stopped liking ice cream. *Or* that there was no place in Hope Mountain to get it.

"HOW WAS THE lamb tagine?" Hayley asked Tony, the local veterinarian, as she cleared dishes off his table.

Tony's light brown hair had a permanent hat crease, and his lanky frame sprawled as he sipped his coffee. "Worth leaving home for." His hazel gaze followed her every movement. "How's that pregnant mare of yours?"

"She's looking fit to burst but otherwise just fine." She totted up his bill and handed it to him. "Molly will take care of that at the cash register."

"If you need any help with the birthing, give me a shout." He moved his toothpick from one side of his mouth to the other. "Are you going to the dance week after next?"

"You mean the fundraiser being held after the memorial service? You bet I am. You?"

"Yep." He rose and reached for his hat, shuffling his feet. "I could pick you up if you like. We could go together."

"Gee, thanks, Tony, but…" Tony was nice but he didn't float her boat, to borrow an expression from Molly.

"You can't wear widow's weeds forever."

"I know, but I don't think so," she said gently. "I'll save a dance for you, though."

"All right. Can't blame a guy for trying." Tony adjusted his hat on his head. "I'll hold you to that dance."

Hayley cleared and wiped the table and carried the dishes behind the counter to the kitchen. Working at the café wasn't so bad. She'd caught up with Tony and a few other folk she hadn't seen in quite a while. But she missed her horses, and Tony's reminder of Blaze set her to worrying what would happen if the mare started to foal while she wasn't home.

She dished the last of the lamb casserole onto a plate, picked up the coffeepot and went over to Dave Green, her ex-client, who'd been nursing a mug in the corner all morning. Lunch had come and gone and he hadn't eaten. Until now she'd been too busy to say more than hello.

She set the hot food in front of him, waving away his protest that he hadn't ordered it. "Eat. Don't argue."

With trembling hands he picked up a fork and took a bite. She could almost feel his hunger and the fierce control as he forced himself to chew slowly. "This is real good. Thanks."

She poured his coffee, studying him closely. He hadn't shaved that day, possibly not yesterday either.

His gray hair was lank, and stains dotted the blue business shirt he'd once worn beneath a jacket and tie. "How's it going?"

"Not bad," he said between mouthfuls. "Had a job interview yesterday."

"Any luck?" If he'd gone in looking the way he did now, there was no way he'd have been successful.

"No, but something will turn up." He took another bite. "I'll pay you back for lunch, I promise—"

"Shh, forget it. It would've just gone to waste." That wasn't strictly true. Molly took leftovers home for her and Rolf's dinner, but Dave didn't need to know that. She dropped into the seat opposite. "Are you seeing another counselor?"

"I'm on a couple of waiting lists. Shouldn't be too long now, three or four months." He ate swiftly, wiping up the sauce with a chunk of bread.

Who knew how low he would sink by then? It was obvious his depression hadn't lifted. Most likely his panic attacks hadn't gone away, either. "My offer to give you therapy privately still stands. You can pay when you get a chance. I'm in no hurry."

"I'm not going to take advantage of your good nature." When she started to protest, he held up a hand. "No, don't. However, if the program's funding is renewed, let me know."

"All right." Hayley rose and squeezed his shoulder. "You take care, okay?"

Dave finished his meal and shambled out. Hayley paid for his lunch out of her own purse. With the lunch rush over and the café empty, she wiped down all the tables and filled the napkin dispensers. Anything to keep busy so she didn't have to talk to Molly.

Every time she looked into her mother-in-law's warm brown eyes she was reminded of Leif—and then of the inscription on the watch. She was terrible at lying and worse at hiding her emotions. Already this morning Molly had gently probed several times to see if anything was wrong.

"Leave that, hon. Time you and I took a load off our feet." Molly put an arm around her shoulders. "You look tired. Your eyes are all red."

"I'm fine. Didn't get a good sleep is all." Between Leif's betrayal, Adam's kiss and her own confused reactions to both men, both her head and heart had been swirling half the night. She'd finally come to the cold realization that any love she'd had for Leif had been destroyed. She was no longer heartsick at losing him, just sad and angry at the wasted years.

"I've got something that will cheer you up." Molly bustled into the kitchen where she'd been busy for the past hour and returned with a chocolate cake dotted with silver birthday candles.

"Whose—?" Oh, God. How could she have forgotten?

"Leif would have been thirty-four today. I wanted

you to come to the house for dinner so we could have this with Rolf but I think you need it now."

"You're always so thoughtful," Hayley murmured. Just the thought of eating a birthday cake dedicated to Leif was enough to make her feel sick. "I'm kind of on a diet."

Molly snorted. "Don't give me that. If you lose any more weight you'll blow away with the next stiff breeze. Now, light the candles and we'll sing."

Her heart sank. "Oh, no, really? What if someone comes in?"

"We'll give them a piece of cake. As long as I have a slice left to take home to Rolf."

Hayley lit the candles, resentful and confused and feeling like a giant hypocrite. Molly's voice quavered and her eyes were shiny as she sang the birthday song, clutching Hayley's hand tightly.

Hayley sang along and if she sounded as if she was choking it was from anger, not grief. She'd never told Molly or Rolf about Leif's earlier infidelities, and she didn't want to talk about his affair with Diane, either. Knowing how highly they esteemed their son she wasn't even sure they'd believe her. She adored Molly and wanted to maintain a relationship with her. That might not be possible if she spoke the truth. But it was hard to meet Molly's gaze over the birthday cake and pretend nothing had changed.

Molly blew out the candles, then cut two thick slices to go with their steaming cups of strong coffee. "Rolf and I dropped by your place yesterday but you weren't home. I left a casserole in the fridge."

Hayley never locked her door—there was nothing to steal—a fact her in-laws were well acquainted with. "Thanks, but I'm not staying there right now. I'm at Timbertop."

Molly frowned over her coffee cup. "Whatever for?"

"I'm giving the girl, Summer, horse therapy. Her father, Adam, kindly offered my horses—and me—room and board in partial payment. He's got grass he wants eaten down and it saves me money. It's a good exchange."

"But why do you need to stay in a stranger's house? You always said you liked your own space. It must be awkward."

"There's a guest cottage." No need to mention she'd moved into the house. "But it is a little awkward. I'll probably go back to the garage today." Though in truth she didn't want to anymore. Blaze was due to give birth any day, and she wanted to be present. And if she was completely honest, she liked being around Adam and Summer.

"If only Leif was alive," Molly said with a sigh. "He'd have had your new house built by now."

Leif was so lax about money, that scenario seemed extremely unlikely. She gazed down at her cup, tracing the pattern of flowers. "I'm not so sure."

"What do you mean?" Molly said. "Leif was good

with finances—why, he paid off his truck in six months—and he'd been saving for the dude ranch for years. He would've built the house first, of course."

Hayley just couldn't let another comment in praise of Leif go by. "He wasn't the great money manager we all thought he was. He spent large sums and didn't tell me about it."

Leif had done most of the banking, at his insistence. After he'd died she'd found that not only hadn't he renewed their home insurance but their savings account also contained a lot less than she'd thought. Plus he'd withdrawn five hundred dollars from their retirement account, and she had no idea what he'd done with it. Most likely he'd spent the money on Diane, a high-maintenance woman.

"What do you mean? How much money are you talking about?"

"Lots." As near as she could tell from reviewing their bills and accounts, a couple thousand dollars over a six-month period was unaccounted for.

"I don't understand." Molly's frown deepened. "What on earth would he spend it on that you didn't know about?"

Hayley fiddled with the end of her braid. Molly would be devastated to know the truth about Leif. Could she really destroy this woman, whom she loved and who loved her like a daughter? Molly had strong moral values but blood was thicker than water. She couldn't bear if Molly were to learn the truth and still made excuses for her son.

The door to the café opened. In walked Adam and Summer.

"Hayley?" Molly pressed. "Tell me."

Summer paused uncertainly between the gift shop and the café, keeping her distance from the jewelry display.

Adam waved to Hayley and started to walk toward her.

Hayley rose and squeezed Molly's shoulder. "It's not important now."

CHAPTER NINE

"CAN I INTEREST you in some pie?" Hayley said, smoothing down the black apron she wore over her slacks and top. "Molly's blueberry is awesome."

Hayley felt Adam's eyes on her every step of his approach. Her own gaze was drawn to him like a magnet. Was it possible that his shoulders were broader and his legs longer than yesterday? Their embrace, brief and chaste as it was, seemed to have awakened a deeper, more intimate attraction.

"Sold, with a scoop of caramel ice cream. Summer"—Adam drew his daughter into the conversation—"is dying for rocky road."

"I am not." Summer came forward reluctantly. "He's the one who insisted we come here for ice cream."

"What would you like, then?" Adam asked.

"Hot chocolate," Summer said, then grudgingly added, "with ice cream. Please."

"Rocky road?" Hayley asked with a smile and Summer nodded sheepishly. "I like your hair like that. Turn around, let me see. The flowers you wove through it are pretty."

Summer spun around to show off her attempt at a French braid and the sprig of yellow acacia. "I couldn't get the top part right. Maybe sometime you could show me how you do yours?"

"Sure." She gestured to the table by the window. "Have a seat and I'll get your order."

Hayley turned to find Molly watching the exchange, her eyebrows slightly raised. Her mother-in-law never missed a thing. Which made her fun to gossip with, but all joy was lost when Molly's eagle eye was trained on her.

She heated the milk for hot chocolate, then moved across to the ice cream freezer. Adam had taken a chair facing the kitchen. Every time her gaze flicked in his direction he quickly looked away and pretended to study the menu. Summer was texting on her phone, oblivious to her father's wandering attention.

Molly noticed, though. She cut a slice of pie and passed it to Hayley to add the ice cream. "He's got his eye on you."

Hayley dropped a double scoop on the plate and pushed a wisp of hair off her forehead. "I don't think so."

"I've got eyes in my head, girl. I'm telling you, he's got an ulterior motive in letting you stay in his cottage."

What would Molly think if she knew Hayley was actually sleeping just down the hall from Adam? Not that anything was going to happen, but someday she'd be ready to go out with another man. Would she be forever worrying about Molly's feelings?

"You need to let him know you're not interested," Molly went on. "Your husband hasn't been dead a year. You're still in mourning."

Her firm tone got Hayley's back up. Maybe she *was* interested. Her relationship with Leif had been troubled for years. She hadn't wanted to admit it to herself, but no matter how hard she'd tried to knit her marriage together with forgiveness and love and sheer determination, it had unraveled like one of her homemade cardigans when she'd realized she'd made a mistake ten rows back.

Where had she gone wrong in her marriage? What was the dropped stitch that threw out the whole pattern? Marrying a man who had an eye for women in the first place—or not knowing when to give up?

Anyway, it wasn't Molly's place to tell her she wasn't interested in a new man. Hayley loved her mother-in-law to bits, but right now she was irritated that the woman assumed she could judge her life and determine her future. A few words about Leif's affairs and she might change her tune.

Hayley moved along the counter and quickly mixed the chocolate into the hot milk. She could tell Molly hadn't fully believed her about the money, and she wouldn't, not without proof. Hayley couldn't supply that information unless she revealed Leif's affair.

"Do you hear what I'm saying, Hayley?" Molly stuck a fork on the plate. "You're a bit naive about men. You didn't even notice that guy hitting on you at the movie night last month."

She'd noticed but pretended not to, because she wasn't interested. And in Adam's case, while he might flirt with her, he was leaving town as soon as he could. On the other hand, what harm could it do to flirt back?

It hit her in the gut that for her own mental and emotional health she had to move on from Leif. She needed to leave behind his betrayal and death and all those bad things that were keeping her sad and angry and guilty. She wanted to be happy again.

"Thanks for the advice." Hayley picked up the pie and hot chocolate and slipped through the gap in the counter. "I'd better get this out before the ice cream melts."

She set the pie and ice cream and hot chocolate before Adam and Summer. "Here you go."

"Yum," Summer said. "Thanks."

Adam dug in his spoon and scooped out a bite. "How's your first day on the job?"

"Really busy over lunch, but we're in a lull." She watched the fork slide into his mouth and noticed how full his lower lip was, how sculpted the upper. His faint beard shadow ran below his cheekbone along an angular jaw. She racked her brain for some

way to prolong the conversation. "How's the fuel re-
duction project going?"

"I didn't get much done today. Had a few inter-
ruptions from work but mostly I was working on
your house plans—" He broke off, noticing a boy
outside on the sidewalk waving, trying to get their
attention. "Summer, is he a friend of yours?"

The boy's brown hair was clean and his school
uniform—different from the Hope Mountain uniform—was neat. But what drew Hayley's attention
were the burn scars on his arms and one side of his
face.

Summer didn't glance up from her hot chocolate.
"I don't know him."

"He seems to know you," Adam said. "Aren't you
even going to look and see who it is?"

"No." Carefully she scraped the foam off the inside of her mug.

Because Summer knew *exactly* who the boy was,
Hayley guessed. He looked to be texting on his
phone now. Summer's phone buzzed. She ignored
it. Adam started to reach for it. Glaring, Summer
snatched it first and turned it off.

Outside, the boy raised and dropped his arms in a
gesture of frustration. Then he put his phone away
and strode around the side of the café.

"He's coming inside," Hayley said.

Adam laid down his fork in the melting ice cream.

"Summer, you'd better tell me right now if this boy has been bothering you."

"Leave it alone, Dad. I can handle him." But Summer paled as the boy advanced on the table. Before he could speak, she said, "Go away. I don't want to talk to you."

"Come on, Summer. Five minutes, that's all I ask." Up close, he had a downy moustache and while his features still had the softness of youth, he looked to be two or three years older than Summer. The faint burn scars on his face only slightly marred his good looks.

Adam got to his feet, looming a good head taller than the boy. "Buddy, she doesn't want to talk to you."

While Adam focused on the boy, Hayley watched the emotions playing over Summer's reddening face. She seemed mortified at the public scene and angry with both the boy and her father. Yet there was a touch of yearning in her eyes when she looked at Steve. That was enough for Hayley.

"Breathe, Summer," Hayley reminded her quietly. "Shoulders." To the boy, she said, "Are you Steve?"

"Yes." He straightened as he turned to face her. "Steve Wright. I just want to talk to her. That's all."

"I thought you moved away," Hayley said.

"I hitched a ride up from Healesville."

"She doesn't want to talk, so you need to leave," Adam said. "No means no."

Hayley touched his shoulder. "Steve's come a long way to see her." To Summer she said, "Why don't you give him five minutes? Your dad can wait for you outside. I'll be right over there behind the counter."

Summer pushed away her empty mug. "Fine."

Hayley tugged Adam away as Steve slid into the chair opposite the girl.

"Where do you get off overruling me in a matter concerning my daughter?" Adam demanded. "And how do you know about this kid? I suppose Summer told you about him in her therapy."

"A little, not much. I wouldn't have pushed it if I didn't think he might play a critical role in whatever demons she's facing."

"What kind of role?" Adam cast the teens a worried glance. "It can't be good. She didn't want to talk to him."

"She does, really. I can almost guarantee that." She couldn't say anything more without compromising Summer's confidences. "Trust me?"

Adam searched her eyes. "And if you're wrong? What if he's somehow hurt her, and will hurt her again given a chance?"

"Everyone gets hurt at some point in their lives. It's how we deal with the hurt that matters. We have to grow up and learn how to live our own lives."

And that was true for her as well, Hayley realized. She'd buried her head in the sand all through her marriage in the vain hope that she would be safe. Look how that had turned out.

Leif's previous affairs were tied to specific circumstances. Like the time she'd been helping Molly 24/7 to get her gift shop and café up and running. Meanwhile he'd screwed around behind her back with an old classmate they'd met at their ten-year high school reunion. The other time she'd been pregnant, and severe morning sickness had left her feeling nauseous day and night and uninterested in sex. The miscarriage she'd suffered at ten weeks added injury to the insult of discovering his dalliance with a bar girl.

With Diane, what was his excuse? There was none. She'd been blindsided. This past year she'd wrapped herself in cotton wool, insulating herself from examining her feelings and her life with Leif. Not asking the difficult questions and facing the answers. Maybe it was time to let the hurt in, let it wash her clean so she could start afresh.

"That's easy for you to say, but she's my daughter and I worry," Adam said. "I know virtually nothing about her private life. I know her best friend is Zoe, but that's about it. She doesn't play basketball anymore. She listens to music I'm not familiar with. I don't know who she hangs out with at school. If there's something you should tell me…"

Hayley was barely listening. Standing in front of her was a man who seemed interested in her and whom she found extremely attractive. Adam was a capable, intelligent man who engaged with the world in ways she could barely dream of. He was dynamic and confident and funny and sexy. Why wouldn't she want to get to know him better?

"Are you okay?" Adam tilted his head, perplexed. "Why are you looking at me like that?"

She pressed the flat of her palm to his chest just above his heart. "Sometimes the only thing you can go on is instinct and what your heart is telling you."

Her heart was telling her she wanted to enjoy a friendship with him despite all the other issues they were each dealing with. And maybe even flirt a little. Or a lot…

Something flickered in Adam's eyes as if he understood exactly what she was thinking.

"Dad?" Summer was at his side, holding something cupped in her hands. "Can we go home now?"

"What? Oh, of course." Adam glanced around. "Where's Steve? What have you got there?"

"He left. He just wanted to give me this." Blinking hard, she opened her hands, revealing a ceramic horse, brown with four white socks and a black mane and tail. "It's just like Bailey."

"Oh, that's so sweet," Hayley said. Steve just went up ten points in her estimation. But she saw Summer's tangled emotions, and her heart ached for the girl. She hoped the figurine would heal more than hurt her.

"That was nice of him, I suppose," Adam said. "Go out to the car. I'll be right there." He waited until Summer left, then drew Hayley farther away from the gift counter where Molly was busying herself and studiously pretending not to listen to their conversation. "You made the right call about Steve."

"Thank you for trusting me."

Adam shot a glance at Molly. "She keeps an eye on you, doesn't she?" When she nodded, he reached for her hand and squeezed it briefly. "I'll see you later."

Her heart kicked up a notch. Her fingers curled into her palm as if she could contain the warmth of his skin. "Later."

ADAM LAID HIS preliminary sketches of Hayley's house on the dining table. It was after five o'clock. She would be back soon. Wine or coffee? She might want a shower first before they went over his drawings. He hoped she would like his ideas. Would they be too citified for her?

Who was he kidding? The nerves skittering through him weren't about the plans. Had he only imagined the look in Hayley's eyes back at the café? Unless he was reading her wrong, the spark between them was close to bursting into flame.

There were lots of reasons not to pursue the attraction—she was in mourning, he was leaving, she blamed him indirectly for the fire that had destroyed her home, she was treating his daughter. All that was drowned out by the buzz of knowing that any minute she would walk through that door.

She'd said she wanted to move back to her garage. He so didn't want that to happen, not when things were getting interesting between them.

Wine, not coffee, he decided. She would want to relax after her first day waitressing, not get revved up.

He heard her truck in the driveway and went out to the veranda to lean against one of the upright posts twined with the bright green leaves and magenta flowers of bougainvillea.

"Honey, I'm home." Despite the self-mocking tone her smile was sunny and her eyes glowed.

"I'm about to open a bottle of chardonnay. Can I interest you in a glass?"

"You're a mind reader." Awareness shimmered between them as the silence stretched. Then she lifted the plastic bag she carried. "Perks of the job. Molly's amazing Thai green curry."

"Excellent. My repertoire of recipes is slim. You were about to find out I'm not the gourmet cook I make myself out to be." He held the screen door open for her to go inside.

"Two-minute noodles?" Hayley said, seeing the empty package on the counter. "Even for a noncook that's bad."

"Summer must have gotten those out."

Hayley set the bag down. "Did she say anything more about Steve, or why she was so angry with him?"

"I've been trying very hard not to be a prying father. Is he a school friend? She's too young to have a boyfriend."

"She's fourteen. She's not too young."

Adam still struggled to see his daughter as a young woman, but that was exactly what she was. "The problem with being a father is knowing what I did with girls at that age."

"Get used to it, Papa," Hayley teased. "It's only going to get worse."

He brought the wine out of the fridge and unscrewed the cap. "She's never mentioned him to me. I called Diane, but she didn't know anything, either. Mind you, Diane gets preoccupied with her own life. Summer's always been a dream child. Getting into trouble is so unlike her that neither her mother nor I were prepared for problems."

"She's still the beautiful child you love. She's just going through a tough time."

He searched Hayley's face. "I understand that your sessions have to remain confidential but you would tell me if there was anything seriously bad or wrong happening with her, wouldn't you?"

"I would find a way to let you know. She's underage and it's part of my duty of care as her therapist." Hayley gave his arm a reassuring squeeze and let her hand linger a moment before she withdrew it. "Where is she now?"

"She went straight to the barn to check on Blaze after school and hasn't come out since."

"I'll go have a quick chat with her. I want to look in on Blaze, myself."

"Before you go…" He pulled over the plans. "Take a look at these preliminary drawings. We can review them in detail later and make whatever changes you like."

Hayley leaned over the table, scanning the plans. "I don't understand what all the buildings are, but I recognize the house." She straightened, her eyes shining. "I'm so excited that you did this for me." She reached her arms around his neck and gave him a hug. "Thank you."

"My pleasure." His splayed fingers circled her slender waist as her breasts pressed against his chest. He breathed in her scent, felt her warmth, and his groin tightened.

Too quickly she eased away, her gaze tangling with his. "I should go see Summer. And Blaze."

Adam slid his hands down her arms to squeeze her hands before letting her go. "Don't be long."

He'd told himself he couldn't hit on a woman staying in his house as a guest. But she'd made the first move just now. Maybe she didn't have any qualms about them getting friendly. On the other hand, maybe it was just a hug. A thank-you. It didn't necessarily mean she wanted him.

While he waited for Hayley to return he put the curry on to heat and opened his laptop to check his email. He answered a couple of quick questions from his assistant about the specs for the Shanghai apartments. Then he opened a message from Lorraine, his boss and founder of the architect firm.

Adam, you know how much I value you. But your continuing absence raises questions about your future at the firm. Are you still interested in a partnership? I hope so. I have exciting plans. Let's get together and discuss.
Lorraine.

Adam's heart raced. Making partner in one of the biggest architect firms in Australia engaged in international development had been his goal ever since his first overseas project ten years ago. His finger itched to hit Reply and give Lorraine an unqualified yes. But he didn't know how long he'd be solely responsible for Summer. Would Diane resume primary care of their daughter once her mother was well? Did he really want her to? What were Lorraine's expectations regarding his responsibilities and workload? Would there be any leeway for his situation? He had way more questions than answers.

He tapped out a reply: Lorraine, I'm definitely still

interested. We should talk in person. His fingers paused on the keys as he pondered the best day for him to go into the city. Or…maybe he could get Lorraine to come out here, see for herself how things were with him. In a more relaxed atmosphere his boss might be more amenable to compromise.

He often socialized with Lorraine and her husband, Graham. Besides, it wouldn't hurt to conduct negotiations on his turf. And the clincher: Graham wrote grant proposals for a living. Maybe he could help Hayley find funding for Horses for Hope.

Why don't you and Graham come out this weekend? I could arrange some horseback riding. Adam.

He hit Send.

Partner at the age of thirty-six. He'd worked his butt off for years for this opportunity. The timing wasn't the best, but Lorraine was a reasonable person. If she wanted him as a partner in the firm she should be willing to discuss options.

He just needed some time. A few more months in which to sort out Summer and Timbertop and wrap up everything so he could move back to Melbourne and take on the responsibilities and privileges he'd been groomed for.

He closed his laptop. Time enough to think about the corner office when the partnership came through. Hope Mountain was his world temporarily, and while he was here, he had to be fully present. He owed it to Summer, to himself and to Hayley.

The screen door banged. Hayley came through the kitchen into the dining area. "Summer's not in a mood to chat, but she seems okay. So is Blaze."

"Good." He handed her a glass of wine. "We should talk about what you said last night about moving back to your own place. I wish you wouldn't."

She glanced at him over the rim. "Because of Summer?"

Their unspoken feelings were making things too complicated. It was time to bring this into the open. He cleared his throat. "Because of you. As you may have guessed, I'm attracted to you."

She froze, her cheeks turning pink.

Hell. "If you're not cool with that, I'll back off." He wiped a hand across his brow. "Regardless, you're still welcome to stay as long as you want. I hope I haven't made you uncomfortable...."

"It's okay." Hayley gave a shaky laugh "I... I like you, too."

He stilled. "You do?"

"Yes, but I'm conflicted." She sucked in a deep breath. "One minute I just want to climb you like a tree...." Her color deepened and her gaze darted away. "The next, reality hits and I'm scared shitless. There are so many reasons it's not a good idea for us to get involved."

"I know, believe me." He blew out a gusty sigh. "What do you want to do?"

She bit her lip. "It's all happening so quickly. I'm not even sure *what* is happening. I want to see where it leads, but I need to go slowly. If that makes sense."

"Slowly. I understand." He continued to hold her gaze, willing her to trust him. "For now, please don't leave, and *definitely* don't leave on my account."

She nodded and said, "I'd like to stay at least until Blaze gives birth."

"Then do that. It's decided."

"Good." She breathed out on a laugh. "I'm going to have a quick shower. Keep my wine cool for me." She ran up the stairs.

"No worries." Adam watched Hayley until she turned on the landing and disappeared down the hall.

So she wanted to climb him like a tree, did she? He'd gotten an instant hard-on hearing that. But she also wanted to go slowly. Fine. Just not too slowly, he hoped.

HAYLEY CAME DOWNSTAIRS, showered and dressed in yoga pants and a loose top, her drying hair in waves around her shoulders. She felt good about her decision to stay, glad for Blaze's sake and excited for her own. It was good that the attraction between her and Adam was out in the open and dealt with.

She'd acknowledged her feelings and at the same time bought herself breathing space.

Adam handed her a glass of wine. She had to admit, it was nice to come home to warmth and comfort and a tall, handsome man who seemed to enjoy making her happy. Except she knew better than to get used to this. Adam was on temporary leave from his regular life where he worked such long hours that he'd neglected his ex-wife and daughter. It was easy to forget that. But why else would Diane have had an affair and Summer be so estranged from him?

"Here you go." He pulled out a chair from the dining table and positioned the architectural drawings where the light was best.

Sipping her wine, Hayley studied the plans in detail. If she'd been excited at first glance, now she was completely overwhelmed. Adam had come up with a complete set of plans for her property. House, stables, a barn, several smaller outbuildings and a large structure whose function wasn't immediately clear.

"You did all this in one day?"

"It's just a rough draft." Adam stood behind her, a hand on the back of her chair. "I'll finish them properly but first I wanted your input."

Hayley pointed to the unidentified structure. "What's this?"

"It's a covered ring where you can do your horse therapy."

She twisted in her chair to look up at him. "Horses for Hope is over. I told you, no more funding."

"But the therapy seems so important to you. You have a special gift. I've watched you work with the horses. You seem…more alive than at any other time. Are you going to accept defeat?" Adam asked.

"I don't have a choice," she said unhappily. "I called every government official, every funding organization I could think of, and hammered them with statistics on the numbers of people still in need. Everyone agrees the program is worthwhile, but no one has the money to reinstate it." She shrugged off her feelings of regret and loss. "It's okay. My long-term goal, my dream, is to build a dude ranch."

She went back to studying the drawings. "This is everything I've ever wanted in a house and stables. Well, everything short of a bunkhouse for the dude ranch guests."

"Where?" Adam picked up a pencil and reached an arm over her shoulder.

"Between the house and the barn."

He made a note in the margin. "Is the dude ranch really your dream? I got the impression it was Leif's goal. You don't talk about it much."

"I've had other things on my mind lately. Trail riding is excellent in this area and it makes sense financially. More sense than a government program subject to funding cuts."

But now that Adam had mentioned it, *was* the

dude ranch her dream? Suddenly she was questioning things she'd taken for granted for years. Her life with Leif had been all about him and his dreams. He'd never given her credit for her horse therapy. In fact, he'd been disinterested and dismissive, insisting she focus on the dude ranch.

Adam, on the other hand, respected her and what she did. He seemed to understand how important the connection between her and her horses was and how fulfilled she was when using her abilities to heal trauma victims. Shame that that part of her life was over, at least for now.

"I could use the ring to give riding lessons," she said.

"You could. You could also use it for private horse therapy if government funding isn't an option."

"Most of my clients are on disability or out of work and can't afford to pay." Mention of payment made her realize Adam's charge-out rate was probably astronomic. "What do I owe you for these drawings?"

"Don't be silly. They're my gift to you."

"Oh, no, I couldn't accept. You've already given me so much—accommodation, feed and stabling for my horses…"

"You don't seem to understand how highly I value what you're doing for Summer. I know we haven't seen a lot of progress yet but there have been small, real changes." His gaze held hers. "I believe in you and what you're doing."

Oh, wow. His belief in her was like an aphrodisiac. She could feel his heat, was drawn by his magnetism. She should stand up, get a drink of water, anything. But she couldn't drag her gaze away from his. Go slow? How, when even with the best intentions she couldn't control her thoughts or the desires of her heart and body?

Suddenly she didn't want to fight the attraction. Reaching out, she slid a hand up his arm.

Adam's eyes darkened. "Didn't we just say—"

"Yes, and I haven't changed my mind, but...I can't help myself." She leaned in close. Their lips met, lingered and parted fractionally. She breathed him in, wine and warmth and man. Her fingers brushed the rasp of his jaw. The very molecules of the air seemed to still around them.

Then he wrapped his hand over the back of her neck and angled her head, claiming her mouth. His kiss stole her breath and she was lost to the sensation of heat and pressure and the slide of his tongue along the seam of her lips. Then the moist rush of heat as he gained entrance. It had been years since anyone but Leif had kissed her so intimately.

Adam didn't taste like Leif. Nor did she want him to. Her love for Leif had gone cold as the grave.

Adam was life. Warmth. He deepened the kiss, plunging his fingers into her damp hair as he explored her mouth with his tongue. She strained toward him, sliding her hands over the muscles beneath his fine cashmere sweater. He was solid, hard and real. He ran a hand up to mold her aching breast, pressing a thumb into her hardening nipple, and she moaned out loud.

"Dad? Hayley?" Boots sounded on the wooden deck of the veranda. The screen door banged open. "Where are you?"

Hayley jerked back, dragging a hand across her tingling lips. With the other hand she smoothed her hair and straightened her top. "Sorry. I shouldn't have done that."

"It's okay." Adam held her eyes for one drawn-out moment, then dragged his gaze away and leaned back. "We—" He shut his eyes and cleared his throat. "We're in here."

Summer entered the room. She glanced from her dad to Hayley. "What are you guys doing?"

"I... Your dad drew some plans for my new house." Hayley's voice didn't sound like hers. She could still taste him, still feel his long, strong fingers caressing her. "We were just going over the details."

"Cool." Summer wandered around to the other side of the table and leaned on her elbows to study the plans.

Hayley felt Adam's knee pressing against hers, a silent message. She couldn't look at him, afraid she would blush or do something equally revealing. By tacit consent they weren't telling Summer that in the past few minutes they'd gone from friends to… something else.

Hayley wasn't quite sure what they were yet, but it was clear that although they'd acknowledged their feelings to each other, Summer mustn't know. She and Adam both agreed on this without even talking about it.

One step forward, two steps back.

"What's that?" Summer asked, pointing to the covered ring that from the aerial view looked like a rectangle and from the side view appeared to be a roof on posts.

Hayley drew breath, blinked. Something else had become crystal clear without her consciously thinking it. "That's a ring for working with horses."

"Cool. Horses for Hope?"

She glanced over at Adam and found him watching her. His belief in her had reminded Hayley that her dreams not only counted, but were possible. She didn't know how she was going to reinstate the program but she had to keep trying.

She smiled at him, full of gratitude. Then she turned to Summer. "Yes. Horses for Hope."

CHAPTER TEN

AFTER ADAM DROPPED OFF Summer at the bus stop the next day he spent the morning with a volunteer crew helping a rancher replace fencing destroyed during the fires. He'd seen the notice at the distribution center and signed up, not quite knowing what to expect. He'd come away with new blisters on his hands and a deeper appreciation of the sheer amount of work done by people who lived on the land. And he'd made new friends among the crew. Already he was starting to recognize more folks when he walked down the town's main street.

Back at Timbertop he ate a quick lunch, then fired up AutoCAD to create a set of detailed architectural drawings a builder could work from to construct Hayley's house.

She had a day off from the café, and although her truck was in the driveway there was no sign of her. She'd probably taken one of the horses out for exercise. As he tapped keystrokes into the computer he found himself listening for the sound of hooves on gravel or her special whistle for Shane.

When Hayley told Summer she was going to try

to continue her horse therapy, he'd been surprised but also pleased to think he might have influenced her. She had so much to give, not just her talent with horses but her ability to connect with people.

What was happening with them was less clear-cut. She'd surprised him with that sensational kiss. He'd have happily gone further if Summer hadn't interrupted them. Once she had, though, he'd quickly shut down and retreated. His reaction had been instinctive but on reflection it wasn't really surprising.

Summer had been the flotsam tossed around by her parents' turbulent love lives. He didn't want to have to explain that he and Hayley were just fooling around. After all, it wasn't like they could have a lasting relationship. The last thing he wanted was to hurt Hayley, but the fact was he was leaving. And to be honest, he was a little gun-shy.

Finally he heard Hayley return, but it was another twenty minutes before she finished with the horses and came inside. She washed her hands at the kitchen sink. "How was the fencing?"

"Good, although my hands have paid the price."

"Let's see." She walked over and reached for his hands, turning them over to inspect the reddened, blistered palms. "I've got some salve. Hang on. I'll go get it."

She ran upstairs and returned a moment later, twisting the lid off a metal tin. Adam held out his hands, and with cool fingers Hayley spread soothing cream over the inflamed skin. He watched her face as she worked the cream in. Either she was really absorbed in the task or she was avoiding his gaze. Was she also uncomfortable with where they'd left things last night?

They hadn't had a moment alone since the kiss, as Summer had become suddenly sociable and hung around until bedtime, chatting to Hayley about dude ranches and riding lessons. Hayley had said good-night first, saying she was tired from being on her feet all day. There'd been no chance to talk privately, much less pursue further intimacy.

"How are the horses?" he asked, avoiding the five-hundred-pound gorilla in the room.

"Blaze is ready to foal anytime. I'm betting she gives birth before another week passes."

"Summer's really excited. She's almost her old self when she's around the horses."

Hayley put the tin of salve down and wiped her hands on a clean cloth. "All done."

"Thanks." He smiled at her and her gaze skittered away. He couldn't avoid the subject of them any longer. "Are we good? Yesterday when Summer came in—"

"Hey, no, that was fine. I get it," Hayley assured him. "It's way too soon for her to know anything about…anything. Excuse me, I'll put this away." Rising abruptly, she ran back upstairs.

So. That had gone well. Not.

He went back to the AutoCAD program, making a few final tweaks on the specs of her house. A few minutes later he became aware of her footsteps again on the stairs and her approach.

She came to look over his shoulder at the plans on the computer. "Am I bothering you?"

"Only in the nicest possible way." Her soft chuckle next to his ear sounded like a forest stream. He wanted to turn around and take her in his arms. Instead, he said, "I'm working on the kitchen right now. Do you like L-shaped, U-shaped or a galley?"

Hayley had few possessions but he could easily imagine her in her new place. A blue glass vase filled with wildflowers on the windowsill, handmade hooked rugs and distressed furniture with the paint sanded back to reveal the grain of the wood.

"U-shaped. When the house is built I'm going to get all new furniture and the latest in modern appliances," she said, almost dreamily.

Huh? He twisted to look at her, trying to see past his preconceptions to who she really was. "I took you for a homemade, shabby-chic kind of gal."

She laughed. "Not in the least. I'm sick of second-hand, worn-out everything. I'm sick of making do. Being here at Timbertop, even for a short time, has made me realize just how tired I am of living tough. I don't need fancy or expensive things, but I want modern conveniences. I work hard outdoors all day long. I like a bit of comfort when I'm done as much as anyone else."

"Totally understandable." This new side of her fascinated him. Yet despite her words, she'd delayed getting material possessions due to pride and a desire to help others before herself. "I'm really pleased you're going to try to continue your horse therapy."

"Your drawings inspired me." After a beat, she added, "Your belief in me was inspiring, too."

"You're the one who's an inspiration." Their gazes met and held, and for a long moment he was lost in her warm blue eyes.

"And," she went on, "one of my old clients came into the café yesterday. He's not doing well. I really want to help him." She sighed and moved across to the window overlooking the valley. "However, it's one thing to say I'm going to try again, but I don't know where to start. Maybe I should hold a bake sale."

Adam drew in a butler's pantry—Hayley would need a place to store her army of small appliances. "My boss's husband writes grant proposals for a living. He mainly targets businesses on behalf of charity organizations. Graham and Lorraine happen to be coming up this weekend. I could ask him to help you."

"Seriously?" She turned, a slow smile spreading across her face.

He'd give her the moon if he could, just to see

that smile. "I can't promise anything, but it's worth a try."

"I honestly don't know how to thank you."

"Don't worry about it."

Did it really matter if they had no future together? How long their relationship lasted was almost irrelevant. He'd been married and miserable and stuck it out for years longer than he should have. Why should he pass up happiness, even if it was fleeting—simply because it was fleeting?

But Hayley had experienced devastating losses. Though she was tough, deep down she was vulnerable. She'd only recently found out her late husband had cheated on her, and Adam knew how painful that was. She needed time to recover. She didn't need him pressuring her into a relationship she wasn't ready for. *She'd* kissed *him,* he reminded himself. But she clearly had qualms, too, or she wouldn't be trying to keep her distance.

On the other hand, the attraction, chemistry, connection—whatever you wanted to call it—between him and Hayley wasn't going away. It was getting stronger, day by day. Minute by minute.

"What are you thinking?" She was watching him curiously, head tilted, a finger twining through the curling end of her long braid.

"I'm thinking about you. And me. I'd like to kiss you again." He rose and walked toward her. This could go very wrong…or it could be the start of something really good.

The tip of her tongue slid across her lower lip. "What about Summer?"

"What she doesn't know won't affect her." He wrapped his fingers around hers, tugging her toward him. "As long as we know what we want. And where we stand."

She looked him straight in the eye. "I know some things I want."

God, she blew him away. For a woman without a trace of coquetry she was incredibly seductive. "I'm not talking about microwave ovens, Hayley." With a lazy grin, he drew circles in her palm. "Why did you kiss me yesterday after saying you want to go slow?"

"I couldn't help myself." She paused a beat. "Why did you deepen it?"

"Same reason. I can't stop thinking about you." He nuzzled her neck as he slipped his other hand around her waist. His lips met the incredibly soft skin behind her ear. "You taste so sweet."

"Do you want to go for a ride?"

Adam drew back, smiling a little. "Really?"

Realizing what she'd said, she colored and pushed him away. "Not that kind of ride. On horseback. I'd like to show you something."

"Now?" It was midafternoon. He had work to do, if not on Hayley's house, then on the Shanghai apartments.

"Why not?" She tugged on his hand. "How often do you play hooky in the middle of the week?"

Well, Diane had often complained that he spent too much time at the office. "Okay," he said. "Let's go."

HAYLEY THREW HERSELF into the familiar routine of bridling and saddling the horses. Getting out of the house was a good idea. She'd been one touch, one kiss, away from melting into Adam's embrace, damn the consequences.

There was the smart thing to do—stay away from him. And then there was what she wanted to do—jump him every chance she got.

But she knew she was vulnerable, and that wasn't a good start to any relationship. She was fresh from Leif's latest betrayal. It didn't matter that he was dead and his affair had been nearly a year ago. It hurt as much as if it had happened two days ago. Part of her wanted to shun men for the next hundred years. Part of her wanted to bolster her self-esteem by sleeping with the first man that came along.

That would be wrong. She wouldn't use Adam. Unless he wanted to be used…

She threw the saddle over Asha's back and ran the girth strap through the ring, tightening it. The horse sidestepped away. "Please, Asha, don't fight me today. You need exercise."

She wished she knew why Leif had cheated on

her. Had he simply lost interest? Wasn't she pretty enough, or fun enough, or thin enough or… What?

Adam was a catch. In the city he'd have his pick of glossy, rich women. So what was he doing with her? Was it simply that he was stuck out here with no other female companionship?

"You're going to squeeze that poor horse's belly in two."

Startled, she glanced up. Adam was at the fence, watching her with a bemused expression. She eased off the girth a little and tied off the strap, straightened the stirrup, then turned to him.

"Do you have a girlfriend? I should've asked before I kissed you last night. I did that without thinking and then you kissed me back…."

"No, I don't have a girlfriend. I wouldn't hit on another woman if I did. I wouldn't do that to her *or* you."

Leif had charmed and teased her out of her suspicions. Adam was different. He didn't try to make light of her concerns.

"Okay, then." She smiled out of relief. "Now that we've got that out of the way, we'd better get a move on if we want to get our ride in before it rains."

"What are you talking about? The sky's clear blue."

"Look at the hills to the west. Clouds are building."

Hayley quickly saddled Sergeant and then held

the bridle while Adam mounted. She lengthened the stirrups by two notches and eyed him with approval as he adjusted his reins. He'd said he'd ridden on his grandfather's farm into his teen years, so he was an experienced rider—but she was still responsible.

"Okay, you're good to go." She slapped Sergeant's neck affectionately. "Don't take any guff from this fella. He's a bit ornery but he's got pep."

Hayley put a boot toe in the stirrup and swung up and onto Asha. The gray mare danced sideways as she settled into the saddle and gathered up the reins. She glanced back at Adam. Yep, he sat a horse real nice; confident but relaxed. In a saddle he seemed more her kind of man than he did in a business suit. "Ready?"

"For anything." A smile lurked in his dark eyes that sent a tingle straight through her. She couldn't keep teasing him.

She set off at a walk. At the end of the driveway, she crossed the paved road and onto a narrow dirt track through burned forest. Blackened, limbless trunks emerged like headstones from the scorched earth. Asha shied at a rabbit and Hayley patted her shoulder, talking to her. Her horse never used to spook at things before the fires.

"This isn't the most picturesque route," Adam commented.

"Just wait. It gets better."

Evidence of the fire made him uncomfortable,

she got that. But if on the slim chance he changed his mind and decided to stay in Hope Mountain for Summer's sake, he would have to get used to it. Catastrophic fires didn't occur every year—or even every fifty years. But they did happen. Fire was a fact of the Australian landscape and played an important role in the ecology of the bush. Every schoolkid knew that.

She twisted in her saddle to speak to Adam. "Did Diane and Summer leave during the bushfires?"

"I tried to get Diane to come to Melbourne the day before. The forecast was for extreme fire danger. She had some appointment that afternoon she couldn't miss. The next day she dithered around packing stuff. By the time she was ready, the roads were closed."

That had happened to a few folk in Hope Mountain. Not everyone who'd waited to evacuate had been as lucky as Diane and Summer. What kind of appointment had kept her there? Hayley wondered. Had she had a date with Leif?

Adam had gone quiet. Was he wondering the same thing?

She was tired of second-guessing and rehashing old conversations and behavior for clues. But the past gnawed at her like a sore tooth. She'd made up her mind to put it behind her. Why couldn't she stick to that?

Impatient with herself, she squeezed her calves and Asha broke into a trot. "Up for a canter?"

Adam nodded, seemingly as eager as she to leave the blackened forest and the dark thoughts in their dust. Hayley leaned forward and loosened the reins, pressing her heels into Asha's flanks.

Asha steadily increased her speed until she was galloping flat out and tears were streaming from the corners of Hayley's eyes. She glanced back at Adam. Arabs were known for speed, and Sergeant trailed by three lengths but his competitive spirit spurred him on, as did Adam's frequent cries of "Gee up."

When the trail began to narrow Hayley reined in Asha, slowing to a trot, then a walk.

Adam drew alongside, patting Sergeant's neck. "Good boy. He's got pep, all right. That was awesome."

"See, I told you it would get better." Hayley nodded at their surroundings. The merely scorched trees had green leaves sprouting directly from the trunks and from the larger branches. Pockets of grass and green shoots emerged from the dirt where the wallabies and wombats hadn't eaten them down.

"Already there's lots of new growth," she said. "In time, it will recover completely. There are seeds in the ground, just waiting for more rain and sun to shoot upward."

"Are you trying to convince me that Hope Mountain is a good place to live?" Adam said.

"That's something you have to decide for yourself. I'm showing you why I love living here." Seeing the regrowth always made her feel optimistic in a way that nothing else could, even all the rebuilding going on in town. If the bush could survive the worst that could be thrown at it, how could she do less?

"Mort came out the other day to take photos," Adam said. "He's preparing a listing, just waiting for my word to put Timbertop on the market. I thought I should tell you."

"That's cool." Was he warning her not to get too invested in him? It might be too late. Already she cared more than she wanted to, more than she knew was good for her.

She turned off the track onto a wildlife trail and went deeper into the forest. The horses walked single file. All was silent but for the twitter of birds, the wind in the upper boughs of the trees and the muffled thuds of hooves. The trail led down a slope. Burned trees and scrubby undergrowth gave way to mountain ash, straight and tall as the mast of a sailing schooner with smooth silver bark. In the understory, luxuriant tree ferns shaded the creek that bubbled quietly between mossy banks.

This was her special place. She'd found it on horseback as a child riding out from her grandparents' house. Ever since then she came here when she wanted to be alone, or needed the healing quiet of the deep woods. Platypuses could be found in the cool, tumbling waters, and if she sat very still, wallabies came out to nibble the tender leaves.

Hayley followed the creek until they came to a natural clearing. She let the horses drink from the creek, then looped the reins over their necks and turned them loose. Adam took a thermos out of the saddlebag and spread a blanket on the bank. Dappled light filtered through the green leaves and made patterns on the backs of Adam's hands as he poured coffee.

He handed her a cup and they sipped, listening to the sounds of the forest. She kept waiting for him to talk and disturb the peace. Finally she realized he wasn't like Leif, who would fill any silence with talk. Would she always judge all men by her late husband? She hoped not. The habits of half a lifetime were hard to break, but she needed to work on that.

Adam lay on the blanket, gazing up at the boughs of the trees. "I should play hooky more often. These trees are amazing. So tall, like skyscrapers."

"Only more beautiful." Hayley lay on her side facing him, her head propped on her hand. "Why did you go into architecture? Did you want to build skyscrapers?"

He laughed softly. "It's a long story and will sound crazy."

She checked on the horses. They were a little ways off, dozing in a patch of sun, sleepily whisking at flies with their tails. "Try me."

"Okay, here goes. My grandmother loved birds but hated to see them caged. So my grandfather made birdhouses for the yard. Lots of them, like a small town, all different colors, shapes and sizes. Then he got fancy, creating multistoried houses with feeding platforms and bird baths nearby."

"Sounds like an avian resort complex. Was there a tiny golf course?"

He chuckled. "No, but that would have been cool. Anyway, as a kid I used to watch the birds with Grandma and we'd make up stories about them as if they were families moving into their new homes and enjoying the view and the amenities. On rainy days for fun I'd draw bigger and better houses on paper, then eventually whole towns of animals living in little houses. The birds up in the trees and wombats and echidnas underground." He paused, smiling as he remembered.

"I love it. Go on," Hayley prompted. "What appealed to you about that, aside from anthropomorphizing bush animals?"

"I liked to think about the birds or animals living in a cozy home with everything they needed around them. I drew in root cellars for the wombats and a dozen bedrooms for the bandicoots."

"You do know bandicoots are solitary creatures and only bear two or three young?"

"Really? There were so many around the farm I

thought they must live in huge packs." He threw her a sheepish glance. "It all sounds nuts, doesn't it?"

"It sounds as if you care more about the occupants of your buildings than the buildings themselves." She loved that this big, handsome, sophisticated businessman had such a strong streak of whimsy. And that he'd trusted her enough to share his childhood fantasies with her.

"I was telling a friend at the café about the plans you drew up for my house," she added. "He asked if you'd be interested in designing a house for him, too."

Adam was quiet.

"There's a ton of work in Hope Mountain for an architect," Hayley went on, but still Adam said nothing. "I guess it doesn't pay as well as luxury apartments in Shanghai."

He sighed and shook his head. "It's not that. I couldn't live here. Hope Mountain is beautiful, I'll grant you that. But this area was never my choice for a home."

"Bushfires as bad as the one last year don't happen often."

"Let's not talk about the fires." Adam traced the line of her cheekbone down to her jaw, then tipped her chin up. His eyes darkened and he lowered his mouth to hers.

His lips were firm and cool. She opened her mouth, and his tongue was warm and tasted of coffee. He pulled her down so they were lying on the blanket, her arms around him and his leg twined with hers. He undid the top button of her shirt and slipped a hand inside, caressing her until her nipple peaked and her breast ached. He pressed closer, and she could feel him hard against her jeans. Sensations stirred inside her that she'd thought dead, or at least dormant.

Part of her wanted to make love to him, badly. It had been so long since she'd felt a man's touch. Not for lack of opportunities, but she hadn't wanted anyone. Until now.

Making love to Adam could be the prelude to something lasting and beautiful. Or it could be nothing more than a brief interlude.

She eased back to look at him. His eyes were warm and very compelling, and his hand cupped her breast as if he was holding her heart. Maybe he was. "What are we doing?" she whispered.

"We're exploring and enjoying the attraction between us." He licked delicately at the corners of her lips, creating little curls of heat that went straight to her breasts and belly. "I think you're awesome. I'd like to spend more time with you, to get to know you." His voice dropped, became husky. "I want to make love to you."

She wanted that, too, and it terrified her. What happened when he made her care for him and then left? But at least he was being honest. He wasn't telling her he wanted forever, and maybe that was okay.

She *did* need to move on, as Jacinta was always telling her. Adam could be the man to transition her from grieving widow to a woman again, with needs and desires. Yes, she might get hurt. But she might also experience something wonderful with Adam. However long their relationship lasted, she knew instinctively it would be good.

Even so, she was still afraid. Trusting wasn't going to come easily, thanks to Leif. But she didn't want to introduce Leif into a moment that was just about her and Adam. So she kissed him again, opening her mouth the way she wanted to open her heart.

His answering kiss was slow and languorous, reaching way inside her, melting her. His hand still circled her breast inside her shirt, his thumb teasing her tingling, taut nipple. Then his mouth replaced his fingers, sucking and drawing her in further. Her breath became shallow and her heart raced. She gave herself up to the moment, moving her hands over his heated skin and hot, hard muscles. Oh, he felt good.

Adam's hand slid down, down, his fingers scraping over her belly and dipping beneath the waistband of her moleskin pants. She stiffened, suddenly reluctant to continue. What was that about? She wanted this. Didn't she? Forcing herself to relax, she allowed him to unbutton her pants, then unzip them.

"Do you like this?" Adam ran his fingers lightly

back and forth across her belly, slowly going lower and lower.

"Yes. Yes, I do," she said, almost desperately. But it was no good. The more she tried to ignore her inexplicable lack of enthusiasm, the more her movements became artificial.

One second she'd been aroused and tight with need, the next she was pushing his hand away. "I'm sorry. I can't. It's too soon."

He let her go and just stroked her hand. "What's the matter? Don't you want me touching you?"

"Yes. No. Oh, I don't know." A tiny spurt of anger came out of nowhere. She tried to damp it down, but it wouldn't go away.

She sat up and buttoned up her pants. "You tell me you want to make love. And yet you're planning on leaving Hope Mountain. Maybe it's different for guys, but I have a hard time reconciling those two things."

"I didn't say it would be easy to leave." His gaze was pained and honest. "I don't know if this—us—will end or if it will go on…. Plenty of things are tugging us in opposite directions. But there's also something drawing us together. I feel it. I think you do, too."

"I do, but…" She hardly knew what to make of him. Unlike Leif, he didn't try to sweet-talk her into seeing things his way. Realizing that punctured her anger like a balloon. Adam cared about her feelings, and he liked and respected her. And there was no doubt he wanted her. That alone was a balm to her bruised ego. He hadn't simply offered her a one-night stand or a fling for as long as he was in town—he'd left the future open a crack. And it was almost enough for a tiny seed of hope to find root and grow, if she allowed it.

She wanted to move forward but was she ready to trust? Despite Leif's betrayal she still believed in love and commitment. Sleeping around or having casual sex was not an option for her. When she went to bed with a man it meant her heart was committed. But right now her emotions were all over the place.

A raindrop fell on her hand and she looked up at the sky. Dark clouds were moving in. "We'd better get back."

They quickly packed up the blanket and cups. Hayley avoided Adam's gaze. He probably thought she was awkward and naive and impossibly unsophisticated.

Before she could gather up Asha's reins, Adam reached for her and held her loosely by the shoulders. He gave her a kiss, a mere brush of the lips, his eyes full of questions. "You said you wanted to take it slow and I didn't listen. I don't want to push you into something you're not ready for."

"I guess I need a little more time. I don't mean

to send mixed signals. My body is as confused as my head."

"That's okay." He kissed her cheek and stepped away.

Hayley swung up on her horse. Asha seemed to sense her internal agitation and danced and snorted along the trail as they rode out single file. She kept a tight rein on the animal as she replayed her and Adam's conversation in her mind. She couldn't make him want something he didn't want. But neither was she willing to push him away.

When the track broadened Adam caught up and rode alongside. Then without warning, he clicked his tongue and loosened the reins, urging Sergeant into a canter. "Race you to the road."

Clods of dirt flew up behind Sergeant's hooves. Hayley gave Asha the signal to gallop flat out. She grinned at Adam as she sped past, his ten-year-old gelding no match for her Arab mare. He grinned and shook his fist.

Hayley laughed out loud. She didn't know what was going to happen between her and Adam. But she felt more alive than she had in a long, long time. Maybe once she got past the memorial service she would know what she wanted.

Maybe then her mind, body and heart would start acting as one instead of tearing her apart.

She could only hope.

CHAPTER ELEVEN

As HAYLEY HAD PREDICTED, rain began to fall. Back at Timbertop they hurriedly put the horses away. Then Adam drove into town and picked up Summer from school. The car's windshield wipers clacked as he drove. His daughter's phone beeped with a new text message every few minutes. She didn't even check the sender ID.

"Someone's trying hard to reach you, Summer," Adam said.

"It's not important." She shut the phone, leaving another message unread.

Adam thought about the boy in the café. He seemed all right, but you never knew. "Is Steve sending you all these messages? You can tell me. I'll fix it for you."

"You can't fix things just by saying you will."

"I could try." He thumped the steering wheel lightly. "Whatever it is that's bothering you, I won't get mad."

"How do you know? You don't know what it is."

"Aha, so there *is* something bothering you."

She paled and turned to the window. Damn. How

come he couldn't talk to his daughter for more than five minutes without getting into an argument?

The rest of the trip was conducted in silence. Which was fine by Adam—he was glad to have a little thinking time. He'd thought he had things with Hayley all sorted out in his head. That they could be intimate—when she was ready—without it affecting their lives and plans. But it wasn't that easy or simple.

He'd been telling the truth when he'd said he wanted to spend time with her. Lots of time. In bed and out. But she clearly wasn't comfortable with a relationship that didn't have a definable future, and he didn't want to make promises he couldn't keep. But he could see how "I'm here for a good time, not a long time" wouldn't be attractive to her.

He parked in front of the house and got out, wincing as he climbed the shallow steps onto the veranda. Shane lay curled up in his basket next to the back door.

"Why are you walking so stiffly?" Summer asked.

"Hayley and I went for a horseback ride." Hayley had told him to stretch afterward and he hadn't listened, instead going straight into town.

"You went riding without me?" Summer's face fell. Shane dropped his ball at her feet. Mechanically she threw it across the yard for him. "You know I've been dying to ride."

"You were at school. You'll get a chance."

"Today?"

"That's up to Hayley. She mentioned she wants you to do some horse therapy this afternoon."

Adam went past Summer and into the house. Hayley was coming down the stairs as he entered the living room. He caught her lightly by the wrists, wanting to make amends for his clumsiness by the creek and restore the closeness that had been growing between them.

"I'm sorry if I came across like a jerk earlier. I don't blame you if you don't want to get involved with some fly-by-night architect who'd rather live in the city than your beautiful woods."

She didn't pull away, but slid her hands into his. "I'm sorry I called a halt so abruptly. I don't mean to tease."

"You've got a right to be wary." He was dying to kiss her but he held back, taking his cue from her.

"Hey, listen," she said. "The memorial service for the first anniversary of the bushfires is coming up. Afterward, there's a dance. Do you want to go with me?"

A date. This was progress. He should have thought of that himself. "Sounds good. Is this something teens would attend?"

"The whole town will be there, from grannies down to tots. If you're wondering whether Summer will want to go, I'm sure she already plans to."

"In that case, I wouldn't miss it." He ran his

thumbs over the backs of her hands. They were soft and smooth compared to her lightly callused palms. "You're different from what I thought when we first met. Not so prickly."

Her eyes looked into his and her voice softened. "It's because you've been so good to me."

"I'm glad you decided to let me help. You needed to let someone in."

"I have Molly and Rolf and my friend, Jacinta…." She trailed away. "But they're people I've known for years." She bit her lip. "You're right. I wasn't letting you in. I can't help it. Trust is an issue."

"Not every man is like Leif."

"I know you're not."

He drew her close and she didn't resist, sliding her arms around his neck and lifting her mouth to his. Her lips were warm and sweet and trusting. He held Hayley tenderly, wanting to prove to her he would never hurt her.

The screen door slammed open. "Hayley, where's the lunge line—?" Summer stopped with a squeak of her rubber sole on tiles. Adam let go and stepped back but not in time. The teen glanced from him to Hayley. "What's going on?"

HAYLEY'S HEART SANK. Busted. She glanced at Adam, letting him take the lead. She wished Summer hadn't caught them kissing but maybe it was better if she and Adam were open about their friendship. After all, she was a widow and he was divorced. They weren't doing anything immoral. They'd barely done anything at all.

"Nothing," Adam said quickly. "Hayley, did you want Summer for a horse therapy session now?"

She glanced at him, eyebrows raised. What, total denial? Oh, she knew they'd already decided not to tell the girl, and really, what was there to tell? She didn't expect him to ask Summer's blessing and start planning a wedding. But still…

"That's right," Hayley said. "Summer, I'll be out at the lunge ring once you change out of your school clothes."

"But…" Summer made a frustrated sound and turned to her dad. "You didn't answer my question. You and Hayley were kissing."

"Never mind that now. You heard Hayley. She wants to get started." He walked past them both and into the study.

"Get changed and come outside, okay?" Hayley said to Summer. "We'll talk."

She went out the kitchen door, whistling to Shane, who fell into step behind her. While she brought out the buggy reins and the padded vest and helmet, she thought about what she would say to Summer.

Adam might not want to tell his daughter what was going on between them, but he had no right expecting Hayley to lie. Honesty between patient and therapist was vital. If she wasn't honest with

Summer, how could she expect the girl to trust her with the truth?

Summer found her ten minutes later at the paddock. She got straight to the point. "You and Dad were kissing."

"There was a little kissing going on, yes," Hayley said calmly, though her heart was beating so hard she could hear it.

"Wow, do you two like each other?" Summer said.

Hayley was taken aback at her eagerness. "Your dad's been really good to me and he's a nice man. Of course I like him." And she was dodging the issue.

"No, I mean, are you and he dating?"

"We're going to go to the dance together, but I'm not sure that could be classified as a date. To tell you the truth, we're just feeling our way. We like each other, but we're being cautious because our lives are so different." She paused. "How would you feel if we were dating?"

"I would love it," Summer said enthusiastically. "I think you're awesome."

"Thanks." She gave the girl a big smile and hugged her impulsively. "I think you're pretty amazing, too."

She hadn't realized how worried she'd been about Summer's reaction to her and Adam being together. It was still a dodgy ethical issue and Adam's reaction stung, but at least Summer wasn't against the idea. "Are you going to the dance?"

"'Course. Zoe's coming here for a sleepover afterward. I haven't asked Dad yet, but he won't mind."

"Will Steve be at the dance?"

Summer froze. "Why?"

"Just curious. He seems like a nice boy. Do you still like him?"

"You didn't tell Dad about him, did you?"

"No, but you're fourteen. Isn't that old enough to have a boyfriend? That's how old I was when I started going out with Leif."

Summer kicked at a clump of grass with the toe of her riding boot and asked casually, "How old were you when you first slept with him?"

Hayley's instincts went on alert. She didn't discuss her private life with her clients, but if sharing her experiences might help Summer open up it would be worthwhile.

"Old enough. Or so I thought at the time." In hindsight fifteen and a half seemed young. Modulating her voice to hide her concern, she asked, "Have you slept with Steve?"

Summer hesitated, a telling pause. Then she snorted. "As if. Thirteen's way too young to have sex. That's what I think, anyway. I'm more interested in horses."

"I happen to agree. But I thought you were fourteen."

"I meant fourteen," Summer said quickly. "I get

mixed up because my birthday wasn't that long ago."
She started to put on the safety vest and hard hat.

"Sure." Hayley eased off. There was nothing to be gained by pressing too hard. But either Summer was genuinely mixed up, or else she and Steve had had sex a year ago. Thirteen was definitely too young, in Hayley's opinion. Summer certainly seemed to regret it, if that was what really happened. Had she been coerced?

"Before we start, tell me how you've been coping with school and life in general since our last session."

Summer shrugged. "Okay, I guess. Sometimes not so good."

"Sounds like you're more aware of your feelings, though."

"Hmm, yeah, sort of."

Hayley was used to working with teens. Patience was a virtue when it came to extracting information. "Can you think of any occasions when you felt angry or anxious and were able to use the techniques I taught you to calm yourself down?"

Summer cast her eyes skyward as she thought. "When we were at the café and Steve came in. He was pissing me off. So was Dad. You reminded me to breathe. That helped."

"Why were you annoyed at Steve?"

"He keeps calling me. I told him to stop months ago."

"Don't you like him anymore?"

Summer made an impatient movement. "Can't we get started?"

"In a minute. I'd like to hear more about Steve. He gave you that figurine. That was nice of him. He seems to care about you."

Summer kicked at the grass again, scowling.

"Do you have mixed feelings about him?"

Her head shot up. "Yeah, I have mixed feelings," she said angrily. "He's the reason my horse, Bailey, died."

Hayley frowned. "What do you mean?"

"Bailey didn't get scared and jump the fence. Steve rode him home from here the morning of the bushfires. He went through an area that was burning. Someone came by in a car. He left Bailey and went with them." Tears rolled down Summer's cheeks. "He just let Bailey go, hoping he would come back home. Bailey never made it."

"I don't understand. Why did Steve have to ride your horse? Why couldn't your Mom or his parents have driven him home?"

Summer pressed her lips together, her eyes and cheeks wet. "No one knew he was here."

Ah. Hayley thought she got it now. "What time of morning did he leave?" Silence. "Tell me. I won't judge."

Summer's chin set at a defiant angle. "Just before dawn."

"So he spent the night with you. Did you two—?"

"We did it once and that was it," she said angrily. "If you tell my dad, I'm never going to talk to you again. I'll tell him the horse therapy isn't working and he'll send you away. You'll never see him again."

Sooner or later, most of Hayley's clients turned their aggression and fears on her. But this time it was personal. She didn't believe Adam would send her away on Summer's word, but she couldn't let Summer try to manipulate the situation.

She cared about the girl. And only a few minutes ago Summer had showed she cared about Hayley. But she'd been hurt somehow and perhaps used, and she had feelings she didn't know what to do with. Hayley knew all this with a bone-deep certainty, because she saw herself staring at her out of Summer's anguished eyes.

The summer she was fifteen, Leif had charmed, coaxed and cajoled Hayley into having sex with him even though she wasn't emotionally ready. She'd tried to get him to wait, but he'd been determined.

"It's all right, you know," she said softly. "Whatever happened, you're still a good person and worthwhile. Did he pressure you?"

Summer cried harder. "No. I wanted to do it. But Bailey's death is all my fault. If I hadn't slept with Steve, he would've left earlier and my horse would still be alive. Steve keeps calling and saying he loves me. But I hate him. I don't know what to do."

"Do you hate him?" Hayley paused. "Or do you hate yourself because you feel guilty for having sex so young? And for Bailey dying?"

Summer didn't answer. A second ticked by. Then another. And another. Finally, she whispered, "Yes."

Hayley put her arms around the girl and just held her, trying to absorb her grief and draw it out. "Neither you nor Steve are to blame for Bailey dying. You couldn't have known what would happen."

"The day was predicted to be an extreme fire danger day."

"The weather bureau is sometimes wrong. And you can't accurately predict which way the wind will gust and carry the embers. There are so many variables. You just don't know."

"I smelled smoke in the air that morning, when Steve left." Summer eased back, misery all over her face. "I knew there was a fire somewhere. And then Steve just abandoned Bailey out in the forest."

"You wouldn't have wanted him to stay with the horse and maybe both would have been killed, would you?"

"N-n-no." Summer's bottom lip trembled.

"Oh, sweetheart." Hayley brushed away a strand of red hair that had gotten stuck to Summer's cheek by tears. "You've got to stop beating yourself up over this. Seriously. I'm glad you told me. I know you feel miserable right now, but later, when you've had a chance to reflect, you'll see things from a different perspective."

"There's something else," Summer mumbled, her gaze dropping. "We didn't use protection."

Hayley did a quick mental calculation. The fires had been nearly twelve months ago. "You didn't get pregnant, did you?"

"No, but…I've been worried ever since that I might have gotten…a disease."

"Do you have any symptoms?"

Summer turned redder and shook her head.

"Well, it's not likely you caught anything. Did you ask Steve if he had any STDs?"

"God, no." Summer looked horrified at the thought.

"Did you see a doctor?"

More shakes of the head. "I'm on my dad's Medicare card. He would see the bill and ask what it was about."

"Couldn't you have talked to your mom?"

"She had no time for me," Summer said bitterly. "She was too busy fooling around with—" The girl broke off, wincing.

There was an awkward silence. "It's okay," Hayley said. "I know."

"My mom shouldn't have done that." Summer looked mortified. "I'm so, so sorry."

"I'm sorry, too." She wiped at the sudden moisture in her eyes. Then laughed ruefully. "We're a sorry pair, aren't we?"

Summer sniffed and then smiled a little. "Yeah, we are."

Hayley hugged her again and left her arm around Summer's waist. "I'm sure there's nothing wrong with you. But for your own peace of mind, I can take you to a clinic where no questions will be asked. How does that sound?"

"Good." Summer wiped her arm across her eyes. "Thanks."

"Okay, now how would you like to work with Asha today?"

"Oh, yes, but I thought she was too hard to handle."

"I'd like you to try her in the lunge ring. You got Major's confidence the last time—you can do this. You'll need to work even harder, dig deeper, to be calm enough to be a leader to Asha. It will hopefully speed up your therapy."

"That sounds good."

Hayley banged on the fence with the oat bucket and the horses lifted their heads from grazing. Asha trotted over, neck arched and silver mane flowing.

"Hello, you greedy thing." Hayley stroked the dapple-gray face plunged into the bucket and snapped the lead to the ring on her halter. She spread the rest of the oats on the ground for the other horses and led the spirited mare out of the paddock and across to the ring. There she turned her loose. Asha trotted off to the opposite side.

"Go on in," Hayley said to Summer. "You know what to do."

"Aren't you coming in with me?"

"Not this time. I'll be right outside the fence. I can get over in two seconds flat if you need me. But you won't."

Summer went into the ring. Asha immediately raised her head. She was a very different prospect from gentle old Major. The girl started slapping the leather reins against her thigh and slowly approached the skittish mare. Asha danced away, tail high, twisting her neck and blowing through her nose.

"Stay calm and centered," Hayley called over the fence. "Don't forget your shoulders. Don't forget to breathe." She climbed onto the middle rung in case she needed to vault over at a moment's notice.

Maybe she *should* be in the ring, but Summer had gained in confidence since the last session, both in herself and in the horses. Hayley wanted to see how much she'd grown. She also wanted to see something else....

Asha ran away, snorting and kicking. Summer followed, steadily slapping the reins. Asha cantered along the outside of the ring, her hooves occasionally flicking the wooden boards of the fence.

Finally the time came.

"Turn around and drop your head," Hayley said.

Summer did so. At this point when Hayley tried working with Asha, the horse always ran away, bucking and tossing her head. Today, she slowed to a trot, then a walk. Then she moved toward Summer's slight figure with her head bowed.

So that was the way it was. Hayley had tears in her eyes, partly of joy for the girl, partly anguish for herself.

"Turn around, Summer."

Summer gave a whoop, her face alight as Asha nudged her arm gently. She looked at Hayley, speechless with wonder. "She came to me."

"She did indeed. You can put her back in the other paddock now, if you like."

Summer led Asha away. Hayley sat on the fence, her world spinning around her. How many times had she heard her clients say, "I don't have a problem but my horse does?" Never once had she thought it would apply to her. She'd had losses, but she'd worked through her problems. She was resilient and strong and she'd moved forward because that was what she did—she was a survivor.

Or so she'd thought. Now the truth was plain to see. Asha didn't have a problem. *She* did.

"Everything okay?" Adam touched her elbow. "I saw you were finished so I thought I'd check on how Summer did."

Still in a wondering daze, Hayley turned to him.

"She got Asha to follow her. She's beginning to open up."

"That's great. Did you learn anything you can tell me?"

Hayley picked at a splinter of wood on the paling, considering the balance between Summer's needs and Adam's. "She feels responsible for Bailey's death. She needs to forgive herself, and she's not able to do that while she fears you'll be disappointed in her for what happened."

Adam spread a hand. "Well, what did happen?"

Hayley regarded him unhappily. "That I can't tell you. I'm sorry. This is awkward for me now that we've become…closer. Normally I'd be at arm's length with a patient's parents."

"How can I reassure her when I'm in the dark?" Adam demanded, clearly frustrated.

"I encouraged her to talk to you about the source of her trauma. All I can suggest is that you continue building trust with her and hope that someday she'll open up."

"With so little explanation it's impossible not to think the worst. Has she been assaulted? Is she suicidal?"

"No," Hayley assured him, squeezing his shoulder. "I'd tell you if she was in danger."

He blew out a sigh. "Well, that's a relief. Where is she now?"

Hayley glanced over at the paddock. Asha was

grazing with the other horses, but Summer wasn't in sight. "She must've gone into the barn." She turned back to Adam. "She questioned me about that kiss. I couldn't deny it."

Adam grimaced. "I handled that badly. Sorry. She caught me off guard."

"She's okay with us dating."

"Really? That's great." His face brightened. "I was worried about how she'd react. She's been through so much this past year, and I don't want anything interfering with her treatment. But since the issue has come up, it's nice to know there's one hurdle out of the way of us being together."

"Only one." Hayley glanced away. "I'm not sure I'm ready for a serious relationship."

Adam put a hand on her chin, turning her face to him. "Hayley, did something else happen during your session?"

"I discovered I still have problems of my own." All the anger toward Leif she thought she'd dealt with had only been buried. The prospect of falling in love with Adam had caused those old issues to well up. Maybe that was why she hadn't been able to make love with him. "I have to deal with them."

"Is there anything I can do to help?"

There was nothing in his face but an open, good-natured desire to make her life better.

She swung her legs over the top rail so she faced him. "Taking me to the dance will be a good start.

I want to let go of the past. But you need to be patient with me...."

Adam lifted her off the fence, letting her slide down his body before giving her a hug and setting her away from him. "Honey, *patience* is my middle name."

"THEY'RE HERE." ADAM WAS filling the water jug at the kitchen sink when Lorraine and Graham's sleek black Lexus pulled up at the back of the house.

Hayley finished arranging the appetizers on a plate and wiped her hands on a towel. "Do I look okay?"

Her simple black cocktail dress from the secondhand shop was years out of date, but Hayley had transformed it into grace and beauty. Her hair flowed in long, loose waves down her back, and even plain black pumps couldn't detract from her shapely calves and slim ankles.

Adam touched her cheek, smiling into her eyes. "You look stunning."

Outside, car doors shut. Adam went to open the door. "Lorraine, Graham. Welcome to Timbertop."

His boss was wearing designer jeans, a sparkly Western-style blouse and high heels with red soles. Her blond hair was shaped into a smooth chin-length bob. She reached a hand out to Hayley. "You must be the horse whisperer."

Adam watched the exchange anxiously. Lorraine

was never anything but gracious, but she could be intimidating.

Hayley gave her a warm smile. "It's lovely to meet you."

Lorraine leaned in to kiss her cheek, then pulled back to look at her. "You do amazing things for that dress. All that horseback riding must keep you incredibly fit."

"I wish I'd worn jeans, too, although you'd never get me in four-inch heels," Hayley admitted easily. "Those Louboutins look awesome on you, though."

"I don't know why I bother. They hurt my back."

Hayley's eyes twinkled. "I've got sheepskin slippers you can borrow." She turned to Lorraine's husband, hand outstretched. "You must be Graham. Welcome to Hope Mountain."

With the greetings done, Lorraine asked, "Tell me, Hayley, how did you bewitch Adam into leaving the city for the country?"

"Come out to the deck and see the view." Linking arms with Lorraine, she winked at Adam over her shoulder. "I'll tell you all."

Adam blinked. Once again, he'd underestimated Hayley. Why had he expected her to act like a hick just because she didn't live in the city and work in an office? She was self-possessed enough to match the most sophisticated of folk.

"Hayley seems nice," Graham said to Adam in a bland understatement as they watched the two women settle into the deck chairs. "I was expecting Annie Oakley."

"She's amazing." He was also surprised at how quickly Lorraine had taken to Hayley. Again he had to readjust his thinking. Why should he imagine his boss would look down her nose? She was married to Graham, after all, an aging hippie who wrote grant requests for charities. These days Graham dressed the corporate part, but he still wore his graying brown hair in a ponytail.

"What will you and Lorraine have to drink?" Adam asked. "The usual?" While he poured wine for the ladies and got whiskies for himself and Graham, he told Graham about Hayley's Horses for Hope program and the work she was doing with Summer.

"Does she work solely with teens?" Graham asked.

"Not exclusively. Although, from what I've witnessed she's great at connecting with young people." Adam related how her government funding had been cut. "She needs a stable source of money. Do you know of any companies that might be prepared to make a sizable donation on an ongoing basis?"

"I can think of one or two possibilities. Once I have a chat with Hayley, I'd be happy to see what I can do." Graham lifted his tumbler. "Cheers."

"I'd appreciate that. The Horses for Hope program is really important to her. And to the community."

Adam sipped smooth twelve-year-old scotch. Was he a fool? By helping Hayley get back into horse therapy, he was ensuring she planted herself ever more firmly on the mountain. And where did that leave him? He'd hoped she might consider spending time in the city so they could explore what they had together. On the other hand, how could he drag her away from the home she loved so much? It would be like planting a wildflower in a hot house. She would wither and die.

"And is Hayley important to you?" Graham gave him a shrewd, amused look.

"She's special," Adam admitted. "But we both know our friendship might only be short-term. Our lives are on very different paths."

"Just like Lorraine's and my lives were on different paths when we met." Graham chuckled. "Next month we celebrate our twentieth wedding anniversary."

"Dad, Dad! Hayley, come quick!" Summer burst through the back door. "Where's Hayley?"

"On the deck. We're having a dinner party, sweetheart," Adam said. "Say hello to Graham. And you should take those boots off in the house."

Summer ignored every word except the first three and ran across the cream-colored carpet to the sliding glass doors, calling for Hayley.

Hayley had heard the commotion and was already on her feet. "What is it?"

"Blaze is having her foal. Come quick!" Summer said. "She's grunting and turning around in circles."

"Excuse me, Lorraine." Hayley hurried after Summer. At the back door she kicked off her shoes and slipped on a pair of gumboots beneath her cocktail dress. "Don't delay dinner for us," she said to Adam. "This could take a while. Go ahead and eat."

"Are you kidding?" Graham picked up the bottle of scotch. "I've never seen a horse give birth. Coming, Lorraine?"

Lorraine followed them out, teetering in her high heels. "I wouldn't miss this for the world."

Adam shrugged and tucked the wine bottle under his arm. Neither would he.

CHAPTER TWELVE

HAYLEY ENTERED THE box stall, her boots rustling the thick straw. Blaze was blowing hard through her nostrils, her sides heaving and straining.

"Easy, girl, easy." She spoke softly, running a hand down the mare's neck, over her taut belly and up her flank. "There's a good girl."

Blaze's tail was raised above a bulging perineum. Her belly tightened with a contraction and a soft white forehoof poked through, encased in a silvery membrane. Thank goodness the foal was coming out the right way around. Another tiny hoof peeked out, then the legs retracted.

"Why is it going back inside?" Summer asked, leaning over the side of the stall. "Are you going to call the vet?"

"There isn't time, but it's normal for the baby to take a few tries to come out." Hayley moved to get out of Blaze's way as the mare lumbered around the stall. The horse twisted her neck and nipped at her own belly.

Summer chewed on her thumbnail, her brow furrowed. "Is this her first foal?"

"No, her second. Don't worry. She knows what she's doing." Hayley covered her concern. Things could sometimes go wrong. Last time Blaze had delivered a stillborn foal. Tony, the vet, had attended that birth and there'd been nothing he could do. It had been heartbreaking. She'd hate for Summer to witness anything like that.

Adam, Lorraine and Graham entered the barn, laughing and talking. Graham topped up drinks to the sound of clinking ice.

"Quiet, please," Hayley said. "Don't disturb Blaze."

"We saw the hooves come out and then go back in," Summer whispered as the others approached more softly.

The mare's legs bent and she lowered herself heavily to the floor of the stall and rolled onto her side. Her flanks heaved with the force of another contraction. The foal's forelegs emerged again and this time Hayley glimpsed a nose.

"The baby's got a white mark on its nose like Blaze, only smaller." Hayley crouched next to Blaze. *Please come out alive, little one.*

"What's happening?" Lorraine whispered. "She's so still and quiet. Is something wrong?"

"No, this is how horses do it," Hayley said.

"They don't yell the hospital down like some women I know," Graham said with a smile in his voice.

"Shh, you." Lorraine swatted at his arm.

"I'm going to take a photo." Summer got out her phone.

"You can use it for show-and-tell at school," Adam suggested.

"What century are you in?" Summer said. "I'm tweeting it." She clicked the shutter, then texted madly. "Right…now."

Hayley glanced at Adam and shared a smile. *Teenagers*.

"Oh, it's coming," Summer said. "I see the head!"

Hayley turned her attention back to Blaze and checked her watch. Ten minutes. So far so good. The foal's ears were flattened and its eyes closed, the dark coat wet and matted. Blaze rested a moment, then continued to push. First the body was delivered, then the hind legs. The coal-black foal lay on the straw, motionless.

Hayley dropped to her knees in the straw and ran a hand over the foal's neck, searching for the carotid artery. Blaze, still lying on her side, reached around with her nose to nudge at her baby.

"It's going to be okay, girl," Hayley said, praying it was the truth.

"The foal is bigger than our full-grown black Lab," Lorraine said, oblivious to the potential crisis. "I can't believe all that fit into the horse's belly."

"You thought delivering a nine-pound baby was tough," Graham murmured as he put his arm around Lorraine.

"Why isn't it moving?" Adam said quietly.

Hayley pressed her fingers into the foal's neck below the jaw while she ran her other hand down its chest with hard, rhythmic strokes. Then she felt a pulse beat beneath her fingertips. *Oh, thank God.* With a flutter, the foal's lungs inflated, lifting the rib cage.

Hayley closed her eyes and released her breath and a prayer of thanksgiving. The tiny life had hung in the balance for only a minute, but it had been one of the longest of her life. Lorraine and Graham huddled together, understanding belatedly that the outcome had been in doubt. Adam had his arm firmly around Summer's shoulders.

"She's alive." Hayley glanced up, her eyes blurring. "A beautiful little filly."

Blaze scrambled to her feet. She nosed Hayley's hand away and started licking her baby all over.

"Why's she doing that?" Lorraine asked.

"To help the blood circulation and to encourage the foal to stand up."

"You didn't do that for Ben or Ashley," Graham pointed out to Lorraine.

"Oh, stop it." Lorraine's face was wet with happy tears.

"She's getting up," Summer said excitedly.

Hayley stepped back to allow the foal space. Blaze whickered encouragement, still licking. Tiny ears flickered. Forelegs splayed, the little black filly pushed herself up halfway before her knees buckled. She tried again. This time she made it to a standing position, her spindly legs trembling with the effort of balance and strength. Then she whinnied, a tiny bleating sound, as if to say, *I'm here!*

Tears filled Hayley's eyes as she laughed and hugged first Summer and then Adam. It had been so long since she'd had something to celebrate. Here was new life, fragile but strong. She felt a surge of hope for the future.

Adam's arms slipped around her waist, and she felt him press a kiss to the top of her head. In the dim light of the stable she leaned into him. Would he be part of her future? She was starting to hope so. Together they watched the foal totter toward her mother, nuzzling along her belly, smelling the drops of milk and searching for the udders.

Soon the foal was sucking lustily. Blaze nuzzled the tiny rump and was batted by a damp whisking tail.

"The white mark on her nose isn't as long as Blaze's," Hayley remarked. "More like a diamond."

"Let's call her Jewel," Summer suggested.

"It's Hayley's horse. She should name her," Adam reminded his daughter.

"Jewel is perfect," Hayley said. Summer's face glowed with pride before she turned her adoring gaze back to the filly. Healing came about in different ways, Hayley reflected. Maybe this little horse was just what Summer needed.

ADAM FLIPPED A fluffy pancake and turned the heat down on the sizzling bacon. The aroma of freshly brewed coffee filled the kitchen. Summer came in through the back door, rubbing her eyes and yawning. He took in her crumpled clothes and mussed hair. "Did you sleep out in the barn?"

"Yup. I wanted to be near Blaze and Jewel." Summer took a piece of bacon off the plate and ate it in two bites. "Jewel's walking really well this morning. She licked my hand and nibbled on my hair. She's so adorable, Dad. I just love her."

"That's great, kiddo. I'm glad it all went well."

Summer grabbed another piece of bacon. "Hayley said she would let me halter-train Jewel. First she has to buy a lightweight leather halter. Nylon's no good, Hayley says, because a foal's neck will break before the nylon breaks."

"Ouch." He plated up the pancakes and poured another set onto the griddle. "Did Hayley stay out there all night, too?"

After dinner she and Summer had returned to the barn to clean out Blaze's stall and put down fresh straw. He'd gone out to say good-night around midnight, stealing a brief kiss while Summer was busy with the foal. He, Lorraine and Graham had turned in for the night shortly after that. He'd lain awake for a while, listening for Hayley's footsteps on the stairs, but he had fallen asleep.

"I think she went to bed around two o'clock. She promised to take Graham and me riding this morning so you and Lorraine could talk business."

"That's good of her." Last night had been purely social. This morning he and Lorraine would get down to brass tacks negotiating the terms of his partnership. He'd been working toward this goal for years and suddenly it was within reach. It was a big moment.

He needed to factor in his responsibility for Summer. If she lived with him in Melbourne they could come back to Hope Mountain now and then to visit. She would miss Hayley and her friends and the horses, but her emotional and mental health already seemed stronger. She could even keep a horse on the outskirts of Melbourne. Once they got settled they could start looking for a well-trained three- or four-year-old.

Summer reached for more bacon but he pulled the plate away. "Go shower and change. You smell like a barn."

"Okay." With a cheeky grin Summer sneaked another piece and ran upstairs as Hayley was coming down. She stopped and gave Hayley a detailed account of the past six hours of the foal's life before heading for the shower.

Adam looked up as Hayley came into the kitchen.

She looked more like herself this morning in tan moleskin pants and a soft blue-and-green flannel shirt. "You're up early considering your late night. How are you this morning?"

"Tired but good. I'm almost as excited as Summer. It was hard to sleep." She took a piece of bacon off the plate and munched. "Can I do anything?"

"Don't eat all the bacon, for a start," he said with a smile.

"I wouldn't do that." Grinning, she nicked another piece.

"Taunt me, will you?" He lunged and she dodged, dissolving into giggles like a schoolgirl. Then he faked her out and caught her, circling his arms around her waist.

"I appreciated your support last night," Hayley said, resting her hands on his chest.

"I didn't do anything." Adam picked up one hand and kissed her fingertips. "You were the one who helped that foal into the world. You're amazing."

Hayley nestled closer till their bodies were touching. "Your presence was strong and calming. It helped *me* be calm."

He pressed a kiss to either side of her lips, then ran his tongue along her mouth until she opened for him. She tasted sweet and salty—totally delicious.

Hayley sighed with pleasure, and dropped small kisses along his jawline. "Lorraine and Graham are moving around upstairs. They'll be down soon. It's nice that your boss came all the way to Hope Mountain. You must be important to her."

He hadn't told Hayley about Lorraine's offer, because he was conflicted over what it would mean to them. He couldn't keep it from her any longer. "She's offered me a partnership. It's a pretty big deal to me." To put it mildly.

"A partnership." Hayley eased back. She pasted on a smile but it barely curved her mouth and definitely didn't reach her eyes. "Congratulations. I'm thrilled for you."

He searched her sober face. "You don't look thrilled."

"Sorry, I'm not feeling very bubbly. I'm tired, is all. Really, it's great. You deserve it, I'm sure." She paused. "What about Summer?"

"I haven't told her yet, but we'll work it out. I'm not going to let it affect my relationship with her." He let a beat go by. "Or you."

Hayley gave him a troubled smile. "I don't know much about your business, but I imagine partners put in even more hours than employees further down the pecking order."

"I mean it, Hayley," he said urgently. "This doesn't have to be the end of us. I can still come out on weekends. Lots of people manage long-distance relationships."

"Adam, I really like you, but we've known each other only a short time," Hayley said in her straightforward way he admired so much but which could be so devastating. "You're not going to change your life on my account, and I wouldn't dream of asking." Her mouth twisted and her eyes were sad. "One thing I've learned this past year is that the future might not turn out anything like you planned or imagined."

He guessed he couldn't blame her for being cautious. She'd still been grieving when she'd discovered her husband had cheated on her. But he also knew that Hayley was special, and if he missed this opportunity to keep her in his life, the chance would never come again. He didn't want to regret that for the rest of his life.

He pulled her into his arms. "All I'm suggesting is that we remain open to possibilities. Can we do that?"

Her gaze searched his face. "You're the one leaving town."

"Long distance isn't insurmountable if both parties are willing to work something out. Melbourne isn't that far away." He squeezed her hands. "Please?"

"Okay." Finally she smiled. "I'm open to possibilities."

Adam leaned in to kiss her again. Just as his lips touched hers, footsteps sounded on the stairs.

Hayley drew back, smiling, her palms sliding over his as she pulled her hands away. "Later, alligator."

Lorraine and Graham came around the corner from

the living room into the kitchen. "Mmm, bacon."
Lorraine took a piece from the ever-diminishing pile.

"Grab a mug and help yourself to coffee," Adam
said. "Breakfast will be ready shortly." Graham, too,
picked at the plate of bacon. With a smile and a
shake of his head, Adam went to the fridge for another package of the tasty meat.

Summer came back downstairs in fresh clothes
and helped Hayley set the table. Conversation over
breakfast revolved around Hayley and Summer's
excited plans for breaking the foal.

Adam kept silent but his concern grew. How long
did halter-breaking a foal take? Would Summer be
around to complete the training? Would she then
want to go on to break the horse to bridle and saddle? From what he recalled of his grandfather's farm,
horses weren't ridden until they were two years old.

His gaze shifted to Hayley. The morning sun lit
her face, casting a glow over her smooth skin and
bringing a gleam into her blue eyes. She would be
worth making the journey to Hope Mountain every
weekend—and more than enough motivation to ne-
gotiate with Lorraine so that he had sufficient time
off. Would it be presumptuous of him to find a corner somewhere in the plans of Hayley's house for a
drafting table exposed to good light?

Hayley's attention was mostly taken up by Summer and horse talk. But every now and then her eyes
strayed to his, quietly assessing. She might enjoy the

amenities of the city. There was so much he'd like to show her and do with her—concerts, plays and fine restaurants. Hope Mountain didn't even have a movie theater. He hoped that now they'd broached the subject of the future she would be pondering these things, too. They would need to compromise, no question.

After the breakfast dishes were cleared away Hayley, Summer and Graham went out to the barn and saddled up for their trail ride. Adam sat down at the dining table across from Lorraine with his laptop booted up so he could refer quickly to the Shanghai development.

Lorraine handed him the prospectus for the project. "Hot off the press."

Adam leafed through the pages, recognizing the apartment complex he'd designed plus conceptual artwork for future residential units located in other rapidly growing Chinese metropolises. "This has grown. It'll take years to complete."

"We've estimated five years, minimum. Flow on work will likely extend into the next decade. We can go over all this in detail later. First, I'd like to discuss your partnership." Lorraine took a stapled document out of her briefcase. "I had Legal draw up a new contract for you."

"This is a great honor, Lorraine. You know it's long been my goal to be a driving force in the company." He paused, wondering how best to word his desire to restrict his hours.

Lorraine's eyes narrowed behind her reading glasses. "Am I detecting a 'but'?"

"Not exactly. I've been preoccupied lately with Summer's needs, but soon I'll be able to devote myself to these exciting new projects. However, I'm hoping that Summer will come to live with me in the new year. I will have to balance my responsibility for her with my work."

"I hope she won't mind moving because I don't just want you to join the firm as a partner, Adam. I want you to head up our new office."

"In Sydney? Wow, that's exciting. I didn't know we were expanding nationally." He prefered Melbourne but Sydney was fine, and Summer would be close to her mother, too. His new package would no doubt cover relocation expenses. He started doing mental calculations to see if he could afford to keep the Melbourne apartment as well as buy a place in Sydney.

"You'll be based in Shanghai."

He blinked. "I beg your pardon? Did you say Shanghai?"

With a laugh Lorraine leaned back. "You should see your face. I understand you're feeling stunned right now. It's a huge undertaking. I've talked it over with the board and the decision was unanimous. You are perfect for the job. And you deserve it for all your excellent hard work. Congratulations."

"Thank you." Shanghai. His heart sank. Melbourne was one thing, but maintaining a relationship from overseas might prove a tad more difficult.

"Now, let me tell you about the package we're offering," Lorraine said. "I think you'll be very pleased."

HAYLEY LEANED ON the paddock fence and elaborated on the basics of her horse therapy program, which she'd explained to Graham last night over dinner. He listened attentively, interrupting her to ask questions now and then, fleshing out the details.

Summer went back and forth from the barn to the paddock, getting Bo, Sergeant and Major saddled and ready for their ride. While Hayley chatted with Graham she kept one eye on Summer, noting how much she seemed to enjoy the task and the responsibility.

"Write up a brief overview of your program, including testimonials if possible, and email it to me," Graham said. "I'll draft a grant proposal over the next week or so and shoot you a copy so you can vet it before I send it out."

"That would be fantastic. What do you charge for that?"

"Don't worry." He waved it away. "I owe Adam a favor. And he'll write you a glowing testimonial."

Graham's eyes went to Summer. "He says you've made amazing progress with his daughter."

"She's coming along really well."

"Hayley, look," Summer called and pointed at Jewel. The foal was peeking out of the stable door. While they watched she took her first tentative steps into the paddock. Her head lifted and her small black tail whisked back and forth as she surveyed her expanded world.

Shane slithered beneath the bottom rail of the fence and crept into the field. He usually kept a safe distance from horse hooves but apparently he had to check out the new filly. Jewel lowered her nose, lipping the dog's head as if to see what sort of creature he was. Shane gave her a friendly lick on the chin. Startled, Jewel jerked her head up and trotted away. She stopped abruptly, all four legs splayed, her small sides heaving with the unaccustomed exertion.

Summer laughed heartily and her unrestrained delight warmed Hayley's heart. The process of healing, begun by horse therapy, had been accelerated by the sheer joy she found in the foal. Jewel had given Summer a new purpose, something to focus on beyond herself.

"Excuse me a second, Graham." Hayley walked over to the girl and touched her on the shoulder. "Summer?"

Summer didn't take her eyes off the filly. "Yeah?"

"If your dad agrees, I'd like you to have Jewel.

My gift to you. You can keep it at my house and I'll help you train—" She didn't get any further.

"Really? Oh, my God, thank you!" Summer flung herself at Hayley, wrapping her arms around her waist. "Dad will say yes. He has to. I'm going to ask him now."

"No, wait," Hayley said quickly. "He's in a meeting and won't want to be disturbed." Damn. Why had she spoken so impulsively? She was an idiot. She should've asked Adam before she offered Summer the foal.

"He won't mind." Summer pulled away from Hayley.

"Summer, wait. We're about to head off. Save it for after the ride." Hayley reached out to grab the back of the girl's hoodie but Summer was too quick.

"I'll only be a minute." She ran off to the house.

"That's one excited girl," Graham said. "I understand Adam's trying to sell this property. Where would he keep a horse in the city?"

"Jewel can stay with me," Hayley said worriedly. "Summer can come and ride whenever she's in Hope Mountain." But she knew Summer wouldn't be content with that. She still couldn't believe she'd given the girl a horse just like that. All she'd wanted was to build on Summer's high. Or was that all? Had she subconsciously been trying to trap Adam into staying? "I'd better get in there."

She ran to the house and pushed through the

screen door, not stopping to take off her boots. In the dining room Summer was chattering excitedly about how Jewel was now her horse, her very own. Adam stared at her, his shock turning to anger.

"Hayley," Summer said, spotting her enter. "Tell him. It's true, isn't it? You gave Jewel to me for keeps."

Adam turned to Hayley with a stony expression. "Yes, tell me. Tell me you didn't give my daughter a horse. Because it's not going to happen."

Remorseful only a moment ago, Hayley now felt a surge of defiance. Adam's uncompromising response didn't allow one iota of negotiating room. A glance at Summer and her heart caught at the girl's open yearning. Hayley's loyalties were being tested. Why should Summer suffer because Hayley had made a dumb mistake? On the other hand, how could she undermine Adam when he'd been so generous and kind? When their relationship had evolved into something not only exciting but also healing for her?

But she could only support one of them.

CHAPTER THIRTEEN

ADAM SHIFTED IMPATIENTLY while Hayley took forever to answer a simple question. How dare she foist this on him out of the blue? She'd put him in an impossible position with his daughter, and in front of his boss, no less. He was already in a quandary over the biggest decision of his life.

"Well?" he demanded.

Hayley straightened her shoulders and cleared her throat. "Yes, I did give her the foal. It's part of her therapy."

"See, Dad? You have to let me." Summer went from pleading to demanding in an instant. "Hayley says so. I won't get better unless I have Jewel. Don't you want me to get better?"

This, from the girl who insisted she didn't have problems. Adam counted to ten, then added another five. He couldn't even look at Hayley right now. His initial reaction to moving to China had been a resounding no, but right now Shanghai was looking like a mighty fine escape from this mess. Then he took in his daughter's anxious face. It wasn't going to be that easy. She might have made progress, but she still had issues that needed to be addressed. He'd never run away from problems. He wouldn't start now.

"We'll talk about this later," he said firmly. "Lorraine and I are discussing something important."

"Your stupid job again," Summer muttered.

"Lorraine, I apologize for my daughter's behavior," Adam began stiffly.

"Don't worry. I've got teens, too." Lorraine waved off the interruption. "Anyway, we were pretty much done. Unless you have any more questions, or want to give me your answer now."

He wasn't ready to say yes to Shanghai. He didn't want to make a decision this important in the heat of the moment, when he was distracted by guilt and anger. "I'll need time to think about your offer. May I have a few days?"

"Take a couple of weeks if you need it." Lorraine began to pack up her briefcase. "I'll leave you the contract and the rest of the material to look over."

Adam turned to Hayley. "We need to talk."

"I left Graham alone with the horses. I should probably make sure he's all right."

"Summer can do that." Adam turned to his mutinous-looking daughter. "Summer?"

"I'll go with you, dear," Lorraine said, steering the teen toward the door. "You can show me how the foal is doing this morning."

Left alone with Hayley, Adam's anger surged with

renewed force. "How could you offer Summer a horse when you know I want to move back to the city and take her with me? You've just made my task an order of magnitude harder and cast me as the bad guy."

Hayley's chin rose another notch and she took a step forward. "I did tell her she had to ask you first."

"You can't do that with kids. Don't you know that?" He took a pace away and threw his hands in the air. "No, of course not, because you don't have kids yourself."

The skin around her eyes tightened and her mouth compressed into a bloodless line. "That was uncalled for."

Oh, hell. He hadn't intended to be cruel but he'd obviously touched a nerve. What if she'd wanted children but couldn't have them? What if she'd, God forbid, lost a child? Suddenly it hit home that she was right—he barely knew her.

"I'm sorry," he said. "But you should've asked me first, without telling Summer what you were thinking. Now she's got it in her head that she not only wants that horse but she *needs* that horse." His tone became strident as he thought about how Summer would use the alleged requirements of her treatment to get her own way. "My life will be a living hell unless I allow her to have it."

"Maybe she should be allowed. Has that occurred to you?" Hayley was hot under the collar now. "You want her to overcome her anxiety and depression and heal. I believe having Jewel will help her do that. It would at least make her happy."

Exactly what Diane's approach would have been—give Summer whatever she wants. "Don't you understand how spoiled that would make her? Diane gave into her way too much."

"I'm not suggesting you spoil her. Just be kind to her. She's so vulnerable. Be gentle. Love her."

His nostrils flared. Hadn't he turned his entire life upside down to be with Summer, to help her, precisely because he *did* love her? "That's monstrously unfair."

Hayley's eyes closed briefly as an agonized expression flitted over her face. When she opened them again, he expected to see contrition. Instead, they blazed fiercely on Summer's behalf. "She's afraid of your anger and of your disappointment. You need to show her that no matter what, you are on her side."

"And you think I can prove that by letting her have a horse? I'm selling this property, remember? Where will she keep it? It's a real live horse, for God's sake, not a figurine."

"She can keep it at my place. I told her that. But you went off the deep end right away, so she didn't get a chance to explain."

"I was planning on letting her have a horse once we go back to Melbourne and board it closer to the city. But now—" He broke off. If he moved to Shanghai that plan was out the window. All his recent plans and hopes and dreams involving Hayley would come to nothing, also.

"Now *what?*" Hayley asked impatiently.

He wasn't ready to tell her about Lorraine's offer. He hadn't decided if he was going to accept. If he said anything now there would be another huge thing for him and Hayley to deal with. "Nothing."

"Look, maybe I should've asked you first if Summer could have Jewel, but it wasn't a plot to force you to say yes," Hayley said, more forceful than defensive. "I may not have kids, but I do know you don't hold out the lollipop until you get the dad's okay. She was so thrilled and so happy about the foal. I wanted to give her something to make that happiness last."

"I thought that's what therapy is about—to enable her to find her own inner happiness. Is she going to chase that foal around the ring until it follows her?"

Hayley shook her head. "Summer has lost so much. I wanted to do something nice for her."

"Something nice is taking her on trail rides. Not giving her a goddamn horse." Adam cleared the papers off the table with jerky movements.

Hayley watched in silence a moment. "How did your meeting with Lorraine go?"

"Fine." He didn't want to talk about it with Hayley right now—he didn't want to talk to her, period.

"Partnership in the bag?" Hayley persisted.

"She made me an offer that is difficult to refuse." He folded his laptop and stacked the documents on top. After his big plea for Hayley to keep the future open, how could he turn around and say he might be moving to another country?

"You're not going to discuss it. Okay. Fine." She turned and started to go, then paused. "By the way, do you still have Leif's watch? I want it after all."

"It's in the sideboard."

She found it and stalked out. A second later, the back door slammed.

Adam felt sick, from anger and adrenaline. In the space of minutes Hayley had driven a wedge between him and his daughter, even though she'd had the best of intentions. And he was keeping a secret that could kill their budding romance.

Hayley was as natural as a wildflower, as skittish as the wild horses in the high country and as prickly as the thistles growing behind the barn. From first to last, their relationship was problematic. What made him think anything would change in the future?

"I FEEL TERRIBLE, Jacinta." Hayley flipped through the dress rack in the Healesville boutique without really looking. "Adam's so mad at me and I don't blame him."

"Who cares what he thinks? Summer's the one who matters, right?"

Summer mattered, but Hayley also cared about Adam. She cared a lot. She avoided Jacinta's gaze. She hadn't told her friend what was going on between her and Adam. What was the point in making their relationship appear more real than it was? Although there was nothing fake about the desire she felt when he kissed her.

And on top of everything else, she couldn't help but wonder what Adam had been hiding about his talks with Lorraine. She knew there was something important he wasn't telling her. She wished he'd just be up front with her. She'd had a partner who was deceitful—she didn't want to ever go down that road again.

"Well?" Jacinta said impatiently, reminding Hayley that she'd asked a question.

"Summer won't be happy with me, either, if she doesn't get to keep the horse. I should've handled it better. I never act impulsively. I don't know what got into me."

Had she been subconsciously trying to keep Adam in Hope Mountain? She couldn't bear to think she would lower herself to manipulation, even subconsciously. If he didn't want to stay for her sake, what was the point? She didn't want to be that woman again, the one who abased herself to keep her man. Not that he was "her" man. The future was so far up in the air it was practically in outer space.

"Quit beating yourself up," Jacinta said. "Being

impulsive now and then isn't a crime." She handed Hayley a dress in a soft sky-blue. "Try this. It's your color and the style would look fabulous on you."

"All right." It didn't look like much—a halter top and a skirt made of a stretchy fabric that went mid-calf—but she trusted Jacinta's taste. She was determined to wear a hot dress to the dance. She wanted Adam to admire her in it. In it? Hell, she hoped he'd want to rip it right off her.

In the fitting room she quickly shucked her jeans and shirt and pulled on the dress. She shook it down, checked herself in the mirror and blinked.

"How is it?" Jacinta called from the other side of the door. "Do you need a different size?"

"It fits like the proverbial glove. I love it." Hayley opened the door and struck a pose. "What do you think?"

"Wow," Jacinta said, her eyes wide. "You look amazing."

"I'm going to buy it." She started to go back inside the cubicle. "Can we have lunch now? I'm starving."

"What about shoes?" Jacinta was like a drill sergeant when it came to shopping. She wouldn't let Hayley stop until she was completely outfitted.

"I'll wear my black pumps."

"You can't ruin that fabulous dress with those chunky shoes. Here, try these sandals." Jacinta handed her a pair of strappy silver high heels.

Hayley grumbled but she had to admit the shoes

went perfectly with the dress. That sorted, she returned to the cubicle and changed back into her own clothes.

Jacinta was waiting by the checkout, her own purchases already paid for. "Do you want to pick me up on the night of the dance or should I come out there? I can't remember whose turn it is to drive."

"I'll pick you up." She finished her transaction, then headed for the door, adding casually, "Adam will be coming with us. That's okay, isn't it?"

"Oh, really?" Jacinta grinned. "Is it a date?"

"No, don't be silly." Hayley set off at a brisk pace down the sidewalk. She knew Jacinta wouldn't disapprove, but there were some in town who might censure her for going out with another man so soon after her husband had died. Leif was a bit of a hero around Hope Mountain.

Jacinta caught up and pulled Hayley to a halt. "Come on, spill."

"Oh, all right. We've been…getting close."

"How close? Like holding-hands close?"

Hayley felt her cheeks warm. "We kissed."

"Oh, my God!" Jacinta hooted with laughter. "Good on you, girl. It's about time you found someone."

"Look who's talking. Who are you bringing to the dance?"

"Don't deflect attention from yourself. Now tell me everything. I want all the gory details."

"I need food if we're going to do this."

Over lunch at a bistro Hayley brought Jacinta up to date. She swirled her fork in the last strands of creamy pasta. "I just don't know where it's heading. I can't see a happy ending. Adam's never going to want to live in Hope Mountain, and I don't want to live anywhere else."

"Long-distance relationships can work," Jacinta said dubiously, taking a sip of wine.

"Maybe, but I want children someday. I don't want my kids to have a long-distance dad." She put her fork down, the last bite uneaten. "Sometimes I wonder if the only reason we're having a romance is purely due to circumstance. We both happened to be in the right place at the right time."

"Serendipity might bring you together but it won't make your relationship last."

No, that would take love, commitment and hard work. Did she and Adam have what it took for the long haul, or was this a spring fling, something she would look back on a little sheepishly when she eventually came to her senses?

"I wonder what Molly is going to say?" Jacinta said with more than a smidgen of satisfaction.

That was what Hayley was afraid to find out.

She signaled to the waiter for their bill. "Before I forget, I need to drop something off at the jeweler."

ADAM SCANNED THE crowd gathered for the memorial service for the bushfires. The residents of Hope Mountain were clustered twenty-deep before a dais next to the cenotaph erected in the public gardens. In the street opposite the park, the bright pine frames of a house under construction contrasted sharply with the blackened timbers of a burned dwelling yet to be torn down. Farther out, the mountains rose around the narrow valley, a reminder of both the isolation that contributed to the tragedy and the close-knit community that had come together to remember their dead.

He spotted Hayley, in a dark skirt and black cardigan over a mauve blouse, standing next to Molly and Rolf. She'd gone into town separately, as she was part of the service.

Summer fidgeted at his side. She wasn't talking to him. When he'd put on a dark suit, she'd expressed her displeasure with him by wearing jeans and a colored shirt.

"You realize you're showing disrespect to everyone *but* me?" he'd told her. "Hayley's husband died in the fires."

She'd given him a shrewd, far-too-adult glance. "I don't know why you'd care about him." Then she'd wrapped a black armband around her pink-and-yellow sleeve. "For Bailey."

His heart ached for his daughter, but she refused

to accept his condolences. Now Adam tried to put an arm around her but she shrugged him off. Then a microphone screeched, drawing their attention to the dais.

Archie MacDonald was the mayor, a tall, red-faced man of about sixty with a comb-over that lifted in the light breeze. He adjusted the microphone and welcomed the townspeople before introducing his wife, Flora, and a grizzled man in a blue suit named Dave Green who was chairman of the memorial committee. Off to the side, the high school band waited to play with the occasional rattle of drums or quiet toot of a horn.

Adam's gaze drifted back to Hayley. Her arms were entwined with Molly's and Rolf's. Everywhere, people were holding hands or had their arms around each other. Hardly any words had been spoken yet, but the chill mountain air was already thick with emotion.

He felt bad about his fight with Hayley last weekend. All week they'd barely spoken, only seeing each other in passing. She always seemed to have something else to do, either at the café or with Summer and the horses. He had work on the Shanghai development that Lorraine had left him. He still hadn't made his decision and it weighed on him, especially when his relationship with Hayley was so tenuous. He hadn't even had a chance to ask her what she'd done with the watch.

"We're not here to mourn," Archie MacDonald began, the remnants of a Scottish accent in his rolling *r*'s. "We've mourned every day of our lives since the fires. We'll mourn for years to come. Today we celebrate. Celebrate the lives of our loved ones and our neighbors, people who lived in this community and will be forever remembered. And now, to read out the names of those who perished, here is Dave Green."

Dave stepped to the microphone with a long sheet of paper and began reciting the names of Hope Mountain residents who had died in the fires. As he read, a boy from the school band put a violin to his shoulder and played "Danny Boy" softly in the background.

The names went on and on. Dave Green's voice wavered more than a few times. When he came to the names of his wife and grandchildren, he had to take a moment to regain his composure. Around Adam, people were crying and holding on to one another.

Hayley's hands were clasped behind her back, and he could see her fingers twisting and untwisting. But her shoulders were straight, and when she turned to comfort Molly as Leif's name was read, her cheeks were dry, though her face was taut with strain. Adam could only imagine what agonies of the heart she was going through. He didn't think for one second that Leif cheating on her made his death easier to bear. If anything, the war between hurt, anger and sorrow made healing even more difficult.

Dave stepped back and Archie called on the minister to lead them in the Lord's Prayer. All heads bowed. The murmur of a multitude of voices reverberated as Adam joined the prayer. He hadn't lost anyone close to him, but the group's sorrow swept through him, making his eyes prick. Summer's head was bowed and this time when he wrapped his arms around her, she didn't pull away.

When the crowd seemed ready to dissolve in tears, Archie came back to the mike and told a joke that his good friend, Harry, who'd died trying to flee the burning mountain in his car, used to tell down at the pub. It was so unexpected that Adam laughed. Many others did, too.

Archie then called on Dave, who told a cute story about his deceased five-year-old granddaughter. The pride and love in his voice when he spoke of little Maggie trumped grief and made everyone smile. Next, a woman talked about the garden her husband had put in last year and how she thought of him as she made soup from the leeks he'd planted. One by one, people mounted the dais and told story after story of their departed loved ones, building a picture of small-town life, of love and laughter and happiness, of quiet lives filled with family and friends. Adam was first moved and then surprised to feel the mood shift from anguish to near euphoria.

Hayley made her way to the stage. Adam tensed. What would she say? Would her anger come out in her voice? Her hurt? Summer glanced at him, a worried frown creasing her forehead. He squeezed her shoulder. "Hayley's strong," he whispered. "She'll be okay."

Hayley cleared her throat and wrapped her cardigan closer, looking so slight she might blow away in the gentle breeze. "Leif loved taking people on trail rides, especially into the high country. He was a natural-born storyteller and he had a million stories to recite around the campfire. Some of them were even true." She paused as a ripple of laughter rolled through the crowd.

"Anyone who went on one of his rides came back raving about the experience. About eight years ago, Dave Green's nephew, Chris, came out from the city. Chris had never been on a horse before. He was nervous and scared but Leif stuck by his side, teaching and reassuring him. By the end of the trip Chris was hooked on horseback riding. He was a regular all that summer. The next year his parents bought him a horse of his own." She paused and let her gaze sweep the crowd. "Chris is now on the Australian Olympic Equestrian Team. It might never have happened without Leif. That's how inspiring my late husband could be."

Adam thought that was the end. Then she found him in the audience and held his gaze. "This memorial service is about celebration. As a community and as individuals we need to be thinking about the future. I know I am, and I know Leif would have wanted that. For years I was part of Leif's dream to build a dude ranch. Lately, I've realized that I need to follow my own dream. I've decided to go into horse therapy full-time. New funding for Horses for Hope looks likely, thanks in part to Adam Banks."

She gestured to Adam and the crowd turned to him and clapped. "Adam thinks of himself as an outsider, not part of Hope Mountain. But through his generosity he's earned a place in all of our hearts."

"Wow, Dad, did you really help her get Horses for Hope going again?" Summer asked.

Smiling and shaking his head, Adam held up his hands in self-deprecation to the applause. To Summer, he said, "It hasn't happened yet. All I did was get Graham to write her a grant proposal."

Hayley was the one with the dream and the determination to achieve it. She was the one making a permanent difference in her community. Unlike himself, contemplating building luxury apartments for complete strangers.

Hayley stepped off the dais and returned to Molly and Rolf. The trio hugged, rocking back and forth. Adam was moved and he admired her even more. Leif had treated her badly, but she'd found the strength to be forgiving enough to talk about her late husband's good qualities.

The high school band started to play "What a Wonderful World" and a girl with wildly curly dark hair sang the words. After the first verse she encouraged the crowd to sing along to the chorus. Everyone linked arms and lifted their voices.

At his side Summer's sweet soprano rang out high and clear. Adam glanced down at her. She met his gaze and grinned. Uplifted by the crowd, the song, his daughter's smile, Adam joined in. It was indeed a wonderful world.

"EXCUSE ME, MOLLY, ROLF—I'll see you tonight. Right now I need to talk to someone." Hayley spied Dave and ran to nab him before he disappeared in the dispersing crowd.

"Dave!" She gave him a hug. "You did really well up there. If you still want horse therapy you'll be first on my list when I start up again."

"Thanks, I appreciate that," Dave said. "Today was good for this town, good for all of us. Chris wanted to be here, but he's riding in an equestrian event in America."

"Actually, Dave, I have something I'd like you to give Chris. Leif would've wanted him to have something to remember him by." She pulled the gold watch from the pocket of her sheepskin jacket. "This was Leif's. Please give it to him the next time you see him."

Dave turned the watch over in his hands, unaware

that the highly polished back had once bore an inscription. The jeweler had done a good job of erasing all traces. "This is an expensive watch. Are you sure?"

"Positive." She hadn't been able to think of anything else to do with it. It would mean something to Chris to have a personal item of his mentor's, and she would be happier knowing it was far away from Hope Mountain. And her.

"Thanks so much. I'll be seeing him in a couple of weeks at my sister's birthday party. I'll give it to him then. I know he'll cherish it." Dave hugged her again. "Take care."

After Dave moved off, Hayley found herself alone at the cenotaph where a single wreath had been laid to mark the victims of the bushfire. She touched a yellow freesia woven into the wreath, releasing its sweet scent. "Goodbye, Leif," she whispered. "You were a good man even if you weren't a good husband. I…"

She wanted to forgive him. She desperately wanted to let go of all the negative emotion swirling inside her. But she couldn't bring herself to say the words. She didn't feel forgiving. She felt anger and grief and shame.

"Hey, how are you doing?" Adam came up to stand beside her.

Her heart did a little flip at the sound of his voice

close to her ear. "I'd been dreading today, but it was okay."

"I'm sorry about last week—"

"Sorry, I was so—"

They both spoke at the same time and then broke off with sheepish grins. Adam slid his arms around her and drew her close. "I was too harsh. I was reeling from my meeting with Lorraine."

Hayley waited for him to say more but he just continued holding her as if he'd almost lost her. She leaned into his solid strength. "I was too rash. I shouldn't have said anything to Summer without running it by you first."

"We'll sort it out," he said into her hair. "I don't know how, but we will."

She soaked up his warmth and generosity, wishing with all her heart she could allow herself to fall in love with him. But she was afraid and weak, not the strong, resilient woman he seemed to think she was.

"I was surprised at how uplifting the service was," Adam said. "Those stories made me cry and laugh at the same time. I can see why this community is special to you."

"You're part of it, whether you see yourself that way or not. I know about you dropping cash in the donation jars around town. And helping out here and there."

"That's nothing," he said, waving it away. "But

you pricked my conscience by thanking me publicly. So I had a word with the mayor just now and made a more substantial donation to the reconstruction efforts."

"Adam, that's fantastic. Thank you. They'll probably name a building after you."

He brushed a strand of hair off her face. "Sounds like they should name it after Leif. I found it hard to hold on to my dislike of the guy when you told the story of him mentoring that boy."

Hayley shrugged. "No one's all good or all bad. Everyone loved Leif."

"You're very generous but it's to your credit." He kissed her lightly on the lips. "Want to get some lunch?"

"Can't. I have things to do this afternoon." She met his gaze. "But I'm looking forward to the dance tonight."

He leaned closer and whispered in her ear, "I'm looking forward to after."

Her pulse quickened at the rough timbre of his voice and his warm breath tickling her ear. "After?"

"I've been thinking about you, about us, all week. It's time we stopped letting our doubts hold us back. Time we stopped circling around each other and found out whether we've got something worth fighting for."

She smiled slowly. "Maybe you're right."

"Dad!" Summer hurried toward them along the path through the park. Zoe followed, hanging back.

Hayley eased out of Adam's arms as the girl came closer. In spite of Summer's endorsement of her as a candidate for her father's affections, Hayley didn't feel comfortable with her seeing them being affectionate. Until Hayley knew where this was going, she wanted to be discreet.

"Can Zoe stay at our house tonight after the dance?" Summer asked.

"Tonight?" He threw a glance at Hayley. "I don't know...."

"We want to be near Jewel. We'll sleep in the barn." Summer put her hands together below her chin. "Please."

"Oh, the barn. I guess that would be okay." He put on a stern expression. "You can't be running in and out of the house all night, though."

Hayley bit back a smile and kept her gaze cast down.

"We won't," Summer promised fervently.

"And don't stay up all night talking."

"Da-ad. We're not nine years old."

Adam turned to Hayley. "Does that mean, of course, they're going to stay up all night talking?"

"I think so," she said, laughing. "You're just not allowed to tell them not to anymore."

"Well, okay then—Zoe can spend the night. Do you ladies want to grab some lunch?"

Summer glanced uncertainly at Hayley. "I, uh…"

"Summer and I have plans," Hayley said smoothly. She glanced at her watch. "In fact, we should get going."

"I'll just tell Zoe it's okay." Summer ran to her friend.

"What are you two up to?" Adam asked.

"Oh, this and that. Girl stuff." Hayley couldn't look him in the eye. Not because she thought she was doing anything wrong, but she was afraid *he* would think she was.

"Okay." Adam looked puzzled but thankfully didn't ask any more questions. "I'll see you back at the house."

"Did I mention we're picking up Jacinta tonight? She doesn't have a date, and I don't want her to have to go alone."

"That's fine. Is she coming for a sleepover, too?"

Hayley grinned. "Over my dead body."

"Good. Not that I have anything against Jacinta, but tonight I want you all to myself." His smile faded. "Is that possible, to have no ghosts in the room?"

She took the open sides of his jacket in both hands and pulled him down for a brief but emphatic kiss. "No ghosts. Just you and me."

CHAPTER FOURTEEN

WHY WAS THE doctor taking so long with Summer?

Hayley leafed through a women's magazine in the waiting room, barely seeing the airbrushed celebrity photos. Earlier in the week she'd brought Summer to the clinic for blood tests. Today they would hear the results.

Hayley kept telling herself Summer was going to be fine. The girl's overactive imagination and guilty feelings had combined to make her think she could have an STD when she more than likely did not.

But what if Summer did have something that needed treating? She was a minor. It wouldn't be right to keep taking her to the clinic behind Adam's back. If he found out she'd kept this from him he would be furious, and rightly so.

Hayley flipped pages. She wouldn't worry about that now.

A door down the corridor opened and Summer came out. "Thanks, Dr. Margolis," she said to the young female doctor.

Hayley rose, scanning Summer's face for clues as to the results of the blood tests, but the girl was remarkably good at hiding her feelings when she wanted to.

"We can go now." Summer headed straight for the exit.

Hayley quickly paid the bill and caught up with her in the gravel parking lot. "Well?"

"I'm clear." Summer burst into tears and buried her face in her hands. The tears were short-lived as she wiped them away and breathed a huge sigh of relief. "That was so embarrassing. I never want to answer questions like that again."

Hayley hugged her. She could guess how excruciating it must have been for Summer to answer the doctor's intimate questions. "Never mind, now. It's over. You did good."

"Thanks for coming with me," Summer said, pressing her face to Hayley's chest. "I couldn't have done it without you."

"If you ever need me again, I'll be there for you." She gave her another hug, then said, "Come on, let's go."

When they were in the car she put the keys in the ignition but didn't start the engine. "You really should speak to your mother about this stuff, though. Next time you see her, talk it over."

"I couldn't. We always fight." Summer slumped in her seat and stared out the side window. "She doesn't care about me."

Hayley's heart twisted. "I know that's not true.

She stayed in Hope Mountain for you, even though there was nothing left for her here."

Summer snorted. "She had nowhere else to live. Dad was at the apartment in the city. She wouldn't have gone there."

"Your mother's a strong-minded individual, kind of like you. She would have found another place to live if she'd wanted to."

"I can't talk to her!" Summer burst out. "I can't forgive her for what she did to my dad. And to you. She and Dad were still married when she started seeing Leif. If she hadn't taken up with your husband, she and Dad might've gotten back together."

Hayley closed her eyes on a stab of pain. She was almost tempted to ask for details of how and where Leif and Diane's affair had started and was conducted. But besides the fact that it was inappropriate to ask Summer, what was the point in torturing herself? No ghosts. She would do herself more harm than good by dwelling on the past.

She took a deep breath and opened her eyes. "I don't think that's true from things your dad has said. I'm sorry. Every child wants his or her parents to be happy together. Sadly, it doesn't always work that way." She paused, then added quietly, "My parents divorced when I was ten. It was really hard."

And maybe that was why she'd attached so strongly to Molly and Rolf, her ideal of a married couple. Her parents' split had come after years of tension and fighting. Seeing Molly and Rolf so loving and strong together had given her hope and, yes, expectations, that she and Leif would have that kind of marriage. Hope that had lasted through multiple affairs. That's how badly she'd wanted the dream.

To change the subject, she asked as casually as she could, "So what now for you and Steve?"

"He wants me to go to the dance with him tonight." Summer's face scrunched in confusion. "I like him, but I'm afraid he'll think I want to go back to the way we were."

"And you don't want to."

"No. He let Bailey go because he was a coward. I get that he was scared and everything…but Bailey died because of what he did."

"He couldn't have known that would happen. And you wouldn't have wanted him to be killed in the fires, would you?" She'd already said this but it bore repeating.

Summer shook her head. "It's my fault—"

"It's not. You made mistakes, you're human. You have to forgive yourself. The fires were a tragedy that was bigger than all of us. Lots of mistakes were made that day and some ended in death. We can't let that poison our lives. Yes, Steve should have gotten his parents to pick him up, but that mistake doesn't make him a bad person, right?"

Again Summer mutely shook her head.

"And you're not bad because you sent him and

Bailey out into the woods that morning. When you're young, sometimes your judgment isn't the best. As for what you and Steve did that night, it's not my place to lecture—"

"The doctor did, don't worry," Summer said drily.

"I'll just say this—when young people are intimate before they're old enough to be responsible for their actions, it can lead to the kind of mistakes you and Steve made that night. And if you'd been older and not so concerned with what your parents would think, you wouldn't have left it so long to see a doctor and find out if you had anything to worry about."

Summer was silent, her head down.

"Do you understand what I'm saying?"

"Yes. But how will I know when I'm old enough?"

"It's hard to give a specific age because everyone's level of maturity is different. The important thing is, when you do make love it should be because you want to, not because the guy pressures you, or all the other girls are doing it, or you think he expects it, or to please him. Or to keep him."

"I don't know if I can even be friends with Steve," Summer said. "Every time I see him, I think of Bailey and I'm angry all over again. I don't know what to do with those feelings. Working with the horse therapy has helped me control them, but they haven't gone away completely."

Oh, boy, could Hayley empathize. She felt like a fraud giving advice, but she had learned a few things recently. If her mistakes could help Summer, she had to try.

"It will take time, but you're doing really well. Maybe it would help if you think about what Steve's lost. You, for a start. Plus he's got scars on his body. He probably feels guilty, too. His life will never be the same as it would have been had he not ridden into the woods that night."

Leif had lost his life. There wasn't a much bigger price he could have paid for his mistakes.

"What if he wants to, you know…" Summer turned pink.

"Tell him exactly how you feel. Be honest. You have a right to define your own life. It's not having sex that empowers a girl—it's being able to choose to have it, or not. If you just want to be friends and he loses interest, then he wasn't the guy you thought he was."

"I guess." Summer sniffed and blotted her nose with a tissue. "Can we get ice cream now?"

Hayley didn't take offense at having her little speech dismissed. She'd given Summer a lot to process. "Sure. After that we can pick up snacks for you and Zoe tonight."

"Oh, Dad will do that."

Hayley shook her head at the casual way Summer took her thoughtful father for granted. She started the car and pulled out of the clinic parking lot onto the highway. On the other hand, it was nice she knew she could count on her dad.

"You're lucky," she said. "Your father's pretty great."

Summer had the grace to look sheepish. "I know."

Hayley smiled to herself. It must be tough being a parent. She only hoped that someday she would get to find out for herself. Maybe, just maybe, if things worked out with Adam...

ADAM CARRIED THE groceries and supplies he'd picked up for tonight into the house. Champagne and soda went in the fridge along with the first sweet strawberries of the season and handmade chocolates. Chips and other junk food for Summer and Zoe he stashed in the pantry.

Fresh flowers on the dining table and more on the dresser in his bedroom. He changed the sheets even though they didn't need it and put fresh towels in the bathroom en suite. He paced through the house, making sure everything was perfect. The moon would be full tonight, so maybe they would have their champagne on the deck, looking over the moonlit valley.

It hardly seemed possible that only a few weeks ago he hadn't even known Hayley. So much had changed in that short period of time—he'd changed. After he and Diane had split up he hadn't thought he would fall in love again for a long time.

Love? Was that what this was? It would explain the buzz of anticipation as he prepared for the evening, how Hayley entered his thoughts a million times a day, the way his heart did that funny somersault whenever she came into the room. He was thirty-six but he was as excited as any eighteen-year-old.

It felt a little odd to be setting out Diane's candles to romance another woman, but, hey, life moved on. She certainly had. When she'd moved out of the apartment they'd both known there was no turning back. He felt badly for Summer's sake, but now he and Diane were free to find someone they were more suited to. He wasn't sure they would ever be real friends. She'd had an affair with a married man, not caring if she caused the man's wife heartbreak. Not acceptable by Adam's standards. But they would be friendly, for Summer's sake.

Now that he was free, would his choice be Hayley? She was very different from his previous women friends, but she had a knack of fitting in with anyone simply by being unapologetically herself. She would be a breath of fresh air among the city-centric architects and engineers he hung out with. And she and Summer had bonded. He was grateful his daughter had a female role model who was so grounded. Diane had her good qualities, but she lived in a bubble of money and privilege that allowed her to be self-indulgent and self-centered.

Tonight he would tell Hayley about Lorraine's offer to head up the office in Shanghai. Maybe by talking it out with her he could come to a decision. He was really torn.

This was his reward, the prize for working long hours over the past decade. But seeing the community of Hope Mountain respond to tragedy with optimism and hope had been inspiring. The life Hayley had here was real. It was the kind of life he'd experienced as a kid on his grandfather's farm. It was the kind of life he wanted for his daughter. Was he willing to give up everything he'd worked for careerwise to stay in Australia, to stay in Hope Mountain? To marry Hayley if she would have him? Or had he spent too long in the city to be satisfied with a simpler existence?

Adam went back downstairs. Everything was ready. He still had a couple of hours before the dance, so he went back to his drafting board and got to work. He'd put in every fireproofing feature known to man on Hayley's house, including sprinkler systems and nonflammable building materials—and he'd done the same for the stables and outbuildings.

As a final touch he drew in a fire bunker where she could shelter in case of another bushfire. Whatever happened between them, he wanted her to never again have to share a dam with snakes while she watched her property burn. Hayley's safety had become paramount to his own sense of well-being.

A couple of hours later Summer burst into the house with a clatter, bringing the aroma of pizza with her. She set the boxes on top of the counter. "Hey, Dad. We're home."

Adam put down his pencil. When was the last time she'd greeted him on entering the house instead of slinking upstairs without a word? "How was your afternoon? Where's Hayley?"

"She's coming." Summer opened the pizza box and got out plates. "We'd better eat it while it's hot."

"I don't know how she has an appetite after putting away a double fudge sundae," Hayley said, coming through the back door carrying a small gift bag.

"What's that?" Adam was dying to ask what they'd been up to all afternoon. Not shopping, if one tiny bag was all they'd come home with. And even the biggest sundae didn't take Summer more than fifteen minutes to demolish.

"It's for Summer." Hayley passed the bag to the girl.

"When did you get this? What is it?" Summer was clearly surprised at receiving a present.

"I got it while we were at the café, when you went to the ladies' room. You've worked so hard and done so well. Open it."

Summer put down the slice of pizza and wiped her hands. "You didn't have to get me a present."

"I wanted to. And Molly agreed."

Summer took out a small box and lifted the lid. Nestled on a black velvet square was a pair of garnet earrings. She looked up at Hayley and her eyes filled. "These are the ones I tried to steal. Is this a horrible joke?"

"No, sweetheart." Hayley pulled her into a hug. "I thought you took them because you liked them."

"I love them. But I don't deserve them."

"I think you do. They're a gift from me." Hayley hugged her harder. "Now stop crying. You don't want your eyes to be red tonight."

Summer wiped her eyes. "Dad, can I keep them?"

"Of course you can. What do you say?"

"Thank you, Hayley." She hugged her again. "And thanks to Molly, too. I'm so sorry I took them. I'll never do anything like that again. I'm gonna try them on." Clutching her earrings, she ran upstairs.

"All's well that ends well," Hayley said.

"So, did you two have a good afternoon?" Adam asked.

"The best." She wagged a finger at him. "Don't ask because I won't tell. I'll just say we had a breakthrough today. I think from now on Summer's going to improve rapidly."

"Well, that's worth celebrating. Do you want champagne before or after the dance?" He stole a kiss, his hand sliding down to linger on her butt. "I have a few other tasty treats to go with it."

Hayley leaned over to open the fridge. "Ooh, strawberries and chocolate. You devil. Definitely *after.*" She went back into his arms and ran a hand up his chest. "I'll try not to tire you out on the dance floor."

"We'll stick to slow dances." Humming a Latin beat, he led her in a mangled version of a tango. Her breasts felt warm and resilient pressed against his chest and he pulled her hips in close to his, letting her feel just how much he wanted her.

Then he slowed and stopped and took her mouth in a long, deep kiss. He wanted her badly, not just in his bed but also in his life. Dancing in the kitchen, making love in the moonlight, watching her eyes open at sunrise, seeing her smile just for him. Finally he pulled away and kissed her nose, her cheeks, her eyes. "We'd better stop before I forget I have a young daughter in the house and drag you upstairs to my room."

Hayley laughed breathlessly, her lips swollen and red, her eyes huge and luminous as their gazes held for a long wordless moment. "I should go get ready."

"I should let you." He kissed her again, his hand sliding up under her shirt to feel her warm skin, up further to cup her breast through her soft cotton bra. Her nipple hardened and he tweaked it between his fingertips. With his other hand he opened her shirt and pressed his mouth to the curving top of her breast, drawing down the bra to slip her nipple into his mouth. He sucked, eliciting a moan and he pressed his aching groin into her hips.

A noise upstairs made Hayley draw back and this time push Adam's hands away. But before she turned for the stairs she gave him a heated look and whispered, "Tonight."

HAYLEY DESCENDED THE staircase, a little wobbly in her high-heeled sandals. Her hair fell loose past her shoulders, curling slightly. In her new dress she felt like a princess.

Adam waited at the bottom looking incredibly sharp in a dark suit jacket over an open-neck shirt and tan slacks. Freshly shaven, hair combed, he was as hot as a model from the pages of a magazine. Simply wow.

"Don't watch or I'll stumble," she said. "Jacinta made me buy these stupid shoes."

"If you fall, I'll catch you. At the risk of sounding sexist, those shoes make your legs look amazing."

"Thank you." She made it safely to the bottom, her cheeks warm from the intensity of his gaze. Self-consciously she twirled, letting the full skirt of her new dress flare out. "What do you think?"

"You're beautiful." He held out his arm. "Summer's in the car, waiting impatiently."

Outside, Hayley slipped into the passenger seat next to Adam. Summer was sitting in the back wearing a short skirt and a stylish but modest blouse. She'd stopped dressing to shock, Hayley noticed.

"You look very nice," Adam said to her.

Summer beamed at him. "Thanks."

"You're welcome." He started down the driveway. "What do you call a psychic little person who has escaped from prison?"

"Oh, Dad, don't ruin it."

"A small medium at large."

Hayley chuckled.

"See, someone appreciates my jokes."

Hayley gave Adam instructions to Jacinta's house and ran inside to get her friend when they arrived. Jacinta piled into the back with Summer.

"Cute outfit," Jacinta said to Summer, then added to Adam, "Thanks for the lift. I've heard so much about you."

Adam met her gaze in the rearview mirror. "Hayley's been telling stories, has she?"

"The whole town has. Apparently you've single-handedly financed the rebuilding of the community center." She gave him an arch glance. "But I notice you haven't gotten a library card yet."

"Jacinta!" Hayley winced. "Adam, turn left at this next street to park in back of the school. It's closer to the gym."

"Zoe and I helped decorate," Summer piped up. "It looks awesome. The band is from Healesville, and they're playing for free because it's a fund-raiser."

Hayley, Jacinta and Summer got out near the entrance and Adam went to park in the gravel parking lot. Hayley waited for him outside. Together they walked into the gym.

Murals of the forest and the town the way it had been before the fires had been painted on huge canvas cloths lining the walls. The lights had been dimmed and there was a bar, in addition to a table with nonalcoholic drinks. A band was setting up onstage. Tables ringed the perimeter of the room, enclosing a dance floor.

"Summer's gone to sit with her friends, and Jacinta's finding us a table." Hayley scanned the room and then waved. "There she is. Oh. Molly and Rolf are at the next table."

"Is that a problem?"

"No, it's just that…" She bit her lip. "This is the first time I've been out with another man since Leif died. It will be tough on Molly, especially."

"Would you rather sit somewhere else? You can find another table and I'll go get Jacinta."

"Thanks, no. I need to face Molly sooner or later."

"Okay, but if you need to escape give me a signal and we'll find an excuse to leave."

Crossing the gym took a while. Hayley stopped to say hello to people who congratulated her on her speech that morning and expressed their condolences. And, no doubt, to eye up her escort for the evening. Adam seemed to know quite a few people, too. Mort, the Realtor; Belinda, from the grocery store; Leanne, from the garden center; members of the fencing crew; Tom, the school principal; and a man Hayley didn't know—Adam told her was a forestry research scientist whose acquaintance he'd made in the line at the liquor store.

Finally they arrived at their table. Hayley was about to sit down when Molly called her over. "Join us. There's plenty of room."

She glanced at Adam. "I don't see how I can say no."

"It's fine. I'll get us drinks. Wine for you and Jacinta?"

"Thanks." Hayley waved Jacinta over. Her friend made a discreet eye roll, but she picked up her purse and joined them.

"It was nice of you to let Adam come with you," Molly said to Hayley, subtly fishing for information. "Although I'm not sure why he'd be interested in our little dance."

Hayley stifled a sigh. There was no point in pretending anymore. "We're here together on a date." She touched Molly's hand and added gently, "I know it must be hard for you to see me with another man, but I like Adam. He's a good man."

"Hayley, my dear, it is hard for me, but I always knew in my heart it was going to happen someday. I have nothing against Adam. I'm sure he's a perfectly fine person. But I don't want you to get hurt. From what I understand he won't be in Hope Mountain much longer. Mort was telling me he'd been out to Timbertop to take photos so he could list the property."

"I know about that. Adam told me himself. But he can still enjoy Hope Mountain while he's here, can't he?"

And there was no reason she couldn't enjoy his company while she had him. If she'd learned anything from the fires, it was that life was short and you had to find your happiness when and where you could. Deliberately going into a relationship knowing it wouldn't last wasn't her way, but maybe she needed to jolt herself out of the past by doing something out of character.

"I know you, Hayley Sorensen." Molly tapped the table for emphasis. "You don't give your heart lightly—I remember how long Leif pursued you in high school—but once you do, you're loyal to the end even when—"

"What?"

Molly drew back, mouth pursed. "Nothing."

How much did her mother-in-law know about her and Leif's marriage? It was on the tip of her tongue to ask but she just couldn't. "You're right, Molly. I don't give my heart lightly and I haven't given it to Adam. That's why I'll be okay when he leaves. But we are leaving the future open to possibilities."

"That's a fancy word for a whole lot of nothing,

if you ask me." Molly shook her head. "He'll take a loss on the property, no doubt, trying to sell in a hurry. I heard his ex-wife ran off to Sydney and isn't coming back."

"Diane's taking care of her mother, who's had open-heart surgery."

"Oh, I didn't know that. Speaks well of her, I suppose," Molly said grudgingly.

Onstage, the band had finished setting up and began to play a snappy country-and-western tune. A few people got up to dance. Jacinta was jiggling her crossed leg, scanning the room for prospective dance partners.

"Ask Tony," Hayley suggested, pointing out the handsome vet standing by the bar. "Nope. That redhead beat you to it."

"Damn. Oh, well, who needs a partner? I'm going to dance by myself." Jacinta got up. "Want to come?"

"In a minute." Hayley wasn't ready to dance, content to watch for a while—the dancers, the band, her friends and fellow townsfolk. The music was lively, the atmosphere upbeat. Laughter and conversation competed with the band. After the emotionally wrenching memorial service, everyone was ready to throw off their sorrow and kick up their heels.

Adam's dark head was bent toward Rolf as they talked earnestly, the older man gesticulating with a rough hand at frequent intervals. Whatever they were talking about was clearly absorbing. And now the conversation was winding down.

Adam clapped a hand on Rolf's shoulder and rose, coming around the table to Hayley. "Dance?"

"Love to." She put her hand in his and together they walked onto the floor. Heads turned their way but Hayley decided to ignore the inevitable wagging tongues. She deserved to enjoy herself.

She should be hardening herself to Adam's departure. Instead she was looking forward to tonight. Summer and Zoe would be in the barn. She and Adam would be alone in the house. Tonight wasn't about commitment and the future. She'd grown up over the past weeks. She could have a relationship without expecting it to last forever. She could make love to Adam and enjoy it, no strings attached.

"Did Molly give you a hard time about being here with me?" he asked.

"She's worried I'll be heartbroken when you leave." Hayley smiled to show she wasn't worried. "What were you and Rolf talking about? It looked very deep."

"We made a stab at football and cars, two ordinarily failproof guy-talk subjects but those didn't pan out. Then we found common ground in a topic dear to both of our hearts." Adam paused, a grin quirking his lips.

"Well?" Hayley demanded. "What topic is that?"

"The best way to stack firewood. Rolf is a 'bark up' kind of guy, just like myself."

She laughed. "Firewood. I don't believe it."

"Cross my heart. We bonded over the intricacies of wood cutting and stacking. Norwegians—and their descendants—can talk about wood for hours. He's going to show me a good place to chop down trees for firewood. The supply I've got isn't going to last a whole winter."

"You're not going to be here next winter."

"Oh, well, it's good to stock up anyway. You never know."

That was true. Hayley smiled. *You just never know.*

HAYLEY SAT ON the bed and slipped off her high-heeled sandals while Adam popped the cork on the champagne. Tiny bubbles of excitement rose in her just like the fizz in the sparkling wine. Candles glowed, freesias poured forth their heady scent, chocolates and strawberries were at the ready. Adam had gone to a lot of trouble just for her. She felt precious and wanted and, dare she say it—loved?

"I hope you don't think I'm trying too hard," he said, pouring the bubbly liquid into flutes. He'd taken off his jacket and rolled up his sleeves. His forearms and neck glowed, tanned and dark against his pale shirt.

"It's wonderfully romantic." She accepted a glass

and shifted a little when he sank onto the bed beside her. "Cheers." They clinked glasses and drank. "Summer and Zoe safely in the barn?"

"All tucked away in their sleeping bags in the hayloft with flashlights, snacks and magazines. I told them they could use the cottage bathroom if they needed it." He met her gaze and smiled. "We won't be disturbed tonight."

He kissed her lips in a gentle brush of his mouth, sweet and cool. Tiny kisses in the corners of her mouth, beneath her jaw, then back to her mouth, this time a little more insistent, subtly demanding entry. She opened to him readily, wanting this, wanting him. She longed to let go of the past and move into the future, whatever it held.

The kiss deepened, intensifying not just her physical response but her emotions. Now she held nothing back in a sensual merging of lips, breath and tongues, a mindless swirl of heat and sensation. She put her arms around his neck and pressed her body against his, seeking more contact.

To her relief, there was no repeat of the doubts that had marred their encounter by the stream, no cooling of the blood when things got hot.

But a drop of cold liquid on her neck made her aware she was still holding her champagne glass. With a breathless laugh she broke apart to set it on the bedside table.

When she turned back to Adam, he was unbuttoning his shirt. He paused, his eyes dark and intent. "Before we go any further, are you sure about this?"

Hayley nodded. Oh, she had questions—about his job and promotion, how long they would have together once he sold the house, how often they might see each other when he was back in Melbourne— but there would be time later to talk. For now she would enjoy the fantasy that he was hers.

She slid her hands up his bare chest, feeling the smooth skin and ripples of hard muscles beneath her palms. He undid the clasp holding her halter top together and the two sides of the bodice slipped down, exposing her bare breasts.

"No bra. I knew it," Adam said. "You've been driving me crazy all night." Reverently he cupped one breast and lowered his dark head to kiss and lick and suck gently on the nipple.

Hayley tipped her head back and shut her eyes, letting out a tiny moan as the pressure increased and the electric sensation shot from her breast to her pulsing core.

His hands moved over her as he greedily sucked first one, then the other breast. Her skin heated beneath his caress as *her* touch became more urgent. She pushed his shirt off his shoulders. He had broad shoulders and flat pecs, a tapered torso and a smattering of dark hair across his chest that ran down to his waistband and disappeared, leading her eye lower to the hard bulge in his pants. As she looked at him, his gaze roamed over her, from her tousled hair to her flushed cheeks to her bare breasts to her waist with the bunched dress still around it. For a long few seconds they simply drank each other in by candlelight.

"Stand up," he said huskily, lifting her hands as he rose.

She pushed her dress over her hips and stepped out of it, leaving her wearing nothing but her panties and high heels. Adam dropped his pants and peeled off his underwear. His erection jutted high, setting her pulse racing and making her instantly hot and wet. His gaze lingered on her breasts and the junction between her thighs.

"You're incredible." He lowered himself to his knees, kissing and licking his way down her breasts, her belly, to her thighs. His hands touched her breasts, her butt and slid between her legs to stroke her through the thin, moist silk of her panties before pulling them down.

She gripped his shoulders as her eyes slitted and lost focus. He kissed and licked and sucked his way back up, pushing her legs apart a little to nip at the sensitive inside of her thighs.

He paused to lick between her legs. "Do you like that?"

She clutched his head in her hands. She would come in seconds if he kept that up. "Yes," she moaned. "But right now I need you inside me. Please."

Adam lowered her onto the bed and left her a moment while he found a condom and put it on. Then his warm weight slid over her. He was so hot and she was so needy, tingling and pulsing and aching. Her legs parted of their own accord and she moaned again as he pushed a little way in, then paused, hard and hot and throbbing.

He bent his head and took a nipple into his mouth, swirling the peak with his tongue, sucking and withdrawing. "Tell me what you like. I want to know so I can do it to you over and over."

She wanted him inside her, pushing hard. But she also loved the stoking of the flames. "Talking. That's what I like. Talk dirty to me."

He pulled back, a grin on his face. "You little minx, really?"

She nodded, twisting a lock of hair as she tried to assess his reaction. Leif had just laughed at her and joked about mucking out stalls. That was his idea of dirty talk.

Adam leaned down and whispered in her ear, his breath hot and shivery. "I'm going to push inside you with my big hard cock until you sigh and moan and cry out and beg me to let you come. You're hot and wet and I love the feel of you so tight and hot around me."

Oh, dear God. "That's it," Hayley moaned. "More."

Adam whispered a stream of naughty nothings in her ear as he slowly pushed inside her, stretching and filling her. And then just as slowly pulled out. He did it again, driving her mad with his words and his hands and his body. He was erotically eloquent, not missing a beat as he filled her ears with sweet, sexy talk, torturing and teasing her with his body, until she was taut as a bowstring, ready to scream with tension.

"Stop, Adam, I can't take any more," she panted.

His eyes sparking, his face alight, he paused, half-way in, pulsing and hot. "But we've only just got started."

"You're very bad," she told him sternly, trying not to break into a grin of delight. Sex had never been fun or whimsical or hot…ever.

"I know. And you love it." A wicked grin stretched across his impossibly handsome face.

"Take me *now*." She lifted her hips and, with both hands on his butt, pulled him home, hard. Her eyes shut on a long wave of pleasure as he filled the hollows inside her, places that hadn't been filled in far too long, stretching her and completing her.

He began to move, long, firm thrusts stroking in and out, stoking her to fever pitch. She matched his rhythm, wrapping her legs around his hips and pushing back. Candlelight flickered over his skin, casting shadows on his muscles and the hollows of his cheeks. Now he spoke to her in low tones, holding her gaze as he whispered intimate phrases, making her feel beautiful and desirable.

Her eyes filled and she couldn't speak, lost in Adam's beautiful, dark eyes as they both moved together, making small adjustments here and there to find the sweet spot. Holding back, then surging forward, higher and higher until finally she gasped and broke open. The sun poured out of her, and the river streamed through her as shards of green and gold and blue danced across her eyelids....

Adam's muscles tightened beneath her fingers as he pumped harder, looking for his own release. She clung, tightening around him. Slick with sweat and heat, he came, too, with a shuddering cry. Then he lowered himself onto her and she wrapped her arms and legs around him, blissed out, listening to his breath slow in her ear and his heartbeat gradually return to normal.

They lay there as the seconds stretched into minutes, and she savored a sleepy sense of well-being. If she were a cat she'd be purring like a train engine.

With Leif she'd had orgasms, pretty good ones, but this was beyond anything she'd experienced before. Adam was a sexy, considerate lover who'd excited her and satisfied her. Her heart was full of awe for everything he'd made her feel. It was huge, almost too big for her to comprehend. Was this love? If it was, then she'd never been in love before. What she'd felt for Leif paled by comparison, like thinking she'd been looking at the sun, then finding out all along it had been a lightbulb.

How stunted her life had been until now. But how wonderful that she'd found Adam before it was too late. Forget what she'd told herself about being fine with him leaving and that having him for a short time would be better than nothing. She couldn't give him up now.

He stirred and eased off her slightly, keeping an arm and one leg over her. She nuzzled his neck and worked her way around to his mouth to claim a kiss. "You are awesome."

"You are." He kissed her lazily, stroking her damp hair away from her temples. "When I get my energy back I'll grab the chocolate and strawberries."

"Allow me." She rolled off the bed and brought back the platter of delicacies along with the bottle of champagne. Raising her glass again to his, she said, "To a night of debauchery and pleasure."

Adam fed her a strawberry and then a piece of dark chocolate, making her eat them at the same time and chuckling when she moaned with pleasure. "You keep surprising me. Here I thought butter wouldn't melt in your mouth and you turn out to be a wanton."

"I am not. And no one from this century says *wanton*." But when had she ever sat cross-legged in the middle of the bed after mind-blowing sex, stark naked, drinking champagne and eating strawberries? She giggled just to think of how far she and Adam had come since he'd driven onto her property all stern and demanding and she'd been prickly and intent on pushing him away. She'd had no idea then that a short month later she would be contemplating a future with this man.

He traced a finger down her bare instep and around to her sole, tickling her. "There's something I have to tell you."

"Oh?" She smiled and popped another piece of chocolate in her mouth. "What is it?"

CHAPTER FIFTEEN

ADAM FELT UNACCOUNTABLY nervous telling Hayley about Lorraine's offer. His plan made sense in so many ways. It was logical and neat. It might not be immediate or romantic, but the important thing was that he thought it would work. With Diane he'd tried bending to her whims to make their marriage last, but he'd only succeeded in hastening the end.

"I mentioned Lorraine made me an offer I couldn't refuse." He paused. Hayley nodded, watching him intently, the half-eaten strawberry forgotten in her fingers. "It was better than I'd expected or hoped for."

"You told me you made partner. I know I wasn't very supportive earlier, but I really do think it's wonderful." Hayley leaned over and hugged him. "Congratulations."

"It's better than partner. I'm to head up a brand-new office in Shanghai. More projects are in the offing. We'll be very busy over there for the foreseeable future."

"Shanghai." Hayley blinked, her smile fading.

"It doesn't mean the end of us, far from it," he

hastened to assure her. "I'll have to put in the hard yards at first. I figure a year or two."

"You mean you're going to live over there?"

"Yes, but I'll be back and forth. When I'm here, I'll be here with you." He searched her face. "If you want me."

Hayley's troubled gaze fixed on the strawberry in her hand as if just now seeing it. She set it aside unfinished on the plate. Then she wrapped the sheet around her, pulling her knees up to her chin. "Shanghai is far, far away. Most of the time you'd be gone."

"It's only until I get the office established and running well. Then I'll ask Lorraine for a transfer back to Melbourne and we can take it from there."

"What if she doesn't let you transfer back?"

"Then I'll… I'll quit and start my own company."

"You could do that now."

"I've worked toward this opportunity for ten years. I can't throw it away."

"No," she said slowly. "I can see that. What about Summer?"

"I hope she'll come with me, but if she chooses to stay with her mother I'll make sure she has a place to keep Jewel." He leaned forward to touch Hayley's knee under the wads of cotton sheet. "*You* could come with me. I would've asked you first thing if I thought there was a chance you would say yes."

Hayley's forehead wrinkled in confusion. "So

you're only asking me now because you think I'll say no?"

"No." He sat back. This wasn't going at all the way he'd hoped. His plan had made total sense yesterday. It still did. Maybe it was because he didn't have a plan B. "I'm not explaining properly. This will be good for us as a couple. I'll make a lot of money and I can help you build your equestrian center."

"That's too grand a name for it," she said, shaking her head. "I just want to help people and work with horses. I don't want your money, Adam. I want you."

"And I want you," he said, increasingly frustrated. Why wasn't she getting it? "I'll come back every few weeks for a couple of days. When you have a slow period you could visit me. I'm sure you could find someone to look after your horses now and then. It's not ideal, I grant you, but it can work if we want it to."

She stared at him, her expression sober and thoughtful. Not joyful and excited as he'd hoped.

"We can email and talk on the phone, spend time together, get to know each other properly," he went on. "I made a mistake the first time around by jumping into marriage quickly. I don't want to do that again."

"Who said anything about marriage?"

"Well, I just assumed—"

"And if you think hooking up with me could be a mistake, why do you want to bother?"

"You're taking everything I say out of context." It was like she was deliberately misunderstanding him. "We came together through a rather unique set of circumstances, Hayley. What if the only reason we fell for each other is because of Leif and Diane? This is the first relationship for both of us after our long-term marriages broke down. You have the additional issue of your husband dying. It's a lot of emotional baggage."

Hayley pleated the sheet against her leg. "And we're dealing with it."

"I don't want to get you on the rebound only to lose you when you fully come into your own again. We have a common bond and understanding because our partners had an affair, but as individuals we come from quite different backgrounds."

Her head shot up. "Values matter, not background. Or at least that's what I always thought. Things like family and fidelity and working hard."

"Yes, and we have all those things in common, including passion. It's because you have a passion for what you do and a determination to pursue your goals that I know you'll understand why I have to accept Lorraine's offer."

"And our passions are taking us down separate paths."

"Temporarily," he stressed. "Taking this job will secure our future. I'm doing it for us. For you."

"No, don't say that. You're doing it because you're

ambitious, and there's nothing wrong with that. Everything you say makes logical sense."

"Well, then?"

She just stared at him sadly and shook her head.

That was it? She was turning him down? A few minutes ago they'd been making love, welded together as if they were one soul in a single body. Now she seemed distant and separate and he felt more alone than when Diane had left him.

"What are you thinking?" he asked.

"I don't know. I need time to process things."

Downstairs, the back door slammed open.

"Dad! Dad!" Summer's terrified voice screamed through the house. "Come quick! The barn's on fire!"

FIRE. SENSE MEMORIES flooded Hayley. Orange sky. Black smoke. The water around her boiling with snakes. Choking on acrid fumes. Choking and spluttering, gasping for air.

"Hayley, are you all right?" Adam had his shirt on and was pulling on his pants.

She fought her panic and forced herself into action. Blaze and Jewel were in the box stall. *Off the bed. Don't think. Just move.*

"Call emergency services," she said and ran back to her own room, putting on a long-sleeved shirt and heavy pants. She ran downstairs to find Adam stabbing at his phone.

"Fire at Lot 68, Timbertop, on the Hope Mountain Road, ten miles west of town," he said. "The barn is burning. Hurry."

Hayley dragged on her boots and a jacket, pulled a beanie over her hair and ran outside. The cracks between the boards on the left side of the barn glowed orange. Summer and Zoe huddled together in the yard, not knowing what to do.

"Girls, fill every bucket you can find," Hayley said on the run. "If you have burlap bags lying around, oat bags, find them. Adam, get the hose by the garage."

A high-pitched whinny pierced her brain and sent terror into her heart. She opened the barn door a crack and slid through. Blaze and Jewel were moving restlessly around the box stall. Flames shot from the loose bales of hay stacked near the tack room, licked along the wooden wall and ignited scraps of hay strewn over the wooden floor.

Blaze whinnied and pawed the floor, her eyes white-rimmed and wild. Jewel's nostrils flared in and out, her small head high as she trotted close to her mother's side. The door to the paddock had been shut, mostly likely by Summer wanting to keep Jewel close while she and Zoe spent the night.

Hayley pulled her shirt over her nose against the smoke and heat and slipped into the stall, dodging the terrified horses. Fumbling with the latch, she dragged the bolt across and pushed open the gate.

Blaze surged past her, into the paddock and Jewel followed. The mare and her foal galloped across the field.

Hayley went back inside, shutting the door behind her. She grabbed the half-full basin out of Blaze's stall and threw the water on the flames. The door opened. Summer staggered in with two sloshing buckets. Hayley emptied them on the fire and grabbed the burlap bags from Zoe.

"More," she said throwing Summer the buckets. "Zoe, help Summer. Find anything you can carry water in." As they ran out, Hayley began to beat at the burning straw littering the floor with the burlap.

Adam appeared with the hose. "Where do you want this?"

"Wet down the walls around the fire," Hayley called above the crackling of the flames. She ran back to the door to intercept Summer, who held another full bucket. "Keep them coming, fast as you can."

Adam handed the hose to Zoe with instructions and ran out again. Hayley had no time to wonder where he was going. The bales were fully ablaze and the wall behind them had caught. Smoke billowed through the barn, thick and black. She threw a bucket of water and retreated, coughing and spluttering.

Summer kept the buckets coming and Hayley carried them to the flames in an increasingly vain attempt to douse the fire. Panic tugged at her, and she fought the urge to drop the bucket and run for the dam. Or get in her truck and drive down off the mountain.

"My iPod!" Summer suddenly shrieked and ran for the ladder to the hayloft where she and Zoe had arranged their sleeping bags for the night.

"No, Summer." Hayley grabbed the girl by the back of her jacket. "Embers might have flown into the hay and could be smoldering. It's not safe."

Summer struggled to get away, pulling with all her strength toward the ladder. "It's got all my school stuff on it and my diary and everything."

Hayley took the girl by the shoulders and brought her face right down to Summer's. "You need to help fight this fire or the whole barn will burn. Understand?"

Two tears rolled down Summer's cheeks. "My backpack is up there, too, with stuff from the doctor."

A siren could be heard coming closer. Thank God. They just had to hang on a little longer. "What stuff from the doctor? You can get more pamphlets."

"Not pamphlets," Summer shouted. "Birth control pills."

"What!?" Adam had returned with a large fire extinguisher.

Hayley directed Summer toward him. "Take her out of here."

While Adam led Summer, protesting, from the barn, Hayley hoisted the heavy canister, primed it to pump and sprayed the flames with retardant foam. She was fighting a losing battle and nearing the end of the canister when the fire truck rumbled into the yard, siren wailing, lights whirring. Four men and one woman poured out of the truck, donning their breathing apparatus. They took over, carrying one big hose inside while using the other to wet down the outside, spraying high up on the roof.

Hayley found Zoe outside on the grass, well away from the barn. Adam and Summer were nowhere to be seen. Probably in the house. She cast an uneasy glance toward the lit interior.

Birth control pills. Oh, boy. She hadn't seen that coming.

"How are you doing?" she said to Zoe. "You look like you could use a drink of water. Come on inside."

Zoe's oval face was smudged with smoke and her brown hair was falling out of its ponytail. "Are the horses okay?"

"They're fine." Hayley barely had the energy to speak. Summer hadn't told her about the pills. Did that mean she was planning to sleep with Steve again? She felt hurt and somehow used.

Hayley went inside, put on the kettle and got orange juice for herself and Zoe. Adam and Summer must have gone upstairs. Should she go up and try to mediate, or was this a golden opportunity for Adam and Summer to finally talk things out?

"Summer's dad is really mad, isn't he?" Zoe said, seated at the breakfast bar. "He practically dragged her into the house. But it's my fault. You've got to tell him."

"What do you mean? Were they your pills?"

"Huh, what pills? The fire was my fault. Summer shouldn't get in trouble."

"How did it start?"

Tears squeezed between the lashes of Zoe's closed eyes. "I smoked a cigarette. I must not have put it out properly."

"Smoking in a barn filled with hay! How irresponsible could you be?" Hayley blurted. "It's lucky no one was hurt."

Zoe sobbed openly. "I'm sorry."

Oh, God. Hayley went and put an arm around her. "Don't cry, it's all right. Was Summer smoking, too?"

"I offered her one but she wouldn't take it."

Adam came downstairs, his footsteps heavy on the carpeted steps. Hayley had never seen him look so grave or so angry. "Summer's in her room. Zoe, you can go up. But I want you girls to go to sleep. The party's over."

"It's my fault, Mr. Banks." Zoe tearfully retold her tale. "I'm so sorry. Are you going to call my parents?"

"Not tonight. Clean up and go to bed. I've set up

a mattress in Summer's room. In the morning we'll assess the damage."

"Okay," Zoe said meekly and scuttled past him to run upstairs.

"I'm going to speak to the firefighters," Adam said without looking directly at Hayley. "We'll talk later."

Hayley followed him out. As Adam went over to the fire truck, where the firefighters were putting away their equipment, she took a flashlight and checked the barn for damage. The tack room, the floor and the wall were charred and smelled strongly of smoke. She peered inside the tack room. One of her saddles was ruined, but the rest seemed okay. She went through the box stall. The front was a bit charred, but it and the fence connected to the barn were intact.

She raised the flashlight across the dark paddock. The beam of light bobbed around until it lit the cluster of horses. She counted heads. All present. Breathing a sigh of relief, she went back to the yard.

The firefighters' faces were rimmed with soot and they'd discarded their heavy jackets even though the spring night was cool. Without their helmets and breathing apparatuses Hayley recognized most of them.

The captain, Don, a fit fifty-year-old with a shaved head, nodded at Hayley in greeting, then carried on with his report to Adam. "The loft didn't catch alight, but the west half of the lower part of the barn is pretty badly burned. Any idea how it happened?"

"The girls were sleeping in there. I gather they were smoking," Adam said.

Don shook his head. "Young idiots. We soaked the place but keep an eye on it for smoldering hay."

"Would you like some coffee, Don?" Hayley offered.

"No, thanks. We'd just as soon be back in our own beds. I'll leave you to it." Don climbed into the truck with the rest of the crew, then they headed off.

"Zoe was smoking, not Summer," Hayley corrected quietly as they walked back to the house.

Adam waved that off angrily. Inside the kitchen he rounded on her. "What I want to know is why you took my daughter to a doctor to be tested for sexually transmitted diseases and didn't tell me."

Hayley's jaw tensed. "I couldn't—not and keep her trust. How much did she tell you?"

"Everything. About being with Steve the night of the bushfires and him taking Bailey. Jeez, Hayley, didn't you think I had a right to know these things?"

"I urged her to tell you. And now she has, finally. That in itself is a huge step forward in her recovery."

"Oh, well, that's a relief," he said sarcastically. "And birth control pills. She's fourteen, for God's sake."

"I didn't know about the pills. She told me she wanted to just be friends with Steve. I agreed that was best considering her age. It's hard to imagine her asking the doctor for them."

"She says the doctor gave her the pills because her periods are irregular. She told you everything else. Why wouldn't she tell you that?"

"I don't know. Maybe she worried I wouldn't believe her when she said she wasn't going to have sex again."

Adam winced. "Please don't use that word in connection with my little girl."

"She's not a little girl anymore. You need to believe her and trust her."

"Why didn't she tell *me* these things?" There was a world of hurt and baffled anger in his voice.

"She loves you so much, Adam, even if she doesn't show it. She is desperate for your approval. She was afraid you'd think badly of her. Afraid you wouldn't love her—that maybe you'd leave her." Adam just stared at Hayley, bewildered and still angry. "Please try to understand. She hasn't loved herself very much these past months. Be kind to her."

Suddenly Hayley was exhausted. In the space of a few hours she'd gone from euphoria over making love to Adam to a scary flatness. He'd *sort of* asked her to consider a future with him, but sort of *not,* as if he was hedging his bets. He wanted to have his cake and eat it, too. If things didn't work out between them, then at least he would have his career and his big promotion. And now he was blaming her for siding with Summer against him when she'd only done what was right and respected the patient's confidences.

When they'd gone up to his room earlier in the evening she'd imagined them cuddling till morning, maybe making love more than once, and becoming intimate in word, deed and feeling. Now they almost seemed further apart than the day they'd met.

"I'm going to bed, too," she said. "In my own room."

Adam rubbed a hand tiredly over the back of his neck. "That's probably a good idea."

Hayley gave him a brief, cool kiss on the cheek and left the room. She waited for him to catch up and give her a warmer embrace. She expected him to, all the way up the stairs. But when she got to the top and turned to look back, he was staring out the darkened window, looking very much alone.

As she felt alone. By the time she undressed she was shivering, and not from the cold. A delayed reaction to the fire. Her experiences that night mingled with the fires of a year ago in flashes of orange flame and banked terror.

She crawled into a hot shower, but even the steaming spray couldn't warm her. She'd done it again, fallen in love with a man who couldn't, or wouldn't, give her his all. Only this time it was worse, because she'd believed in Adam and thought he was different.

At first she hadn't dared to hope he would stay.

Then he seemed to make attempts to become part of the community. Making love had shown her how deep and strong her feelings were for him. Of course she'd hoped he also loved Hope Mountain. She'd wanted him to be happy here and naively thought that all he had to do was get to know the place to feel its special beauty.

But his pie-in-the-sky version of the future had a feeling of unreality about it—gone a year or two, back every few weeks. He'd have one foot in each country, committed to neither. Whereas she lived with both feet firmly planted in Hope Mountain. Why should she take a chance on him when he wasn't taking a chance on her?

Maybe Adam was right. They both had baggage weighing them down. Both were afraid to take a risk. She was afraid and she freely admitted it.

Adam wasn't the same as Leif, she knew that. But she was still the same woman who wanted a home, family and a loving husband. What she didn't want was to be so desperate that she submerged herself and her own needs for a facsimile of those things. She wanted the real thing.

It was time she went back to her own home. It might only be a garage, but it was hers. She knew who she was there.

ADAM WOKE TO the sound of horse hooves clopping on gravel below his window. He rubbed his gritty eyes and sat up in bed, blinking away the cobwebs and trying to shrug off the pervading sense of gloom that had dogged his uneasy sleep.

It all flooded back. Hayley's lukewarm response to his proposal. The fire. Finding out his daughter had had sex at the age of thirteen. And now she was taking birth control pills. Even though the reason wasn't that she was planning on having more sex, as a father it was hard for him to accept. He felt as if he'd missed out on her childhood, and now it was too late.

She'd sobbed in his arms last night. He'd held her close, murmuring reassuring words, torn between anger, frustration, guilt and an aching love. It cut him to the quick to think Summer was so afraid of disappointing him that she'd buried her pain, buried it so deeply she'd become emotionally sick. He'd forgiven her, of course. He would forgive her anything—she was his daughter.

Now, hopefully, she could forgive herself.

All that hadn't stopped him from taking out his frustrations and guilt on Hayley.

A horse whickered. He got up and went to the window. Placid old Bo was wearing a bridle and a long lead clipped onto his saddle. Hayley was attaching the other end of the lead to Asha's halter. While Adam watched, she headed back to the paddock and brought out Sergeant and Major.

She was leaving, and taking her horses with her.

He yanked on his jeans and ran downstairs shirt-less and barefoot, hopping over the gravel drive. "Where are you going?"

Her glance held a flash of something indecipher-able before she turned away to clip Sergeant's rope onto a saddle ring. "Home. I'll leave Blaze and Jewel here for now, if you don't mind. I talked to Summer this morning and she's happy to take care of them. The grass has grown at my place while I've been gone, and I can supplement that with hay."

Adam didn't give a damn about the horses right now. "What about us? What we talked about last night—the future, everything?"

Hayley walked Major around to the other side and attached his rope to another saddle ring. Sergeant, Major and Asha were now tied to the back of Bo's saddle, strung out in a fan. "I need time to think about what I want, Adam. And from the sound of your plans, I'll have plenty of time to do just that. When you know what you want, then maybe we can talk again."

"You can't expect me to give up my dream job to sit up here on a mountain, twiddling my thumbs."

"No one's asking you to do that."

"So what's the problem exactly?"

"If I have to tell you, you won't get it."

"Try me. You owe me that much."

Hayley busied herself checking Bo's girth strap. Finally she looked up at him, troubled. "Do you love me? You never once mentioned that. I wasn't sure if you wanted to marry me or manage my business."

Adam shifted uncomfortably, aware of the gravel digging into the soles of his bare feet. "Yes, it's true I offered to finance your rebuilding. What is that if not an expression of love and commitment?"

"Is it?" She gave him a sad smile. "You're very generous, but I wonder if your offer wasn't your way of easing out of a relationship you're not ready for. When your marriage broke down you bought Timbertop for Diane to live in, away from you. You're a good man. You find ways of letting people down easily."

"No, that's not true." Was it? "I do...love you. I'm just not sure yet if we've got what it takes to make a life together. What's the harm in taking things slowly?"

"No harm." She led Bo a few steps forward, taking up the slack on the ropes attached to the other horses. "That's why I'm going back to my home. While you figure things out I'm going to get on with my life."

"But, I assumed you'd stay here and we would figure it out together...." He was floundering. "Didn't you enjoy last night? I mean, until the fire."

Hayley rested a hand lightly on his chest. It felt as if she was touching him for the last time. Her bright blue eyes were huge and shiny. "It was the best night of my life. You're not the problem, Adam.

You're strong, honorable and kind. The truth is, I'm not as brave as everyone thinks I am. I'm afraid of getting hurt again."

She stood on her toes and brushed his lips with hers. Then, as if she couldn't help herself, she opened her mouth for a passionate but brief kiss that tortured him with the knowledge of all he was losing. All *they* were losing.

He tried to tighten the embrace but she slipped out of his arms, turned away and vaulted onto Bo's broad back. "Thank you for everything, Adam. Goodbye."

With a cluck and a dig of her heels, she urged Bo into motion and whistled for Shane. Asha, Sergeant and Major surged forward. Adam jumped back, out of the way, swearing as his tender feet landed on the sharp rocks.

Hands clenching with impotence and frustration, he stood and watched as Hayley walked out of his life. She was right; he hadn't offered her anything except maybes.

Hayley deserved a man right here, right now. That was something he'd never been very good at. He was a dreamer, always building toward a future but never living in the present. It was how he'd gotten as far as he had in his career—continually striving to catch the carrot dangling ever out of reach.

When the last horse's twitching tail disappeared

behind a bend in the driveway, Adam limped inside the house.

Hayley wasn't a carrot, but she was definitely out of reach. And he wasn't going to give up striving for her.

He got Summer and Zoe out of bed to help him clean up the barn. When Zoe's mother came to pick her up, Zoe confessed again, shedding new tears. Her mother had given her little comfort and fully supported Adam's wish that the girls not be allowed to see each other for two weeks. That set off more tears from Zoe and a token protest from Summer, but the punishment was fair and they knew it.

Now, hands on his hips, Adam scraped a boot toe across the charred floor and surveyed the damage to the barn. Summer was in the box stall brushing Jewel. It was all fixable, and he could do most of the work himself. Carpentry would give him something to do instead of brooding over Hayley's sudden departure.

"Summer, come here and hold the end of this tape measure."

She ducked through the door and grabbed the end of the tape. "Why did Hayley leave?"

Adam noted the measurement and moved to the other wall. "It was time. Her pasture has recovered and she wants to be in her own home."

"It's a garage," Summer said bluntly. "Why would she live there when she can be in a house with us?

Did you guys have a fight? You better not be mad at her for taking me to the doctor. I didn't tell her about the pills because I know she's uncomfortable keeping stuff from you and I didn't want to add to the secrets."

"It's not about you," Adam said. "She didn't like my plans for the future."

"What plans? Are you selling Timbertop?" Summer asked, agitated. "You said you'd wait until school was over. But I thought that if you and Hayley got married or something, we'd stay in Hope Mountain."

Adam tucked away his pencil and notebook. He'd hoped he and Hayley could tell Summer together what the next few years would look like. But that wasn't happening, and he could no longer put off talking to Summer. "Let's sit down. There's something I have to tell you."

They perched on the metal box containing sacks of oats and grain. "Firstly, I've let you down and I want to make it up to you. You are so important to me. Hayley said you were afraid I wouldn't love you if you did bad things. That's not true. I might be angry and disappointed, but I would never stop loving you and I would never leave you. Do you believe me?"

Moisture filled Summer's eyes. She nodded mutely.

Adam gave her a hug and just held her for a moment. Then he eased away. "I've got exciting news."

He told her about the offer to head up the Shanghai office. How he'd been working toward this his whole life and now that he had the opportunity he couldn't pass it up.

"I don't get it. You'd rather go live in China than be married to Hayley? You chose work over her?" Summer's voice rose. "You did that with Mom, too, so she went and found someone else."

"It wasn't quite that simple. Your mother and I had other differences. Hayley and I are both goal-oriented and hard workers. She understands. Over time, we'd get to know each other and figure out if we'd work out long-term."

"Did you even ask her to marry you?"

"We've both been through difficult relationships. We need to take it slowly. I told Hayley I'd be back for periods of time and she could visit Shanghai whenever she wanted." He put his arm around Summer's shoulder. "It's up to you whether you live in Sydney with your mother or with me, but I hope you choose me."

Summer jumped up, shrugging off his arm. "If it was up to me I'd live here in Hope Mountain with Hayley."

"That's not going to happen, sweetheart. I'm sure she'll be happy for you to visit."

"You're an idiot, Dad." Tears spurted from her eyes. "You say you want to spend time with me. And I can tell you really like Hayley. But instead of just being with us, you're running away to China.

No job is more important than people. I'm only a kid and even I know that. What are you afraid of?"

"Summer, you shouldn't talk to me like that."

"Someone's got to tell you the truth," she shouted. "When Mom and I lived with you I saw how tired you were, how crabby. You worked at night and on the weekends, and you didn't even seem to enjoy what you were doing. Now you want to do the same thing in a foreign country. But up here you've been different, laughing and relaxed and having fun."

"Grown-ups can't have fun all the time."

"But you *never* have fun. It'll be worse in Shanghai because you won't know anyone there." Summer's face was drawn and white. "I don't want to live with you if it's going to be like that. Work is just an excuse for you not to have to deal with people."

Her words hit him with a jolt. "That's not true."

She turned on her heel and ran out of the barn.

His gaze dropped to his hands. He didn't recognize them anymore. Callused and dry, the nail broken on his right index finger, they were no longer the hands that tapped computer keys far into the night, or wrote budgets or did any of the myriad tasks associated with being a high-level architect. Where had he gone off track?

He looked around the mote-filled barn smelling of burned wood and smoke. Somehow he'd made a shambles of his life up here on Hope Mountain.

What was he doing wasting his time pounding nails into boards when he had real work to do?

He got off the hay bale and brushed his jeans. He had to stop navel gazing and look over the prospectus Lorraine had sent him so he could talk about it intelligently when he phoned to accept her offer.

Back in the house he got himself a cup of coffee and sat down with the drawings, site report and budget analysis. This was his comfort zone. This was what he understood, what he'd groomed himself for over the past five years.

But the figures and numbers swam before his eyes and his mind drifted. He sat there for thirty minutes and couldn't concentrate for a second. Was Summer right—had work taken over his life? And not just work but jobs that had little to do with the creative bent that drew him to architecture?

Certainly as his marriage had deteriorated he'd worked longer and longer hours until his life revolved around the office and the projects he was working on. He and Diane never should have been together in the first place, and that was what had led to him working too much, not the other way around.

But now that they were divorced, was he still using work to withdraw from people? Not just any people, but Hayley?

Logic told him that what he'd proposed made sense for two people recovering from troubled relationships. A cautious approach was only smart.

So why was no one but him happy about it?

The doorbell rang. Relieved at the distraction, he got up to answer it. Passing the mirror above an occasional table, he glanced at himself. And was shocked anew. Happy? You'd never know it from the grim downturned mouth, the twin creases between his eyes and the drawn face. His hair was a mess and he hadn't shaved yet this morning.

The doorbell rang again. He shook his head to clear it.

Molly was on the doorstep bearing a covered basket that smelled delicious. She seemed taken aback by his appearance but quickly rallied. "I hope you don't mind the intrusion. Hayley used to come for breakfast on Sundays. She hasn't since she moved in here, so I brought over some fresh scones."

"She's not here. She moved back to her place."

"That was sudden. She seemed so happy here."

They'd all—he, Summer and Hayley—been happy for a time. Until he and his good intentions screwed things up.

"We, uh, had an accident last night. The barn caught fire. That might have had something to do with it." It didn't, really, but it was a convenient excuse.

"Oh, dear. I hope no one was hurt. Are the horses okay?"

"Yes, everyone's fine. So are the horses."

"Well, I won't disturb you. I'll carry on to Hayley's, but I'll leave a few scones."

She bustled into his kitchen and deposited six scones on a plate and scooped half the cream she'd brought in a covered container into a bowl. "Do you have jam? I know what you bachelors are like. Oh, and here's the local newspaper. Don't know if it's delivered out here. Some interesting items in the local government ads."

"No, the paper isn't delivered. Thanks. And yes, I've got jam." He bit back a smile at her motherly nature.

She gave him a worried look, searching his face so hard it made him shuffle his feet. "Don't give up on Hayley. She's not as sure of herself as she appears. And she's been through a lot. Not just with the fires."

"I know. I won't rush her. She needs time."

"Really, you think so?" Molly tipped her head. "I think she needs… What do they call it in books? A grand gesture."

"What do you mean?"

"Just think about it." She gave him another worried stare. "Now, you take care of yourself. You've been through a lot, too. Are you really selling Timbertop?"

"I can't live here."

"Because of the fire danger?"

"Because of Diane."

Molly nodded. "I understand." Then she surprised him by giving him a hug. He was also surprised by how much he needed it and how his eyes pricked as he embraced the woman's plump figure. They drew apart a moment later, him slightly abashed, her brisk and tart.

"Now eat something. Tell Summer hello from me." She went to the door and paused. "Oh, and Adam? If you hurt Hayley, you'll have to answer to me."

He found a wan smile because he could see she was half joking, trying to put a spark in him. "I know better than to cross you, Molly."

CHAPTER SIXTEEN

HAYLEY WAS GLAD to be back in her garage. The familiar concrete block construction brightened by colorful knitted throws and dusty Persian carpets were *cozy,* not depressing. She refused to even think that *D* word. Or indeed, any of the *D* words—*discouraged, defeated, demoralized.*

"We're made of sterner stuff, aren't we, Shane?" With one arm around the dog's neck, she sat on the couch and sipped a cup of lemon-and-ginger tea. Shane licked her chin as if to say yes, they were.

Hayley mentally ticked off things to be thankful for: the horses were back in their paddock, busily chomping down the new growth of spring grass; she had a small but steady income at the café with the prospect of more to come as her horse therapy started up again; Graham had sent her a text message yesterday, which she'd only just read, saying the response to her grant proposal so far was promising. He hoped to be able to give her good news later in the week.

Hayley put down her cup and took up her knitting. She'd been secretly making Adam a sweater for

Christmas. Now she didn't know if he would even be in Australia then, but she would keep knitting.

Because other things were definitely looking up. The building contractor she wanted was finally available. He'd looked over Adam's drawings and pronounced them "doable." Work would start on her new house next week, commencing with leveling the site.

Shane barked excitedly and jumped off the couch to scratch at the door. A moment later Hayley heard the car. *Adam.* Heart racing, she stuffed her knitting down the side of the couch.

When the knock sounded she ran her fingers through her hair. "Come in."

The door opened. Molly entered, carrying a cloth-covered tray. "Here you are. I can't keep track of your comings and goings. I've just been to Adam's house looking for you. I had to leave him half of my fresh scones. Poor man looks like he's been run over by a truck."

Hayley's heart rate took a nosedive, along with her spirits. Covering her disappointment, she retrieved another teacup and some plates. Her stomach rumbled, and she realized she hadn't eaten today. "These look fabulous. I don't have any jam, though. Haven't been shopping yet."

Molly fished two containers out of her huge handbag, one of whipped cream, the other of her own raspberry jam. "Why did you come back here? I thought you would stay at Adam's until you got your place built, or at least until he sold his. It's so good for the horses."

"Did he tell you about the barn catching on fire?" Hayley slathered a scone with jam and cream.

Molly nodded. "I don't think that's why you left."

"I really don't want to talk about it." She took a big heavenly bite.

"Well, I do. I was thinking about your comment that you and Adam aren't serious. I hope you didn't feel you had to pretend not to care about him because of me. Watching you two dancing last night, I could tell there's a whole lot more to your 'friendship' than giving each other a helping hand."

Suddenly Molly's delicious scone tasted like cardboard. "It doesn't matter anymore. It's over."

Molly ignored that. "I want you to know that if you do care about him, love him, then you have my blessing."

Hayley's eyes pricked. Molly's approval meant the world, though it was too late.

The older woman rested a papery dry hand on Hayley's. "This is hard for me to say because I loved my son, but don't let Leif put you off getting married again."

"Wh-what do you mean?"

"I know he ran around with other women." Molly's eyes were dark with sorrow. "Maybe I should've said something, but I thought you must have known—

and truth be told, I didn't want to rock the boat. You were the best thing that ever happened to Leif. Oh, he was a charmer, but he wasn't steady, not till you came along. Rolf tried to talk sense into him but he didn't listen."

"I can't believe you knew," Hayley cried. "All this time I was trying to keep it from you, to protect your feelings. I didn't want to lose you from my life. I thought you'd be angry with me if I sullied his name."

"I would never have been angry with you!" Molly seemed incensed at the very idea. "I was angry with Leif that he would treat you so shabbily. I never understood why you stayed with him, but I didn't want to question it too deeply for fear you'd leave him."

"I thought about it several times, but I always compromised." She was sick of compromising—look where it had gotten her.

"Leif hurt you," Molly said. "Please don't let him ruin the rest of your life by making you afraid to take another chance on love."

"But, Molly, I *am* afraid. Neither my parents' marriage nor my marriage worked out. I don't want to get hurt again." Too agitated to sit still, Hayley paced to the sink to wash the jam from her fingers. "Adam's proposal wasn't much of an offer. I said I'd think about it."

"But you really meant no."

"That's right." She bowed her head, her wet hands

resting on the edge of the sink. Adam had asked her to give up her safe cocoon of solitude for uncertainty.

Molly came up behind her and put her arms around her. "It's normal to feel afraid," she said gently. "What isn't right is to know you're hurting and broken inside and not try to make yourself better."

Hayley should know that better than anyone. She'd even acknowledged it that day she'd realized Asha didn't have a problem but she did. She'd been no different from Summer or any of her clients who buried their problems instead of facing them.

She had to ask herself now what she always asked them: *If you don't confront the pain and take risks, are you prepared for the consequences? Are you willing to live with dysfunction and unhappiness?*

She could be happy on her own—she had no doubt about that. But she wanted more. She wanted love and to share her life with a man who made her laugh and feel like she wasn't alone. She wanted children. Was she prepared never to have a chance at having a family? No.

Maybe it wouldn't work out with her and Adam. Maybe she would take the chance and fall flat on her face in six months or six years. But maybe it would work out, maybe she would find that perfect union of body, mind and soul with someone she trusted with her whole heart. She had a hunch

Adam could be that man, but she'd never know if she didn't take a risk.

Daring was also a *D* word.

It all boiled down to one question: What was the point in being safe if she couldn't be with Adam?

She turned into Molly's arms and gave her a long hug. "Dearest Molly. I don't know what I'd do without you."

Molly blinked as she eased away. "I hope neither of us ever have to find out."

As she saw Molly out, a quote she often told her clients came to mind: *Everything you want in life is on the other side of Fear.* She'd never thought it would apply to her. But it did. She was going to break through that fear and go after what she wanted. Adam.

ADAM FINISHED HIS coffee over the local paper. Summer had scoffed down three scones in almost as many minutes and gone back up to her room to finish a homework assignment.

Ah, this must be the ad Molly had referred him to. The Shire council was calling for tenders to design and construct a new community center. The center was to incorporate meeting rooms as well as recreation rooms and an indoor swimming pool. Ambitious, but no doubt the council was hoping to convince people to stay in the area.

He'd never designed anything like a community

center. It appealed to him, though. He could picture kids like Summer and Zoe playing volleyball in the gym. Hayley's knitting circle might even use the facilities. And his favorite winter exercise was swimming laps.

He wouldn't be here next winter.

The thought sobered him.

But, hey, he'd be in Shanghai, the exotic and mysterious East. Suddenly the idea of living in a multistoried box surrounded by a bunch of other multistoried boxes was deeply depressing.

He wandered outside. There was still a faint odor of charred wet wood, but overall the air was fresh. The trees and mountains rose up around him, not brooding and claustrophobic, but friendly and sheltering. The view over the valley of the town strung along the river and the farms dotted with cows, horses and sheep was sensational.

There was only one view better than his. Hayley's. No wonder she loved Hope Mountain.

He finally got it. Surrounded by the living forest and the mountains, he understood the appeal deep down in his bones. A man could breathe here. He could dream under that vaulting blue sky. He could balance life and work. He could have space for himself and time for a family. He could find love, happiness and contentment. He'd had moments of all three in the past month, tantalizing glimpses of what life could be like.

But to get that, he'd have to let go of his career dreams, his ambitions—partner of a big firm, CEO of an international architectural office. Suddenly those dreams seemed dry and dusty. He'd be chained to his desk practically 24/7 in a foreign land among strangers. Yes, he might make friends—if he found the time.

He already had friends here—Hayley and Molly and all those people in the town. When he'd first come to Hope Mountain he'd thought of it as a backwater, of little interest. Now he realized he'd barely scratched the surface of what it had to offer. Yes, it was a fire-prone area and people were at the mercy of the weather. He still didn't like that aspect. But if he planned well, he could minimize the danger.

Because what was the point in being safe if he didn't have Hayley? That was what all his logic and rationalization couldn't dismiss. He loved her, in a forever kind of way. He wanted to marry her and have children with her. He wanted to bask in her loving kindness and wisdom—in her smile. He wanted to grow old with her.

What had Molly said? Hayley needed a grand gesture. He got that now, too. Oh, he could tell her how he felt, but talk was cheap. He needed to *show* her he was committed to her *and* Hope Mountain. He laughed out loud. Now that he understood the problem, the solution was easy.

He grabbed his car keys and headed out.

HAYLEY PARKED AT a skewed angle in front of Adam's place and jumped out of her truck, ran onto the porch and stabbed the doorbell. Adam wasn't Leif. And she wasn't the same woman who'd married a ladies' man thinking she could change him. Nor was she the same woman who kept quiet when she should have spoken up. She wasn't the woman who put her man's needs ahead of her own. She wasn't a woman who let fear stand in the way of happiness.

She was a woman who knew what she wanted and wasn't afraid to ask for it. She was a woman who had a lot to offer the right man. She was a woman who loved Adam Banks with all her heart—and she was going to tell him so.

Impatiently she jabbed the bell again.

Summer opened the door. Her face brightened. "Hey, Hayley."

"Is your father here? I need to speak with him."

"He went into town to get some documents. He's all fired up about something."

For a moment her resolve faltered. The documents must have to do with his new job in Shanghai. Maybe Lorraine had sent a contract special delivery to the post office. Or Mort had found a buyer for Timbertop. Her mind could conjure half a dozen scenarios.

No, no, no. *Everything you want in life is on the other side of fear.* She was a woman who broke through fear.

"Do you want to come in?" Summer said. "I'm doing homework but I can take a break."

"Thanks, but it's important I see your dad right away. I'll see you soon, though."

"Okay. See you later."

Hayley drove through town slowly, checking both sides of the street and the side roads for Adam's dark purple Mercedes. Finally she spotted his car, parked outside Mort's realty office. Her heart sank.

She got out of her truck and went inside. Mort was at the front desk, doing something on the computer. "Hey, Mort, have you seen Adam? His car's out front."

"He was here a few minutes ago. He's gone down the street, heading north, I think."

"Thanks." She hurried down the sidewalk, checking shop windows as she went. Even though it was Sunday, most businesses were open, taking advantage of the trickle of tourists and day-trippers who'd begun to find their way back to Hope Mountain and the surrounding hiking trails.

Still, many other shops were empty and locked, their owners having sold up and moved out—these she only gave half a glance. So when she hurried past the darkened travel agency it took her a moment to register the movement inside.

She checked her long stride and backtracked to cup her hands against the glass and peer in. Adam was pacing the interior of the empty shop. She opened the door and went in. Her heart sped up. This was it, the moment she found out what she was really made of.

She didn't ask him what he was doing, although she wanted to know. She couldn't risk getting sidetracked. "I've been looking for you."

"Really? I was coming to talk to you once I finished here." A slow smile spread across his face and he walked toward her.

She met him halfway and huffed out a breathless laugh. "Me first. Or I might chicken out."

He tucked back a strand of her hair. "I'm all ears."

Her heart was slamming against her rib cage and she couldn't catch her breath. *Shoulders down. Breathe out.* She found the scrap of calm she needed to begin. "I love you, Adam Banks. I want to marry you, and I want you to live here in Hope Mountain with me." With each sentence she sped up. "I don't want some half-assed fly-in-fly-out relationship. I want a solid, everyday marriage where we sleep together in the same bed every night."

"Hayley—"

She held up a hand. "I know. You have your big job overseas. I can handle you going on business trips but not for too long, or too often. You can work from here and let someone else run the show in Shanghai."

"Can I say something?" He wore a bemused smile.

"Just a minute. In return for you doing that, I will

love you and be true to you and do my best to be the kind of woman you want in your life. Someone to share your interests and dreams, whatever they are. But I have my own dreams. I hope you can respect that."

"Are you finished?"

"I think so." She scratched her head. "Well, what did you want to talk to me about?" Her gaze dropped to her hands. "Are you selling Timbertop?"

"What? No. At least not yet." He held up a dangling set of keys. "This is what I wanted to show you. And this." In his other hand he had a sheaf of papers.

"I don't understand."

He gestured to the narrow office with the pale blue carpeting and a travel poster of Rome clinging crookedly to the far wall. "This is going to be my new office. Adam Banks, Architect, Residential and Retail Design." He shook the papers. "And this is my tender application for the new community center. If I'm successful, I'll be off to a head start. If not, there's plenty of other work to be done in Hope Mountain. I'm thinking of specializing in fireproof homes."

Hayley struggled to take it in. "What about Shanghai?"

"I called Lorraine this morning and turned down her offer. I told her I would consult on a part-time basis, but that it was time for me to go out on my own."

"Congratulations." Hayley finally found her smile. "That's wonderful." She hesitated. "Does this mean you're staying in Hope Mountain?"

He set the keys and papers on the floor, then took both her hands in his. "I'm going to try to do this right, but I'm a bit nervous so bear with me."

Hayley was nervous, too. Would he say what she longed to hear? Or was he letting her down gently?

His fingers tightened on hers. "I love you, Hayley Sorensen. I love you so much I can barely contain my feelings. I've realized I don't want to be away from you for any period of time. I trust you with my heart, and that's something I haven't trusted anyone with for a long time."

"Oh, Adam." Tears welled and her heart ached for the pair of them, yet she was optimistic, too. They'd come through the hard times, and as far as she could see, there was nothing but happiness on the horizon.

He sank to one knee. Hayley smothered a giggle and glanced over her shoulder, hoping no one was looking through the window. It was romantic and silly and she loved it.

"Will you make room for my drafting table in your new house? Will you make room for me in your life? In short, will you marry me?"

"Didn't I just tell you I wanted to marry you?"

"Yes, but I thought I should ask."

"You're such a man. But you're *my* man." Smiling, she tugged on his hands. "Now get off your knee and kiss me."

"Yes, ma'am. I can see who's going to wear the pants in this family."

"You'd better believe it." Hayley pulled him into her arms and rose on tiptoe to claim his mouth. With his strong arms around her, all her doubts and fears melted away as happiness flooded her heart.

Adam eased back but slid his hands to her hips, keeping her close. "Let's go tell Summer. I can't believe I'm actually excited about the thought of living in Hope Mountain but now, thanks to you, there's nowhere else I'd rather be. I can't wait until we start working on your new house."

Hayley couldn't believe she'd ended up with Adam Banks, of all people, but now she couldn't imagine being with anyone else in the whole world. They were both in it for the long haul, and he and Summer felt so right for her. At last she would have the loving family she'd always longed for.

She pressed her face against his chest and hugged him tightly. "You mean *our* new house."

* * * * *

LARGER-PRINT BOOKS!
GET 2 FREE LARGER-PRINT NOVELS PLUS
2 FREE GIFTS!

HARLEQUIN

super romance

More Story...More Romance

YES! Please send me 2 FREE LARGER-PRINT Harlequin® Superromance® novels and my 2 FREE gifts (gifts are worth about $10). After receiving them, if I don't wish to receive any more books, I can return the shipping statement marked "cancel." If I don't cancel, I will receive 6 brand-new novels every month and be billed just $5.69 per book in the U.S. or $5.99 per book in Canada. That's a savings of at least 16% off the cover price! It's quite a bargain! Shipping and handling is just 50¢ per book in the U.S. or 75¢ per book in Canada.* I understand that accepting the 2 free books and gifts places me under no obligation to buy anything. I can always return a shipment and cancel at any time. Even if I never buy another book, the two free books and gifts are mine to keep forever.

139/339 HDN F46Y

Name _____ (PLEASE PRINT) _____

Address _____ Apt. # _____

City _____ State/Prov. _____ Zip/Postal Code _____

Signature (if under 18, a parent or guardian must sign)

Mail to the **Harlequin® Reader Service:**
IN U.S.A.: P.O. Box 1867, Buffalo, NY 14240-1867
IN CANADA: P.O. Box 609, Fort Erie, Ontario L2A 5X3

Are you a current subscriber to Harlequin Superromance books
and want to receive the larger-print edition?
Call 1-800-873-8635 today or visit www.ReaderService.com.

* Terms and prices subject to change without notice. Prices do not include applicable taxes. Sales tax applicable in N.Y. Canadian residents will be charged applicable taxes. Offer not valid in Quebec. This offer is limited to one order per household. Not valid for current subscribers to Harlequin Superromance Larger-Print books. All orders subject to credit approval. Credit or debit balances in a customer's account(s) may be offset by any other outstanding balance owed by or to the customer. Please allow 4 to 6 weeks for delivery. Offer available while quantities last.

Your Privacy—The Harlequin® Reader Service is committed to protecting your privacy. Our Privacy Policy is available online at www.ReaderService.com or upon request from the Harlequin Reader Service.

We make a portion of our mailing list available to reputable third parties that offer products we believe may interest you. If you prefer that we not exchange your name with third parties, or if you wish to clarify or modify your communication preferences, please visit us at www.ReaderService.com/consumerchoice or write to us at Harlequin Reader Service Preference Service, P.O. Box 9062, Buffalo, NY 14269. Include your complete name and address.

HSRLP13R

LARGER-PRINT
BOOKS!

HARLEQUIN *Presents*

PASSION
GUARANTEED
SEDUCTION

GET 2 FREE LARGER-PRINT
NOVELS PLUS 2 FREE GIFTS!

YES! Please send me 2 FREE LARGER-PRINT Harlequin Presents® novels and my 2 FREE gifts (gifts are worth about $10). After receiving them, if I don't wish to receive any more books, I can return the shipping statement marked "cancel." If I don't cancel, I will receive 6 brand-new novels every month and be billed just $5.05 per book in the U.S. or $5.49 per book in Canada. That's a saving of at least 16% off the cover price! It's quite a bargain! Shipping and handling is just 50¢ per book in the U.S. and 75¢ per book in Canada.* I understand that accepting the 2 free books and gifts places me under no obligation to buy anything. I can always return a shipment and cancel at any time. Even if I never buy another book, the two free books and gifts are mine to keep forever.

176/376 HDN F43N

Name	(PLEASE PRINT)	

Address		Apt. #

City	State/Prov.	Zip/Postal Code

Signature (if under 18, a parent or guardian must sign)

Mail to the **Harlequin® Reader Service:**
IN U.S.A.: P.O. Box 1867, Buffalo, NY 14240-1867
IN CANADA: P.O. Box 609, Fort Erie, Ontario L2A 5X3

**Are you a subscriber to Harlequin Presents books
and want to receive the larger-print edition?
Call 1-800-873-8635 today or visit us at www.ReaderService.com.**

* Terms and prices subject to change without notice. Prices do not include applicable taxes. Sales tax applicable in N.Y. Canadian residents will be charged applicable taxes. Offer not valid in Quebec. This offer is limited to one order per household. Not valid for current subscribers to Harlequin Presents Larger-Print books. All orders subject to credit approval. Credit or debit balances in a customer's account(s) may be offset by any other outstanding balance owed by or to the customer. Please allow 4 to 6 weeks for delivery. Offer available while quantities last.

Your Privacy—The Harlequin® Reader Service is committed to protecting your privacy. Our Privacy Policy is available online at www.ReaderService.com or upon request from the Harlequin Reader Service.

We make a portion of our mailing list available to reputable third parties that offer products we believe may interest you. If you prefer that we not exchange your name with third parties, or if you wish to clarify or modify your communication preferences, please visit us at www.ReaderService.com/consumerchoice or write to us at Harlequin Reader Service Preference Service, P.O. Box 9062, Buffalo, NY 14269. Include your complete name and address.

HPLP13R

ReaderService.com

Manage your account online!

- Review your order history
- Manage your payments
- Update your address

> ### We've designed the Harlequin® Reader Service website just for you.

Enjoy all the features!

- Reader excerpts from any series
- Respond to mailings and special monthly offers
- Discover new series available to you
- Browse the Bonus Bucks catalog
- Share your feedback

Visit us at:
ReaderService.com